"Was there something else you wanted to say, Reno?"

"Yeah," he answered, "there is something else."

Roberta let go of the doorknob and pivoted, facing him squarely and studying the odd expression in his dark blue eyes.

"I was just thinking it's kind of nice—" his words were slow and deliberate "—both of us having our preconceived notions out of the way." He leaned close, bracing his forearm against the jamb behind her.

"Yes?" Her spine brushed lightly against the door as she took a tiny step backward.

"I've been thinking—" he moved even closer "—that maybe I was wrong, insisting that things be strictly business between us. I've been trying to think about business, of course... but there's a certain part of my mind that keeps wanting to find that place on your neck."

"What place?" she asked, her voice sounding breathless, as Reno lifted his free hand. He reached out, his thumb tracing a leisurely, provocative path down her throat.

"That sensitive spot I found yesterday morning," he murmured. His fingers grazed the back of her neck.

Bobbie swallowed hard. And when his thumb brushed her skin again, she jumped.

"Yeah," he whispered. "That must be it...."

Dear Reader,

Magic. It dazzles our senses, sometimes touches our souls. And what could be more magical than romance?

Silhouette **Special Edition** novels feature believable, compelling women and men in lifelike situations, but our authors never forget the wondrous magic of falling in love. How do these writers blend believability with enchantment? Author Sherryl Woods puts it this way:

"More. That's what Silhouette **Special Edition** is about. For a writer, this Silhouette line offers a chance to create romances with more depth and complexity, more intriguing characters, more heightened sensuality. In the pages of these wonderful love stories, more sensitive issues can be interwoven with more tenderness, more humor and more excitement. And when it all works, you have what these books are really all about—more magic!"

Joining Sherryl Woods this month to conjure up half a dozen versions of this "special" magic are Robyn Carr, Debbie Macomber, Barbara Catlin, Maggi Charles and Jennifer Mikels.

Month after month, we hope Silhouette **Special Edition** casts its spell on you, dazzling your senses *and* touching your soul. Are there any particular ingredients you like best in your "love potion"? The authors and editors of Silhouette **Special Edition** always welcome your comments.

Sincerely,

Leslie Kazanjian, Senior Editor
Silhouette Books
300 East 42nd Street
New York, N.Y. 10017

BARBARA CATLIN
Mr. Right

Silhouette Special Edition

Published by Silhouette Books New York

America's Publisher of Contemporary Romance

To Dad and Mom:

Without your ever-constant
love and support,
I never could have fulfilled
my life's dream.

I love you both.

Special thanks to Anne Parsons—
for her patience and understanding
when I needed them the most.

SILHOUETTE BOOKS
300 East 42nd St., New York, N.Y. 10017

ISBN: 0-373-09519-8

First Silhouette Books printing April 1989

Printed in the U.S.A.

Books by Barbara Catlin

Silhouette Special Edition

Prisoner of Love #303
Smoky's Bandit #488
Mr. Right #519

*coauthored as Maranda Catlin

BARBARA CATLIN

admits to being an ordinary person who loves to write, a woman whose dream to be published by Silhouette Books before the age of forty became a reality "just under the wire, which is the way I seem to handle almost everything in life." A single parent to two active teenagers, Barbara says one of her favorite sounds is "the roar of those school buses rolling away each weekday morning, while my back is pressed against the door and I'm clutching that first cup of coffee." She and her "usually wonderful" children—a daughter and a son—live in Texas.

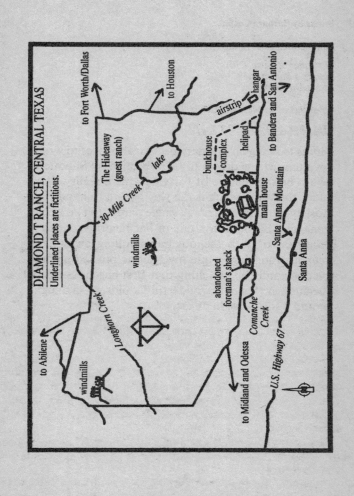

DIAMOND T RANCH, CENTRAL TEXAS
Underlined places are fictitious.

to Fort Worth/Dallas

to Houston

to Abilene

The Hideaway
(guest ranch)

lake

airstrip

hangar

bunkhouse
complex

helipad

to Bandera and San Antonio

30-Mile Creek

windmills

main house

Santa Anna Mountain

abandoned
foreman's shack

Santa Anna

Longhorn Creek

Comanche
Creek

windmills

to Midland and Odessa

U.S. Highway 67

Chapter One

Roberta Powell threw her sling-backed pump at the mahogany credenza across the office. As the shoe hit the wall, the two-inch heel flew one way while the rest of the pump took off in the opposite direction.

Shocked by her own uncharacteristic behavior, Roberta retrieved the shoe. Clutching it in one hand, kneading her tense neck with the other, she turned and limped over to the window that took up the entire side of the room.

As the owner of Powell Property Developments she'd been instrumental in the planning stages of many of the building projects she could see from her office on the outer edge of Dallas. Because of her involvement in its growth, the wide expanse of skyline usually had an exhilarating effect on her. But today was anything but usual.

Today her office felt like a cell, its view nothing more than an elaborate prison yard of high rises and sprawling commercial complexes.

"Darn!" she muttered, glaring at the mauve snakeskin weapon in her hand. Those pumps had cost a fortune even on sale, and they couldn't even hit a target. She'd only knocked over *two* of those offensive birthday cards.

Roberta grimaced at the sound of the door opening behind her, then forced a smile as she pivoted and watched her extremely young, extremely efficient secretary enter the office. At the look of unadulterated amazement on Heather's face, Roberta quickly put on the defective shoe, squared her shoulders and hobbled back to her desk.

"Miss Powell?" the young woman asked, still gawking at her from across the room. "What was that loud thud I heard?" Her puzzled gaze darted around the office. "Are you all right?"

"I'm fine, Heather. It was just a little accident. My shoe...slipped out of my hand." She tried to appear casual as she gestured toward the chip her once-high-heeled pump had taken out of the plaster. "Please have someone fix that wall, will you?"

Heather continued to study her employer with unabashed confusion and curiosity. "Are you sure you're okay?"

"Yes, I'm fine. Really." Adjusting the hipline of her silk dress, Roberta sat down behind the desk and raised her chin, attempting to muster some of her usual dignity. "Why are you staring at me, Heather?"

"I'm sorry, Miss Powell. It's just that I've never seen your hair sticking up like—" She glanced away, then back at her boss. "I've never seen your hair looking quite the way it does right now."

"Heather," Roberta said, reaching up as nonchalantly as possible to smooth the dark, chestnut-brown layers that fell just to her shoulders, "will you please call me Roberta? I know you feel it's a matter of proper office procedure, but Miss Powell seems so formal."

And so *old*, she added mentally. Heather had only been working for Roberta a few months, but the "miss" routine was suddenly beginning to grate on her nerves. Okay. So Roberta had *underwear* that was older than Heather. So what?

"Yes, Miss... Excuse me. Of course, Roberta." Heather made a face as if the name went against all the respect-your-elders training that had been drummed into her as a child. Then she moved forward to put a stack of folders on her employer's desk. "You asked me to bring these files to your attention today." When Roberta looked at her questioningly, she added, "It's Thursday. Remember?"

"I remember." Her hazel eyes shifted to the display of birthday greetings on the credenza. "How could I forget?"

"Isn't it wonderful?" Heather asked, her voice bubbling with enthusiasm. She crossed the room to rearrange the toppled cards and add several new ones to the lineup. "I don't think I've ever seen so many cute birthday cards. You must be thrilled!"

"Yes, I'm—" Roberta forced another saccharine smile "—tickled pink." Sure, she told herself. At twenty-two, Heather could still afford to be enthusiastic about birthdays. Heather didn't have to worry about things like spotting her first gray hair, which for Roberta had cropped up miraculously, and appropriately, that very morning.

"Do you need anything before I start my filing?" Heather asked. "Can I order a sandwich for you?"

"No, but thanks anyway. Hold my calls for a while, will you?"

"Yes, Miss Powell."

"Roberta," she corrected, trying not to grit her teeth as the young woman headed for the door. "Please?"

"Certainly... Roberta." Heather shut the door behind her.

Her birthday, she reminded herself once again, rolling her eyes toward the ceiling. If she had to read one more of those "cute" cards, she was going to scream.

None of the greetings were duplicates, yet they were all the same: Things like, *Don't worry, sweetie. It's the age of recycling.* Or a cartoonish drawing of a tropical setting with the inscription, *So you're 21 today, huh?,* and on the inside, *Welcome to Fantasy Island.* Much as she appreciated her friends caring enough to remember her birthday, she wondered if they'd all forgotten the old adage, "The truth hurts."

She also wondered why she'd had such resentful thoughts about Heather a few minutes before. The young woman was conscientious and extremely bright, the best secretary Roberta had ever had. It wasn't Heather's fault that she was barely old enough to qualify for a valid driver's license, that she was model-thin and nubile and had a flock of muscular young admirers standing in line to cart her off to lunch every day.

Roberta glanced down at herself. Well, at least there was one thing she still had going for her. If womanly curves ever came back into vogue, *she'd* be ready. Unlike poor little Heather, who'd find herself standing out in the proverbial cold, shivering for lack of enough meat on her bones.

And why, she wondered, didn't that thought make her feel any better?

Roberta pushed the intercom button. "Heather?" she said. "I apologize for sounding like an old ... for sounding like a bear. I'm just not feeling well today."

"No problem," the young woman answered promptly. "Can I get you an aspirin or something?"

"I've got some in here, thanks." Roberta released the intercom button. "All right," she muttered aloud, holding up her arms in a gesture of surrender. "I'll admit it!"

Leaning back in her swivel chair, she continued her self-confession internally. It wasn't that she felt like an old woman; thirty-five wasn't old. What she did feel like was an old maid.

There. She had said it.

The issue had been churning in her mind since last night, when a spot on the late news had pointed out that the average person thinks of himself as being nine years younger than he actually is. Roberta had asked herself her age, and her brain had shot back, "Twenty-six." At that very moment it had dawned on her that without even noticing the passage of time she had become a spinster. And that she was incredibly and disgustingly *average*. Her life was nothing but one big average rut.

As of a couple of hours ago, Miss Roberta Louise Powell—with the emphasis on the *miss*—was officially thirty-five years old, and what did she have to show for it?

Nothing. Absolutely nothing of any emotional value.

If this office was a cell, Roberta admitted as she glanced around the room, it was probably one of her own making. She had let a bad experience scare her into postponing her personal goals, something she never would have done with her career goals. She'd taken the area of life where she felt secure and pulled it snugly around her, as if her work could protect her from the hurts and realities of the emotional world outside.

"Congratulations, sweetie," she mumbled, her eyes lowering. "You've done exactly what you set out to do."

Roberta lifted the stack of folders her secretary had left on her desk, holding them up in the air as if she were mentally weighing their importance in her life.

Yes, she admitted, dropping the files. She wanted more than this. Another seven-figure sale had closed yesterday, but that real-estate deal certainly hadn't been there to snuggle up with last night.

In the womanly sense of the word she was still almost as inexperienced as she'd been in her teens, attending a private school for girls, or even in her early twenties, attending a private college for women. Yet in the business sense of the word she was every bit the seasoned professional. Every bit the matron.

When it came to her career she'd made a habit of not letting anything hold her back. She had made her own luck through hard work, concentrated effort and energy. She had put herself in all the right places—joining professional organizations, signing up for courses and workshops, assertively gathering accounts—so that she was visible when opportunities arose.

Roberta smiled a slow, deliberate smile and abruptly tilted her chair upright.

"That's it," she said aloud. Why wouldn't those same principles apply when it came to finding a man? *The* man?

Of course, she assured herself. All she had to do was use her well-developed sense of logic, along with some hard work, concentrated effort and energy. She would stop feeling sorry for herself and simply use her head—make a in the right place at the right time. Somew perfect man for her; all she had to wa

Still grinning, Roberta glanced at the Heather had deposited on the desk. H work, she decided, so why not take the r could go home and plan her strategy.

A knock sounded on the door, and she looked up as her secretary entered and approached the desk.

"Uh, Roberta?" Heather asked, handing her a piece of correspondence. "Your trip to the Diamond T Ranch is coming up Monday. Here's the letter of invitation, in case you'd like to read it again before you—"

"Darn! I'd forgotten about accepting this." Talk about rotten timing, she added silently, her gaze skimming the vaguely familiar, pale blue stationery.

The Diamond T had been a well-known Texas fact for as long as Roberta could remember. It was an enormous ranch, one of the largest in the state, and still a working ranch.

According to the rumors she'd heard, the Diamond T had been suffering financially ever since the death a couple of years ago of Jubal Tanner, the family patriarch. Apparently the rumors were true: the invitation, extended to her and "several other prominent real-estate developers," asked for proposals on how to market a few choice parcels of land.

Heather cleared her throat and asked, "Would you like to take a few minutes to dictate your itinerary?"

"No," she answered, looking up from the document in her hand. "Not really."

"But Monday is two business days from today," Heather pointed out, "and that's when you always like to work up your itinerary."

"My, my," Roberta said under her breath. "I am in a rut, aren't I?" She tilted her head. "Tell me, Heather. Am I always so predictable?"

"Well, I wouldn't exactly say that," the young woman answered timidly. "Methodical, maybe. But there's nothing wrong with that."

Roberta had to smother a laugh. Despite Heather's tender age, she had a marvelous sense of diplomacy.

"In honor of my birthday," she said, smiling, "I think I'll omething really wild and crazy. I think I'll throw caution wind and go without an itinerary this time."

" Heather replied, "if you're sure."

itive."

Heather left the room, and Roberta sighed as she turned her attention to the correspondence still in her hand. This trip was coming at a time when she wanted nothing more than to make drastic changes in her life, but dependability wasn't one of the qualities she hoped to change. Since she had already accepted the invitation, she would simply have to look upon the assignment as a postponement of her search for the right man.

Yes, she would get this responsibility out of the way first, and then—

The heir to the Tanner empire apparently needed a few lessons in responsibility himself, Roberta mused, glancing at the bottom of the letter. Instead of the invitation being extended by him, as she would have expected, it had been written and signed by a woman who worked for him. Noticing the string of titles under the signature, Roberta wondered if the poor woman did windows, too.

A vision suddenly popped into her mind—a picture of an efficient young employee who looked a lot like Heather. But this particular girl was chained to her desk, trying to keep the ranch from going to wrack and ruin while her boss was out cavorting somewhere, a woman on each arm, his palms turned up while the family fortune sifted through his fingers. . . .

Roberta shook her head, smiling as she erased the vision from her mind.

Good grief, she thought, reading the typed lines beneath the beautifully penned signature. Beyond being Mr. Tanner's assistant, the woman was also the manager of the Hideaway. That in itself had to be an unbelievable job; a place like that couldn't possibly run by itself. Situated on one corner of the Diamond T, the Hideaway was the most exclusive guest ranch in Texas.

Distractedly scanning the body of the letter, Roberta's eyes widened as she realized the invitation included nearly a full week's stay at the renowned dude ranch. When the invitation had first crossed her desk several weeks before, sh⁓ had accepted with the intention of staying a day or two, pre⁓
proposal, and rushing back to Dallas.

But why rush back? she asked herself. When it ⁓
ting herself in the right place, who was to say wh ⁓
might be?

Business was at a point where she could leave things right now, she decided. Maybe a working vacation was exactly what she needed. If she arrived at the ranch a few days early it would give her a chance to size up the place and collect some ideas, to get a jump on the other developers who'd been invited. After all, that was how she had managed to succeed in the property development business: by staying one step ahead of the competition.

Yes, she told herself as she tucked the letter of invitation underneath her clutch bag, she would drive down tomorrow instead of taking Mr. Tanner's private plane Monday morning. That way she could submit her proposal at the beginning of the organized festivities and then spend a few days just having fun.

And looking for her man!

Within minutes she had called her close friend and business associate, Judith, and made the necessary arrangements. As she hung up the receiver, Roberta felt a tremendous sense of relief.

Relief, she realized, wasn't exactly the right word. She felt just plain frivolous all of a sudden. On this vacation she wouldn't rule out anything. After her work was done she might even leave the Hideaway and go somewhere more exciting. Judith had met a wonderful man on her trip to the Cayman Islands, Roberta reminded herself, grabbing her bag along with the invitation and file folders before starting for the door.

If she hurried home, she thought, maybe she'd have time to drag out her trusty exercise bicycle and sweat a few millimeters off her thighs by tomorrow morn—

Almost tripping, Roberta took off the heelless shoe. Oh, well, she consoled herself, they'd never been very comfortable anyway.

In keeping with her oddly impulsive mood she chucked the damaged shoe into the wastebasket. Then, shrugging her shoulders, she took off the good one and tossed it into the basket, too. Her parking space was in the basement, so she wouldn't have to walk on the scorching, mid-August pavement. And she would probably look less conspicuous in her ng feet than teeter-tottering on one heel.

Besides, for once in her life she honestly didn't care what anybody thought even if they did notice.

Heather glanced up from her filing as Roberta placed the stack of folders on the edge of the reception desk.

"Judith Cavanaugh is filling in for me while I take an impromptu vacation," Roberta informed her. "We'll handle it with the same procedure we used when she took off a couple of months ago."

"But, Miss . . ." The young woman simply stared at her.

"No buts about it. Furthermore, I want you to promise me you'll take three-hour lunches the whole time I'm gone. All right?"

"Why, thank you, Roberta. That'd be great!"

"Good. I'll be at the Diamond T for about a week. Here's the telephone number." As she came around the desk to jot the number on a pad, she noticed the strange expression on Heather's face as she looked down and saw Roberta's bare feet. "I'm not sure where I'll be after that, but I'll check in with you." Grinning, she put down the pencil. "I may have an important meeting with Mr. Right."

"Wait a minute," Heather said in a fluster, holding up the pad her boss had just written on. "What's *Mr. Wright's* telephone number?"

"I don't have the slightest idea," Roberta answered on her way out the glass double doors. She glanced back over her shoulder and smiled, enjoying her private joke. "But I'll let you know as soon as I find him."

"Did you say something, Annette?" Reno Tanner asked.

The Hideaway's manager laughed as she gave his arm a grandmotherly pat. Reno had known the diminutive, silver-haired woman for over half of his thirty-four years. Their relationship was close and comfortable, far more than employer and employee, and the fact that the sixtyish Annette seemed to grow younger by the day never ceased to amaze him

"Yes, dear," she whispered. "I said, 'You hate tail parties. Don't you have anything better to do night?' And then I asked, 'Why, at seven o'clo ning, are you out to lunch?' And *then* I said—"

"Sorry, I was distracted." With his glass of bourbon and water Reno gestured beyond the far end of the oak bar. "Who's that woman?"

Ever since he'd entered the lounge—intending to talk with Annette about the real-estate fiasco he'd agreed to let her set up for him for the following week—his attention had been riveted to the statuesque woman standing across the crowded room with a group of four other guests. Predinner cocktails were a nightly ritual at the Hideaway, and people dressed in a wide range of clothing: anything from the Western apparel he had on to the after-five number the woman across the room was wearing. But for all it mattered, Reno decided, she could have shown up draped in an old flour sack. Against her style, her striking good looks and sophistication, no one else stood a chance.

"Which one?" Annette turned her attention to the small group, all sporting the white-on-black name tags that identified them as guests. "Oh," she commented, her voice teasing as she asked, "you mean the curvaceous, dark-haired woman in the green cocktail dress?"

"Yeah." *That's not a dress,* Reno added mentally. *It's more like a weapon.* The front of it was enticingly modest—enough to kick a man's imagination into gear—but when she'd turned to the side a moment before, he had noticed the dress was virtually backless. And his imagination shifted into overdrive.

"She must have checked in this afternoon," Annette said. "I don't recognize her."

"Alone?" Reno caught the woman's eye and smiled at her as she looked his way. She smiled briefly, then went back to her conversation with the quartet of elderly people—two married couples who'd been annual visitors for a number of years. "I mean, did she check in alone?"

"I'm not sure. I've been handling various crises since lunchtime, so I haven't even looked over the new arrivals' registration cards. When we're through here, though, I'll make it a point to welcome her."

"Don't bother." He realized the woman's brief smile had probably been one of friendliness, maybe one of mild feminine interest. But he wondered if it could have held something ⁓r to promise. Or invitation. Probably just his overzealous imagination. "I know you've been busy, Annette. Why don't I play host for a change?"

"Okay, Reno," the guest ranch's manager stated flatly. "I give."

Still staring at the woman across the room, Reno had a sudden urge to take her arm and lead her out onto the veranda, to touch the silky-looking chestnut waves that brushed the top of her bare, perfect shoulders. "Hmm?"

Annette tilted her head and glanced up at her boss, smiling slyly. "I've never known you to take such an active interest in any one guest. Is she the reason you're here?"

"What?" After a few seconds, when Annette's words had registered, Reno tried to recall his original purpose.

"No," he said at last, "I wanted to talk about the developers who'll be here next week." His gaze, diverted for only a moment, roamed back to the woman across the lounge. He found himself wondering if her skin was as smooth as he imagined it would be, if she would taste even half as good as she looked.

"Great!" Annette commented, interrupting his thoughts. "I take it you've read the bios I worked up on them, then."

"No. The file's on my desk, but I haven't had a chance to look at it yet."

"And whatever happened to your usual philosophy: no time like the present?"

"Why don't we talk about this tomorrow morning, Annette," he asked distractedly, "around ten, ten-thirty? Those bios have waited this long. I think they can wait a little longer, don't you?"

"Fine, dear. No time like the future."

He heard Annette's wry answer as he headed for the bar, stopping to set down his half-empty glass before he moved toward the group of five.

Reno extended his hand and greeted each of the four older people. At last he turned to the woman in the emerald-green dress. Her appearance was even more regal up close, yet there seemed to be no attitude of snobbery about her. Nothing that said, "You can look, but don't touch."

"I don't believe we've met," he said, clasping her hand in both of his. "I'm Reno."

He kept his hold on her, reluctant to let go as he enjoyed the stark contrast between the firmness of her handshake and the softness of her skin. "Welcome to the Hideaway," he added. "I hope you're enjoying your stay with us."

"Yes, I am." Her eyes glanced at their hands, almost hesitantly, and then back up at him. "I'm Roberta Powell."

The color of her eyes, he guessed, would have to be called hazel. But they gave a whole new meaning to the word. Next to her dark, chestnut hair, the light amber shade of her eyes was startlingly perfect. And the green flecks in them were... That dress, he decided, had to have been made to show off their brilliance.

Despite her stature and the high heels she wore, she was still several inches shy of his six foot three. But he liked the way she kept her head held high and her chin lifted. He liked the way her line of sight moved back up to his and stayed, unwavering.

"Is it Ms. Powell?" he asked point-blank. "Or Mrs.?"

"Neither one, actually. It's Miss Powell. And you?"

"Divorced, actually." Smiling, he managed to curb an impulse to wink.

Her eyes widened, registering a look of surprise, and Reno's smile broadened as he watched her cheeks take on a vivid shade of pink.

"I mean, your name. You're Mr.—?"

"Please. Call me Reno." There was a certain, unexplainable quality about her, a look of almost shy curiosity coupled with a warmth that seemed to be waiting just beneath the surface. If he had to sum it up in words he would have to say she looked somewhat reluctant. And at the same time, both interesting and interested.

"We're very informal around here," Reno continued. Finally releasing her slender hand, he gestured toward his blue-for-staff name tag. "First-name basis, remember? Why don't I call you Bobbie?"

Yes, he reaffirmed silently. Even though her demeanor spelled worldliness, there was an air of youthful innocence about her—a naive innocence, maybe?—that made Bobbie suit her much better than Roberta. This woman, he decided, was definitely a study in contradictions.

"No one but my..."

Her voice trailed off for a moment, and she touched the corner of her mouth with the tip of her tongue. The movement lasted only a split second, but Reno wondered if she had any idea how appealing, how sexy and inviting she looked.

"Yes," she finally answered, that soft, radiant smile back again. "Please call me Bobbie, Reno. I think I'd like that."

No, he decided, she didn't realize how sexy and inviting she looked. And the fact that she didn't realize it made her that much more appealing.

Reno glanced to the right, noticing the two older couples had disappeared and wondering when they'd left. Only a dozen or so people remained in the once-packed lounge.

"Will you join me for dinner, Bobbie?"

"Thank you, but no," she answered quickly. "I've decided to forgo dinner in favor of a good night's sleep." She took a small, backward step. "I had a long drive today, and I'm anxious to see the ranch. Is the stable open early in the morning? At say... seven-thirty?"

"Seven-thirty's no problem," he answered, wishing she hadn't stepped back from him, hoping she'd move closer so that he could take in more of the sheer, flowery fragrance drifting in the air around her.

"Wonderful," she said, smiling. "Good night, Reno."

"Night, Bobbie."

He no sooner let the words go than she turned and vanished, leaving him trying to figure out the conflicting messages he'd gotten from her. He could've sworn she'd searched his hand for a wedding ring, and her statement about being single wasn't exactly subtle—yet she'd been shocked when he'd come back with his own marital status. She had turned down his dinner invitation almost before he'd asked, but then she'd plainly told him when and where he could find her the following morning.

Reno shoved his fingertips into the front pockets of his Levi's and headed for the lobby. Once there, he crossed to the far end, turned a corner and passed through the door marked Private.

Walking beyond the offices that lined the hallway, he stopped in front of the elevator. His hand moved to the recessed key-pad on the wall to the right, and as soon as he punched in the correct series of numbers, the double doors glided open.

Yeah, he decided, stepping inside. The woman he'd just met was definitely intriguing. When it came to Miss Bobbie Powell, there was only one thing Reno Tanner knew for sure: that he couldn't be sure of anything.

When the elevator came to a stop on the second floor, Reno walked down the hall to his office. Not bothering to shut the door behind him, since the entire upper floor was his personal domain, he took his place behind the huge, custom-made oak desk that had belonged to his granddad, then his dad, and now him.

Still puzzling over Bobbie's actions, he raked his fingers through his dark hair and then leaned back against his clasped hands. He crossed his ankles as he propped his feet on the corner of the desk, resting his boots on a stack of papers to avoid scratching the well-tended luster of the desktop.

Out of the corner of his eye, he spotted the red file folder Annette had left on his desk days ago. And she'd been bugging him to read it ever since.

His gaze fixed on the set of longhorns mounted on the wall, Reno let out a long, weary sigh. As far as Annette was concerned, he'd made no secret of how much he dreaded the upcoming week's visitors. He'd rather have five days of digging fence-post holes than five days with those real-estate developers hovering around his property like a flock of hungry vultures. Land had no meaning to those people.

No meaning at all, he reminded himself for the umpteenth time, except for its obvious commercial value and the resultant boost to their commissions. That alone was enough to keep his instinctive resentment toward them alive and festering.

Leaning forward, he picked up the folder and noticed yet another of Annette's notes clipped to the front of the file. The notation started out with, "I think you'll be pleased with the six I've selected."

Pleased? he thought as a short, bitter laugh escaped him. True, he appreciated Annette's diligence and sincere effort.

She'd insisted on taking care of all the initial work: gathering names and qualifications, narrowing the field to six and then doing the actual inviting. Yeah. As always, he was pleased with Annette. But he damned sure didn't have to be pleased with the situation or the people themselves.

They didn't belong here, he told himself, settling back and crossing his ankles again. They wouldn't fit in. He'd be willing to bet not one of them had ever worn a pair of old blue jeans or seen a roundup except in a cowboy movie. Or ridden anything more spirited than an exercise bike. *Hell, they probably didn't even sweat when they did that.* He could just visualize them: the men wearing freshly pressed summer suits, the women impeccably outfitted except for their sensible walking shoes....

His eyes scanned the second paragraph of Annette's latest directive: "And about my offer, I've decided I won't take no for an answer!"

He couldn't help laughing as he thought of the way she'd been trying to coax him into letting her take charge of the developers once they arrived Monday. He had to admit it was right down Annette's alley; nevertheless, this was his problem and he would see it through.

Reno smiled at her signature on the note: Aunt Ann, the term of endearment he sometimes used for her. Although she'd been his mother's dearest childhood friend rather than her sister, Annette had always seemed like an aunt. And even though he hadn't met her until he was in his teens, they had always shared a special fondness for each other.

He could still remember his initial impression of her. Even then he'd towered above her, and because of her size and her prematurely gray hair, she had reminded him of a tiny angel wearing a silver halo. But he'd soon discovered that despite her demure appearance and a heart of gold, Annette had the soul, constitution and stamina of a drill sergeant.

Balancing the folder across his thighs, Reno opened the file and frowned as he went through the reflex action of unsnapping his cuffs and rolling up his shirtsleeves. Then he glanced at the top sheet of paper. The first bio pertained to some woman from Houston.

The fact was, whether the six developers were men or women or an odd assortment of both, he didn't want them on his ranch. It was that simple.

Unfortunately, he reminded himself, it couldn't be avoided.

Reno leaned against his hands again, tilting the big swivel chair. The only thing left to hope for now was that one of the six developers could come up with a reasonable proposal, an idea to market the parcels in a way that would do justice to the land itself as well as everyone involved. If that didn't happen, he wouldn't sell. He would simply... what?

That was what really irked him: the fact that he might be forced into taking another even less desirable route. The fact that he would soon be at the mercy of six people who, for all he knew, might be altogether merciless.

Because Reno had grown accustomed to having complete control over whatever was his, this whole proposition rubbed him the wrong way.

He flipped to the second page in the file. Another woman, he noticed, this one with a San Antonio address.

Reno shook his head and laughed as his mind conjured up another vision: Annette—appearing meek and angelic—in front of a row of six unsuspecting women, each carrying a handbag stuffed with fat commissions, each decked out in a stylish suit and a pair of tan clodhoppers....

Shaking off the vision, he slapped the folder shut. Why *not* let Annette ramrod the festivities? he asked himself. She'd have the nebulous half-dozen whipped into shape in no time, and it would probably serve them right.

And besides that, Reno thought as he abruptly lifted his eyebrows and smiled, as of first thing in the morning, he just might have better things to do with his time. Much better things.

Yeah, he decided, pitching the file into a desk drawer. He would talk it over with Annette when she came by tomorrow morning, and if she was still enthusiastic about taking over, he'd let her do just that. He could hold his initial meeting as soon as the developers arrived, go over his general objectives and turn them loose. Then he'd be able to devote some energy to other, more interesting projects—depending on how long

Bobbie was planning to stay. Lord knows he needed a diversion.

Maybe the upcoming week wasn't going to be so bad after all, Reno decided. When it came to the perplexing Miss Powell, he realized there were actually two things he could be sure of: what he was going to do now, and where he'd be at seven-thirty in the morning.

Picking up the telephone, he punched the extension for the front desk and asked the clerk to dictate the information he needed from her registration card. Checked in today; approximate length of stay, one week.

Perfect, he told himself. Couldn't be better.

Reno pressed the numbers for room service. Smiling, he recalled the expression he'd heard his granddad use more times than one. *If you can't get in the front door, go around to the back.*

Chapter Two

"But I didn't order room service," Roberta said. "There must be some mistake."

"No, ma'am." A freckle-faced, uniformed teenager stood on the porch outside her cabin, a large tray poised on his shoulder. "Compliments of the Hideaway."

"Well, how nice." She ushered him into the sitting area, a room that would have to be called the parlor. For all its rustic charm, her private bungalow was surprisingly elegant.

As he placed the tray on the coffee table, Roberta thanked him and reached for her wallet. But he held up his hand, refusing the tip she extended.

"My pleasure, ma'am. Enjoy your dinner."

"I'm sure I will," she answered, watching him head for the door. "It smells wonderful."

"Yeah," the boy said, grinning from ear to ear. "We've got the best cook in the state." The gangly redhead stood with his hand on the doorknob. He blushed as he added, "'Course, she's my mom. But that's the truth—I swear."

"I'll bet it is." Roberta smiled in return. "Thank her for me, will you?"

"Yes, ma'am," he said, beaming with pride as he left the cabin and closed the door.

Roberta lifted the silver domes one by one, taking in each delicious aroma. The Hideaway was known for pampering its visitors: nonetheless, she wondered who was responsible for sending the multicourse meal.

Remembering the table assignment she'd received while checking in, Roberta realized what must have happened. The waiters probably made a practice of sending trays to guests who were absent from the dining room.

That was more than likely the explanation. But she preferred to let her imagination conjure up a more exciting alternative. Foolish as it seemed, she wanted to think the handsome cowboy she'd met only an hour before had something to do with sending her the lavish meal. After leaving the cocktail party she had returned to her cabin, kicked off her high heels and started putting away her things. And while she'd gone through the motions of unpacking, Reno had occupied most of her thoughts.

Why had she turned down his dinner invitation? she chided herself again.

She had promised herself she would be bold on her vacation, even during the working part of it, and she'd gotten off to a good start by wearing her most daring dress. It was the only after-five dress she owned, in fact, that absolutely required going braless.

Turning to the side, Roberta glanced at her reflection in the mirrored wall. She sucked in a long, deep breath of air and stretched to an outrageously straight posture. Not bad, she thought, for a mature woman of thirty-five.

Roberta released her breath in a rush, smiling halfheartedly as she reverted to her usual stance. Rolling her eyes, she turned away from the mirror. *Sure,* she told herself as she carried the tray to the bedroom. It was undoubtedly Reno who'd sent dinner to her; the man was probably captivated by women who turned down his dinner invitations, couldn't form coherent sentences and refused to wear bras even though they needed them.

Yes, she thought dryly, she'd no doubt mesmerized him with her charm and sophistication. In fact, there was only one portion of her fascinating half of their dialogue that she could remember clearly, and thank goodness she hadn't finished the sentence: "No one but *my daddy* calls me Bobbie." Boy, that one would have given him a good laugh.

She had to admit, though, that she liked the deep baritone of his voice—especially the way it sounded when he called her Bobbie. And she also had to admit that he was the most appealing man she'd encountered in years.

"Correction," she said aloud. Reno was the most appealing man she'd encountered in her entire lifetime. And maybe that was the problem. As soon as he'd taken her hand in his, her stomach had started doing flip-flops and her heart had seemed to jump straight into her throat.

She couldn't deny the fact that physical attraction was part of it. His size and bearing alone were impressive, not to mention that gorgeous tan and the darkest, most beautiful blue eyes she'd ever seen. But there was more to it than that. During their short yet seemingly endless conversation she'd felt as if they were the only two people in the lounge. For a fleeting moment, she'd even thought he might be feeling the same way.

Because of her silly schoolgirl reaction to him, and despite the fact that she was starving, she'd turned down his invitation, actually frightened of being alone with him in a crowded dining room.

Roberta set the tray on the bed, then started closing her empty suitcases and putting them away. Why she'd been afraid to be "alone" with Reno was exactly what had puzzled her for the past hour. She'd had dealings with plenty of corporate types, plenty of men who were sure of themselves, but all of them put together would have a hard time coming up with the easy, quiet confidence this one rugged-looking man seemed to possess. Reno was calm and direct, and for some reason she hadn't known exactly what to think of him. Or even how to act in his presence.

One thing was certain, she decided as she put the last piece of luggage on the closet floor. The next time she saw him—and she would make it a point to see him again—she would put forth her usual composure instead of rattling on like some goggle-eyed adolescent.

Roberta closed the drapes, then slipped out of her dress and hung it carefully in the large closet. Taking her new black teddy from its padded hanger, she held up the filmy piece of silk and lace and suddenly wondered what had possessed her to buy it. She'd made two stops before leaving Dallas: one to pick up a handful of Caribbean brochures from the travel agency and another to purchase this half a handful of fluff from the boutique next door.

She couldn't help laughing out loud as she tossed the tiny garment across one of the king-size pillows. When she couldn't even muster up the courage to have dinner with an attractive stranger, she reasoned, how on earth could she hope to get any use out of that sexy little thing?

Opening the dresser drawer, Roberta opted for a soft, thin nightshirt. Her wry frown changed to a smile of resignation. White cotton had always suited her better than black lace, she decided, and probably always would.

A sudden realization came to her as she pulled on the nightshirt, and her smile brightened. There was a valid reason for the way she'd been acting tonight. A valid reason for her lack of courage.

"Of course," Roberta said, grinning with enthusiasm as she grabbed a notebook and situated herself on one side of the huge bed. For too many years she'd conditioned herself to put business first, above all else. She should have known she couldn't mix business with pleasure. She would simply get this proposal under wraps; then she'd be in the right frame of mind to get on with her personal mission.

Crossing her legs in a lazy version of the lotus position, Roberta ate ravenously from the dinner tray in front of her. Between bites of succulent crab cocktail she jotted a list of what she need to do over the weekend.

Thanks to driving in along the ranch's main road instead of using the Hideaway's direct entrance, she had already seen a lot of the Diamond T. The ranch seemed to be totally self-contained, including its own impressive airstrip. And despite the roughness of the land itself, there was a raw, awesome beauty about it, a magnificence that couldn't be denied.

Even though she was already excited about coming up with a proposal, Roberta couldn't help feeling a twinge of regret that any of the grand old ranch had to be broken off and developed. Most ranchers, she knew, were fierce in their determination to hang on to their land. For most of them, selling would be considered only as a last resort. They were diehards who'd sacrifice anything and everything else they had before they'd give up a single acre.

But there were exceptions to every rule, she reminded herself, and apparently the young Tanner heir wasn't the dedicated, responsible rancher his father had been.

Realizing she wouldn't be able to resist the slice of hazelnut torte, Roberta forced herself to leave more than half the dinner uneaten. She moved the tray onto the luggage rack at the foot of the bed, then picked up the dessert plate while going over her notes. Satisfied that her list was complete, she traded her notebook for the stack of travel leaflets on the nightstand and glanced through them as she enjoyed each and every morsel of the rich cake.

Returning the gold-rimmed china to its place on the tray, she spotted a note that had been underneath the dessert plate. She picked up the card and traced the handwritten message. The words were simple—"Sweet dreams"—yet they seemed too personal for a waiter.

Maybe Reno *did* send her dinner, she thought, smiling as she tucked the note into the nightstand drawer. And even if he hadn't, what could it hurt to let herself think he had?

Roberta covered herself with the cool, crisp sheet, opening the Cayman Islands brochure and studying each of the lush, tropical pictures as she snuggled deeper against the comfortable bed. Even though she wasn't sleepy, she closed her eyes for a moment. Long enough to visualize her perfect man against a Caribbean backdrop.

She could picture him clearly, as if she were standing with him on the beach, touching his tanned face, his firm jaw, his beautifully cleft chin. The color of the sea behind him was pale and washed out in comparison to the deep, dark blue of his eyes.

The warm sand brushed against her foot as she took one step back from him. He was tall and lean and muscular, with shoulders so broad they almost defied her to wrap her arms around them. And he looked every bit as good in swimming trunks and bare feet as he did in jeans and cowboy boots....

"Reno!" one of the little boys called from outside the stable. "Mom said we could ride till nine this mornin'. Is that okay with you?"

"Fine," he told the oldest of the two. "Just be sure to check in with her as soon as you're back."

The boys nodded as they took off, and Reno turned toward Renegade's stall in the far corner of the stable. He led the black stallion out and threw the saddle blanket over the horse's sleek back. Hoisting his saddle from its resting place, he slung it over.

"Easy, Renegade," he said, calming the restless animal with a firm hand. "Easy."

"Good morning, Reno," he heard from behind him.

He recognized her voice immediately: it had a soft, earthy quality about it, and he couldn't remember anyone making his name sound quite the way she did. Turning, he watched the morning rays of sunshine catch in her long chestnut hair as she entered the stable. If anything, he thought, she looked better in the light of day than she had the night before.

Reno tipped his straw Stetson. "Morning, Bobbie."

Green was definitely her color, he decided. Even in the icy-light pastel shade of the tailored blouse she wore now, those green-flecked eyes were gorgeous. With the sun behind her she looked more inviting than mint juleps on a blistering summer day.

Beyond that, she made a pair of designer jeans look more appealing than any fashion model ever could, thanks to the fact that she wasn't the straight-up-and-down model type. From what he'd seen of this woman, she had all the right curves in all the right places.

Smiling, he glanced at his watch. "Seven twenty-nine. Are you always this punctual?"

"No, not always. As I said last night, though, I'm anxious to see the ranch and—" She closed her mouth in midsentence, as if she were trying to compose her thoughts.

Reno turned to finish saddling his horse. "Just give me a second here," he said as he adjusted the cinch, "and I'll—"

The stallion stomped and whinnied, interrupting him.

"Am I supposed to choose my own horse?" he heard Bobbie ask. "Or is that part of your job?"

"Pardon?" He turned to face her again.

"I—I'm afraid I don't know the routine yet. This is my first ride here." She paused for a moment and then straightened her shoulders. "Do I tell you which horse I want you to saddle, or are you supposed to recommend one for me?"

He'd been mistaken for a stable hand plenty of times, and it had never bothered him before. In fact, as a rule he didn't want people knowing he owned the place. The Hideaway's first-name policy was intentional; it kept everyone on a friendly, personal level while eliminating the kind of complications he'd run into a few times in the past. But this time, Reno decided, he would make an exception. For some reason he wanted this particular woman to know who he was. And there was no time like the pres—

"I want to follow the rules, of course," she was adding now, "but if it's all right with you, I'd like to choose my own mount."

More contradictions, he decided, puzzling over the exact wording of her statement. Was she concerned about following the rules, or did she fully intend to break them and make her own?

"Actually, Bobbie," he replied, "it'd be best if I chose one for you." Moving into the third stall, he reached to put a halter on the dapple-gray mare. "I think you'll like Lady Lee. She was—"

"Wait a minute," she said, her voice half a pitch higher all of a sudden. "I hate to be a bother. Since he's already saddled, why don't I just ride that one?" She gestured toward Reno's horse. "Renegade. Right?"

"Right," he answered, then shook his head. "But no. Not a good idea."

He watched as she lifted her chin. Thanks to those expressive hazel eyes, with their flecks now looking more like green fire, he could sense her indignation before she spoke.

"But I'm an experienced rider. I'd really prefer a more spirited mount."

"Oh?" he asked, raising his brows. "And just exactly how experienced are you?"

"Well—" She inched her chin even higher in the air. "I'll admit it's been a while since I've ridden. But I can certainly handle something more than the proverbial old gray mare!"

"Fine," he said, "then you can have your pick of any of the other horses in the stable."

"Why can't I ride Renegade?"

"Because he's my horse," he answered, his tone polite but firm. "And nobody rides him but me."

"All right," she said quickly, her eyes searching the long row of stalls. "Then I'd like to ride that one."

"Blaze?" he asked, following Bobbie's line of sight to a mare whose very name belied her metabolism. "I don't think she's right for you. How about—"

"No," she said, moving toward the stall. "I'm sure Blaze and I will get along fine together."

Her spark of temper seemed to disappear as quickly as it had flared up, leaving him more intrigued by her than he had been the night before. She reached over the door of the stall, smiling while she talked softly to the docile mare and stroked her neck.

If she kept that up for a few more seconds, Reno told himself, Blaze might just doze off. He toyed with the idea of telling her the pet name all the stable hands used for the lazy mare. But for the moment, he decided—keeping an eye on her while he finished the last of his saddling—he would let her have things her own way. For the moment.

Watching the smooth, rubbing motion of her hand, Reno imagined how it would feel if Bobbie were giving *him* a few strokes on the neck, whispering a few sweet, throaty nothings in *his* ear. He grinned, realizing a nap wouldn't be anywhere on his list of priorities, and moved to slip a halter over Blaze's head.

"Okay," he said at last. "If you insist."

Reno saddled the mare and led both horses out of the stable. He reached for the stirrup strap, adjusting it while his gaze ran the length of Bobbie's legs. Not that he couldn't have gone by memory, but . . . Moving to the right side of the mare, between the two horses, he glanced up to see Bobbie's cheeks turn that enticing shade of pink as he adjusted the other strap. It had been a long time since he'd seen a woman blush as easily as she did, he thought. Too long.

"There," he said, tugging at the leather. "That should be about right."

Almost before he could get back around the horse, Bobbie had a boot up to the stirrup, ready to swing into the saddle. "Here," he offered, moving behind her. His hands touched her waist and then slid down to cup her hips. Yeah, he told himself, she felt every bit as good as she looked.

"Thanks," she said, her voice sounding flustered as she gathered the leather reins into both hands.

He stood there a moment, pretending to check the stirrup length while Bobbie pretended to be unaffected by the touch of his hand on her lower leg. Nice to know, he decided, that her voice had a tendency to give her away.

She fidgeted, then went on in the same, slightly higher pitch. "If you'll just point me in the right direction, I'll—"

"Against the rules, I'm afraid." He rounded her horse again. "No one rides alone."

"But—"

"No exceptions," Reno said, mounting the stallion in a swift, easy movement. "In case of accidents." He kept his eyes on hers when he added, "Snakes, mountain lions, things like that."

Touching the reins, he turned Renegade and watched Bobbie's green-and-gold eyes widen as she stared at the rifle he'd sheathed to his saddle.

"Well, I guess that makes sense," she said finally. "But I plan to stay out most of the morning. Are you sure you have time?"

"I'm all yours," he answered, smiling as he took the lead heading away from the stable.

Once his meeting with Annette was out of the way, he'd gladly spend another six or seven days with Bobbie. He was damned tired of being holed up in that office. Damned tired of poring over the books, his stomach tied in knots while he stewed over the financial problems that had started shortly after his dad's death and grown steadily worse ever since.

Yeah, he thought. When it came to Bobbie Powell and figuring out which direction she was coming from, he had to admit he still had a long way to go. But he had a strange feeling that if he was lucky enough to spend some time with her, he could at least get a decent start. In fact he'd be willing to bet that, given a week's time, they could both stay occupied quite nicely. Maybe they could even break a few rules.

As soon as they reached the riding path—a narrow, inconspicuous trail rarely used by the guides—he gestured for Bobbie to take the lead. He watched her closely, realizing she hadn't exaggerated about being a good rider. Considering the fact that she'd mounted the horse with ease, along with the way she held the reins and the way she tried to post in the Western saddle, a couple of things were obvious. First, she'd had plenty of formal training in English, not Western, riding. Second, from this angle she looked good. Real good.

His smile broadened as he added a third item to the list: he had definitely put those first two items in the wrong order.

It took a minute to coax Renegade into staying behind Blaze's slow walk, but the path would widen in another hundred yards or so.

Reno eased back against the saddle. Yeah, he decided, the leather groaning beneath him. They'd do things her way for a while longer. But as soon as the path widened, he intended to take the lead—maybe not literally, but at least figuratively—and in the meantime, he would simply lean back and enjoy the spectacular view.

Roberta grimaced and rolled her eyes skyward. Try as she might, she couldn't seem to prod Blaze into going any faster.

But maybe she should be grateful; with Reno riding behind her for the moment, at least he couldn't see her face.

Where was all that composure she'd vowed to flaunt when she saw him again? All Reno had to do was look at her, and she took leave of whatever senses she'd ever possessed!

If only he'd stopped at just looking at her, she might have been all right. But he'd driven her crazy with that wonderful, male scent of his. And then he'd touched her. Maybe she ought to feel darned lucky that, when he'd given her that innocent little boost into the saddle, she hadn't fainted dead away and fallen into his arms.

Then again, she thought, his hands might have lingered a bit longer than necessary. It would be nice to think his gesture had been more than gentlemanly....

Ridiculous, she told herself. She was being ridiculous and unreasonable again, just like she'd been when he started to saddle that old gray mare for her. There was no reason for her to get so defensive.

Where was her usual sense of practicality? After all, the Hideaway had insurance requirements to meet. No one was allowed to ride alone, and they certainly wouldn't want guests riding horses they weren't equipped to handle. How could she fault the man for following the rules?

The only person she could fault was herself, Roberta decided, for wasting her vacation when she'd promised herself she would look for a man. Here she was, alone with a man who seemed absolutely wonderful. And what was she doing? Instead of taking advantage of the opportunity to find out more about him, she was wasting precious time acting defensive about her riding ability and her age.

She smiled at Reno as he rode up alongside her. She'd heard the two little boys call him by name; more than likely they weren't his. But asking about them would surely bring on talk of a more personal nature.

"Cute boys—" she cleared her throat, trying to regain her normal tone of voice "—the ones who rode off from the stable just as I arrived. Are they yours?"

"No. I've been married, but unfortunately, I never had any kids." He tilted his head. "You?"

"Almost. But no."

"Almost?" he asked, a puzzled look on his face.

"I . . . I was talking about marriage, not children. What I meant was, I came close to getting married once. I've never come close to having children."

"Never?"

When he raised his eyebrows and grinned, she realized the implications of what she'd said. "What I mean is—"

"I know what you mean," he said.

His laugh was playful and teasing, not offensive, and she liked the sound of it. Glad that he'd jumped in before she could bury herself any deeper, Roberta found herself relaxing enough to smile back at him.

"Whose boys are they?" she asked.

"They're the cook's. Her two youngest."

Remembering the teenager who'd delivered the tray the night before, Roberta decided to find out once and for all if Reno had anything to do with sending dinner to her. "The cook?" she said. "How many children does she have?"

"Four. All boys, from nine on up to sixteen."

"Is the oldest one tall and lanky," she asked, "with coppery red hair and lots of freckles?"

"Yeah, that's Wayne. You know him?"

"I met him last night," Roberta answered, watching Reno closely, "while he was on duty. I hadn't ordered dinner, but he showed up on my doorstep with a tray from room service."

Reno's gaze stayed on her as he lifted the crown of his straw hat. His hair, even with bright rays of sun darting across it, was the deepest shade of brown she'd ever seen. She found herself wishing she could run her fingers through it, to see if it was as soft and thick as it looked.

After brushing his forehead with his arm, he replaced the hat and adjusted it. When he didn't say anything, she filled in the silence. "We only spoke for a brief moment, but he seemed like a nice young man. Very polite."

Roberta paused, giving Reno another opportunity in case he wanted to own up to something. But he only smiled and nodded, and she had no choice but to drop the subject.

Darn, she thought. She should have known. The waiters probably had an endless supply of those handwritten cards, all with the same intimate-sounding message.

They rode side by side, rounding a bend and heading toward a creek in the near distance. Roberta tried to coax her horse into a faster pace, to no avail, while Reno managed to hold Renegade back with what seemed like very little effort. And when Reno caught her stealing an occasional glance, she pretended to be enjoying the view provided by Mother Nature instead of by him.

What was there about him, Roberta wondered, that made him so appealing? He wasn't handsome in the classical sense of the word, yet a mere glimpse of him was enough to take her breath away. She watched him raise his head, the corners of his eyes crinkling as he squinted into the fiery morning sunlight. The way he looked right now, sitting majestically in the saddle, it was as if the whole sky...and the world...were his.

He was as rugged-looking as the land around him, and she couldn't remember ever seeing a man who looked so right, so at home in natural surroundings. But even against an urban setting, she decided as they reached the creek, that rakish grin of his could stop traffic.

"What's over there?" She lifted her face to indicate the scruffy terrain on the opposite side of the bank.

"The Diamond T," he answered. "This creek's the dividing line between the Hideaway and the working ranch."

Spotting a path on the other side, she noticed the shallow portion of the creek that led directly to it. "I'd like to see it," she said. "We can cross here, can't we?"

"We could, but I don't think you'd be interested."

"Yes, I would. That's exactly what I want to see."

"I doubt it," he told her. "There's not much to look at, unless you're wild about cattle and grazing land."

"But I am." Taking the lead into the shallow water, she turned her head to smile at him. "I used to visit my grandparents' farm when I was a little girl, and I always loved helping my grandma with the milking."

Reno's look appeared to be one of disbelief.

"Really," she assured him. "They had two cows."

"I'm talking about herd after herd of beef cattle. That's not exactly the same as a couple of milk— Watch it, Bobbie!"

"What?" Roberta turned her head, facing forward just in time to realize what was happening. Blaze had moved into a lope, at last, only to be heading enthusiastically for deep water.

Pulling at the reins didn't do any good. She managed to get out of the saddle, landing feetfirst in the creek just before Blaze plunged into the water beyond. The huge animal set off waves that sent Roberta rocking back, and the cool water splashed her face as she ended up on her bottom.

"Oh," she groaned, wiping her eyes before she tried to stand up. But her struggling was futile—thanks to drenched jeans and full boots—and she finally sat back, crossing her arms while the water lapped around her breasts. She looked behind her, at the horse wallowing happily in the creek, and then back at Reno.

"I take it you're all right," he stated. In the couple of seconds her fall had taken, he had dismounted and was already pulling off his boots.

"Yes," she answered, "I'm fine." He started to remove his socks, taking what seemed an eternity, and she noticed the grin on his face. No, she decided, that was a smirk! It would've been embarrassing enough if this had happened to her in private, but with him here laughing at her...

"I'm just fine," she repeated. "No thanks to you, I might add." Glaring at him, she flung out one arm and pointed behind her. "That—that animal is nothing but a lazy nag! Why didn't you warn me about her?"

"I tried." He stopped his chore midsock and stood up straight as he looked her in the eye. "If you'll remember, I told you she wasn't right for you. But you were hell-bent on riding her."

"Hell-bent?" she asked, her tone incredulous as she clasped her arms in front of her again. "That's going a little far, don't you think? All I liked about her was her name, for heaven's sake. And come to find out, even that's a joke! How on earth can you call her Blaze?"

"Most of us don't," he said, tossing aside his sock. "If I'd thought it would do any good, I would've told you what we call her."

"And what exactly," she asked, "might that be?"

He informed her of the mare's nickname as he hung his hat on the saddle horn and started into the creek.

"Days?" she asked, her voice rising as she watched him wade toward her. "Why? Because it takes her *days* to get you from here to there?"

"Pretty close," he answered, laughing, "but spelled the other way. It's D-a-z-e, since she's usually in some kind of a stupor."

"Oh, thanks," she exclaimed. "I hate to spoil your fun—but maybe you could stop laughing long enough to help me out of this creek."

He reached for her, but she kept her arms locked in front of her. "We won't get anywhere like this." She pulled back, wrenching away from his grasp. "My jeans and boots weigh at least a ton."

Without another word Reno turned and straddled her legs, lifting one at a time to remove her soaked boots. He tossed them onto the bank and then pivoted to face her again. "You want me to help you out of your jeans, too?"

"No."

"Then shut up and stop arguing with me. You've been fighting me—one way or another—since the minute we met." His tone was firm. Steady and matter-of-fact.

She clamped her mouth shut as he reached for her arms, lifting her up. They stood in the water, his strong hands still holding her as she slowly raised her eyes to meet his. They were indigo blue, even darker than she'd thought.

"You're right," she finally said. "I guess I have been acting . . . a little obstinate."

"No," he said, his eyes pinning hers, "you've been acting downright horsey." He pulled her closer, and she could feel his warm breath caressing her face as he spoke. "Now why don't we stop fighting? I think we can find something better to do than argue with each other, don't you?"

"I—I'm—" Her lips were only inches from his. She couldn't concentrate on his questions, not when she had so many of her own: like why, all of a sudden, couldn't she breathe? And exactly when had this strange, burning sensation started, this heaviness that was brewing from somewhere deep inside her?

"What do you say, Bobbie?" He smiled then. A slow, tender, searching smile. "Give me half a chance, and I think I can manage to get on your good side."

And how, she wondered, when they were standing in only a foot of water and she couldn't even breathe, could she feel as if she were drowning in the warm, masculine scent of him?

As he tilted his head to hers, she opened her mouth. But no words came out. And in the same moment, she realized that her heart must have gone haywire right along with her breathing. Her pulse seemed to be completely erratic, stopping one moment and throbbing the next.

If this was what dying felt like, she thought she would go willingly. Right now. Right here in his arms.

A jolt of awareness raced through her when she felt the touch of Reno's bare foot, under the water, as it brushed against the side of hers. His hands slid around her back, bringing her firmly against the length of him. Her arms moved up to circle his neck, involuntarily, and she threaded her fingers through the hair at his nape. It was soft, just as she had known it would be.

Feeling the warmth of his inner thigh, the heat and strength of his body pressing against her softness, she lifted her mouth to his. His breath was hot against her lips as he whispered her name.

Time seemed to stand still as he kissed first one corner of her mouth, then the other, then . . .

His mouth came down on hers. Fully, completely, branding her with the taste of him. And in his kiss she felt both gentleness and strength. Infinite tenderness, along with sheer, uncontrolled hunger.

He was warm. Wonderful and hard and warm. And when his lips teased their way to the curve of her throat, playing relentlessly with her exploding senses, Bobbie realized this couldn't be anything like dying. Never had she felt more alive than she did at this very moment.

He brought his hand to her hair, his fingers brushing it back and lingering, his thumb caressing the sensitive spot in front of one ear as his deep voice and hot breath whispered against the other. "Did you?"

"Did I . . . Did I what?"

He lifted his face, his blue eyes locking into her gaze as he smiled. "Have sweet dreams?"

"It *was* you," she murmured.

Watching his smile broaden, she felt her cheeks grow warm. He'd probably known she'd been fishing during their earlier conversation. But if he hadn't, he certainly did now. "You sent me dinner?"

"Uh-huh."

"It was wonderful. Thank you." Wondering now if he could look into her eyes and read her thoughts, Bobbie turned her head. With her temple she skimmed the dark, tempting V at the opening of his shirt. The hair was crisp, yet it had some of that same softness.

The pulsing beat of his heart felt so strong. So right. "And yes," she said at last. "I had sweet dreams."

Reno lowered his chin, stroking her hair for what might have been a few seconds or several minutes; she couldn't be sure. But when she raised her head again, the blatant desire she saw in his eyes made her realize that this moment, even though it seemed like an elaborate dream, was real. He was here with her, holding her in his arms, touching off feelings she'd never experienced before. Feelings she suddenly ached to explore and understand.

"Have dinner with me tonight," he said, the invitation more a statement than a question.

His gaze held hers as he smoothed her cheek with his hand. And the heat of his touch seemed even more intense than the flaming Texas sun.

"Yes," she answered. "I'd like that."

"Good. I'll pick you up at eight." His hand moved, tracing a slow, sensual path down her arm. She watched the muscles of his throat constrict as he swallowed hard and then took a slow, deep breath.

"Meanwhile," he added, sounding almost regretful, "I guess we should head back. I have a meeting to go to in a while, and you probably—" He glanced down, his gaze raking her body, and grinned as his eyes met hers again. "Unless you're planning an afternoon of water polo, I imagine you'd like to change clothes."

"No more water sports for the rest of the day," she said, laughing. "I think I've had my quota."

Before she knew what was happening, he had swept her into his arms and was starting toward the creek bank.

"Reno! Put me down. You'll—"

"Bobbie?" he asked, his eyes fixing on hers as he stopped dead in his tracks. "Are you arguing with me again?"

"No, but I'm too..." She stared up into his smiling, unflinching gaze, blinking once as she swallowed the air that had become trapped in her throat. "No. I'm not arguing."

"Good," he said, lifting his dark eyebrows. "That must mean we're making progress."

He shifted her weight then and headed for the bank, where he helped her put on her wet boots before he started back into the creek. Smiling, she watched as Reno went through the process of separating Blaze from the water she seemed to enjoy so much.

How could it be? Bobbie asked herself. Thirty-five years old and never been kissed.

Never like that, anyway. When he'd kissed her, nothing else had seemed to matter or even exist. She'd forgotten everything: her drenched clothes, her bruised ego after being tossed into the creek, her usual concerns about dignity and propriety.

Dear Lord, she thought all of a sudden. Her dreams last night had been sweet, but they had also been vague. Tonight, after this, she would probably need to be hooked up to a respirator!

Realizing she was holding her breath, Bobbie let out a lengthy, audible sigh as she recalled her brother-in-law's prediction a long time ago about her meeting a nice country boy someday. If this was what Joe Sinclair had been talking about, if this was what people meant by ''country living''...

Maybe the corporate type was all wrong for her. A three-piece suit didn't necessarily make a man—she knew that from experience. Years before, she'd learned it the hard way.

Perhaps that had been her problem. Maybe, because of what Harrison had done to her, she'd become leery of all men who appeared to be in his league. Maybe when it came to the high-rolling executive types her business brought her into contact with, she could never set aside her suspicions long enough to start trusting them.

She had to admit she'd let herself become distrustful of men in general, and it had all started with the actions of one man when she was fresh out of college and extremely naive about love. But the future was wide open. And thanks to thirty-five years of living, her eyes were wide open, too. She was able to weigh things more carefully now, able to use her sense of logic to judge a man's character.

And Reno seemed like a man who could be trusted.

Yes, Bobbie decided, smiling as she watched him lead the mare toward her. Reno seemed like the kind of man who just might be Mr. Right.

Chapter Three

Reno stared at the bio sheet in his hand as he pounded on Bobbie's cabin door a second time. Getting no response, he used enough force on the third try to raise the dead.

Still no answer.

He wadded the paper into a tight ball, flexing his left fist around it as he checked his watch. Almost five o'clock. She'd have to come back at some point, he told himself. And when she did, he'd be waiting for her.

After raking his fingers through his hair, Reno propped his right hand high against the doorjamb. Why the hell hadn't she been up-front about it? he asked himself again. Why the hell hadn't she told him who she was and what she wanted from him?

Simple, he thought, his mind supplying the answer he hadn't wanted to face: because his instincts about real-estate people had been right all along. Because a big commission was a big commission, no matter what she had to do to get it.

But it was one hell of a disappointment to think of her that way. A faceless, nameless real-estate tycoon was one thing. But he'd thought, until he spotted her name on one of the bios he'd put off reading till only a few minutes ago, that Roberta Powell was something special.

Well, she might not be special, but there was one thing he could say for her. She sure wasn't dumb. She'd shown up three days early, making it a point to be in the right places at exactly the right times.

Bobbie had dangled the bait last night, he decided, and reeled him in this morning. Appropriate, too, since they'd been in the middle of the creek.

Then again, it wasn't the first time a woman had played him for a fool. But at thirty-four, and considering the track record he'd had with women in the past, he damned well ought to know better. His most recent experience alone should have been enough to teach him something. During three years they'd been together, Glendelle had certainly pulled more than her share of deceitful little tricks.

If anything, he told himself as he sank down onto the glider swing and propped his boots on the porch railing, Bobbie Powell had done a better job on him than Glendelle ever had. Bobbie had played him just right. And maybe if his head hadn't been in the clouds, he would have spotted the signs: the green weapon; the innocent, hesitant smiles that always seemed to follow that come-and-get-me look in her eyes; playing hard to get just long enough to get him really interested.

Dammit, who was he kidding? He wasn't nearly as angry with her as he was with himself for being taken in again—and, worse yet, for still being interested.

Interested, he thought with a bitter laugh. The word itself wasn't nearly strong enough. He hated to admit it, but the last thing in the world he wanted with Bobbie Powell, even now, was a business relationship. But that was the way it would have to be. And now that he knew the score, he might as well start getting used to the idea.

Still flexing the muscles of his hand around the wadded paper, Reno bent his leg and set the swing into motion. The first thing he needed to do was to stop feeling like a sap. He wasn't the first man who'd been a sucker for a pretty face, and he certainly wouldn't be the last. From the minute she arrived she'd been dogging his heels, and considering the trap she'd set for him, he could hardly be . . .

Recalling this morning's scene in the stable—and the way she'd made it a point to interrupt him before he could mention who he was—Reno stopped the glider, wondering why the devil he should be mad at himself. Who'd she think he was, anyway? Some ignorant plowboy who was still pickin' the straw out of his hair?

Okay, he told himself, leaning forward and pushing his elbows against his knees. If that was what she thought of him, he'd let her think it a while longer.

Bracing his chin on his clasped hands, Reno decided it was just as well she wasn't around. Eight o'clock would come soon enough, and he was downright curious about her next strategy.

He'd be willing to bet he could call at least some of her moves. She'd probably be running late, needing help with the zipper of some sexy little number that was equal to the green one if not better. Dripping, no doubt, in that perfume that sent his hormones racing like some pubescent kid's.

Yeah, he decided, a smug, ominous frown on his face as he stood up from the glider. He'd show up at eight, the simple, unsuspecting country boy dressed in his store-bought clothes, to see just how far she'd take this spider-and-the-fly routine. And then he'd let her know Reno Tanner wasn't the easy mark she'd taken him for.

"Bitch," he muttered under his breath, turning on his boot heel before he bounded down the porch steps. "Sneaky, conniving . . . beautiful bitch."

Five till eight.

Bobbie turned toward the mirror, taking a deep, calming breath as she clasped her dress and adjusted its draped bodice.

She had to admit she'd never felt this jittery about a dinner date. But she wasn't normally running late, either. Being prompt was something Bobbie had always prided herself on, yet she'd completely lost track of time earlier in the day. After changing into dry clothes, she'd checked out one of the guest ranch's Jeeps. She had covered only a small portion of the

Diamond T, but between driving and stopping and taking notes, she hadn't realized how late it was when she started back to the Hideaway.

Dabbing an additional trace of perfume behind each ear, Bobbie studied her reflection in the mirror. The black dress she'd chosen to wear was simple, with a loose, wrap-front bodice that tapered into a form-fitting waistline and skirt. As she glanced at the dress's V neckline, which was low enough to be enticing without telling all, she realized she felt especially feminine. And with the silk-and-lace teddy underneath it, she felt more than feminine.

But not one bit ladylike, she added mentally, a smile touching her face as the thought came to her. If she had to put it into words, the feeling would have to be called seductive.

And uncharacteristic. And very, very nice.

As she grazed her bottom lip with a touch of gloss, Bobbie found herself thinking once again about Reno's kiss. And once again, she found herself wondering what he would be like as a lover. Surely making love with an honest, unaffected man like Reno would be different from what she'd experienced in the past.

A knock sounded at the door, and Bobbie shook her head as she picked up her necklace, a narrow rope of black silk with a pendant: a gold outline of a heart that would rest just above her plunging neckline. With trembling fingers, she tried unsuccessfully to open the rope's delicate clasp as she padded from the bedroom to the parlor.

She opened the door, her eyes busy taking in the sight of Reno as she stood back and allowed him to enter.

"Hi," she said, no other conversation coming to mind as she watched his tall, lean frame move through the doorway. He was outfitted in a Western-cut suit of the darkest shade of blue. Or was it black? She glanced from his vest to his eyes and back again. Yes, she decided. It was dark, dark blue. And with those eyes of his, he looked breathtakingly handsome in it.

"Hi," he said in answer, his gaze traveling up and down her body with an excruciating slowness that left her feeling self-conscious. "You look absolutely..."

Absolutely *what*? her mind screamed. Why didn't he finish the sentence? Instead, he only glanced from her stocking feet to the pendant dangling from her hand.

"You're not ready yet," he stated. "What a surprise."

His voice was steady, the same deep baritone. But there was something different about it.

"I'll only be a minute," she said, studying the smile on his face that now seemed to be guarded, trying to decide if it had been a hint of sarcasm she'd detected in his tone. "I hope that's all right."

"No problem," he answered. "I'm just surprised you're not ready. After all, you were right on time at the stable this morning."

Not knowing how to respond to his comment, Bobbie glanced toward the bar. "Why don't you—"

"Fix us a drink?" he asked, finishing the question for her.

"Yes. That would be nice, if we have time."

"Of course we do," he answered. "The night's just beginning, isn't it?"

"Uh, sure." Smiling nervously, she tilted her head toward the bedroom. "Well. I'll be with you in a minute."

Leaving the bedroom door open, Bobbie slipped into her high heels as she listened to the tinkling of ice cubes against glasses. Was it her imagination, or had his tone been bordering on patronizing?

"How does bourbon and water sound?" he called out.

"Perfect," she answered. "But make mine weak, will you please?"

"Absolutely."

Bobbie moved to the dresser as she continued to puzzle over Reno's odd behavior. It wasn't just his tone that was different, she decided. He'd been studying her closely ever since he arrived. And his steady gaze had seemed cautious—more watchful than appreciative. Almost as if he were the cat eyeing the proverbial canary.

As she tried to calm her shaking fingers long enough to clasp her necklace, Reno appeared with two glasses in hand.

"Here," he said, setting them on the dresser before moving behind her. "Something tells me you could use some help with that."

She tipped her head forward and to the side, gathering up her hair in a loose array as his fingers worked the clasp. He leaned closer then, his hands moving to caress her upper arms, and she felt the brush of his soft, warm breath against her neck. A delicious shiver of anticipation raced through her body when she heard him inhaling the scent of her perfume. Her neck tingled from the nearness of his lips, and a faint, guttural sound escaped from somewhere deep down inside her as she waited for his kiss.

It was slow, sweet agony... driving her beyond the edge of patience. Never had she wanted anything as badly, as urgently, as she wanted the touch of his lips against her skin.

"This dress," he murmured, "definitely has the desired effect."

With a nervous laugh, she turned to face him. "What?" she asked, her voice a mere whisper.

His expression had changed to a look of blatant anger. He stood before her, feet planted firmly apart, and scowled down at her as he spoke.

"Why didn't you tell me you were a real-estate developer?"

"What... what difference does it make?" she asked, more confused by his question than she had been by his sudden anger.

He caught the edge of her dress, his thumb and forefinger rubbing up and down along the black fabric that fell from her shoulder. "Not very professional, is it? Trying to seduce me and then—"

"Seduce you? Why..." Her chin shot up as she glared at him. "Why, of all the nerve. Just who do you think you are, talking to me like that?"

"You know damned good and well who I am, Bobbie." His blue eyes seemed to catch fire as he took her by the arms, backing her against the wall. "And I'll tell you right now, you're dead wrong if you think one little kiss is going to make a difference. I won't be swayed by that incident in the middle of the creek this morning."

Her mouth flew open again, but he kept on talking.

"In fact, I've got news for you." His words were quiet, almost to the point of sounding dangerous. "If anything, your conduct will sway me to *turn down* your proposal. This is strictly business, and I assure you—"

"Proposal?" she asked, stunned. Her hand flew up to her face. "Oh, dear Lord," she moaned. "You're not . . . You're Jubal Tanner's son? You're Reno *Tanner*?"

"None other. And you can cut the act, Bobbie. I'm not blind."

She felt her body stiffen in an instinctive flood of self-defense and rage. "What's that supposed to mean?"

"That means this isn't the first time I've ever been deceived." His voice was smooth and level, but his eyes burned into hers as he went on. "That means I know when a woman's trying to get me into her bed, especially when she wants something tangible in return."

She struggled to break from his grasp. But despite her sudden burst of adrenaline, he held her almost motionless.

"Why you pompous, self-centered—" Never! she thought. Never in a million years would she let that cad know she'd actually wondered what it would be like to make love with him. "I've got news for you, too, Mr. Tanner. One little kiss is all it'll ever be! I wouldn't share a bed with you if you paid me—in cold, hard cash or a *hundred* business deals. So don't flatter yourself."

Physically she was no match for him. But in an act of mental defiance, she lifted her face and continued to glower at him. "Now let me go."

He loosened his grip slightly, still pinning her to the wall. And his eyes still held their spark of flame.

"If you didn't know who I was," he asked, looking her up and down before meeting her eyes again, "then why the hell did you show up three days early? Without announcing yourself to me or to anyone on my staff?"

"Because, Mr. Tanner, I wanted to get a feel for the ranch. Because I wanted to pay my own way until I was officially invited to be here. Because I'm a businesswoman—first and foremost—and I take my profession very seriously. And regardless of what you think, mine is *not* the oldest profession in the world!''

When his hands relaxed suddenly, Bobbie broke free and took several quick steps away from him. She spun around to face him again, her hands flying to her hips. And despite the short distance between them, her voice rose to a near scream. ''I have a long list of clients because I'm good in real estate— not in the art of seduction.''

The last word of her statement registered as soon as she said it. Bobbie's jaw dropped open, her hands still on her hips and her tone incredulous.

''And just exactly who's been trying to seduce who? In the middle of that creek this morning, I don't recall holding a knife to your back! I don't remember forcing you to pull me out of the water and into your arms.''

''What did you expect me to do?'' he yelled. ''Let you drown?''

''Drown?'' she asked, her eyes wide, her words dripping with angry sarcasm. ''Well, you'll simply have to pardon my naïveté. I thought you were kissing me—not giving me mouth-to-mouth resuscitation!'' She stomped from the bedroom through the parlor and flung open the door.

''Do me a big favor,'' she added, one hand on the knob as she stood aside. ''If it ever happens again, let me drown!''

''Fine,'' he said, heading for the open doorway. ''No problem.''

''Good night, Mr. Tanner.'' She slammed the door after him, pushing her spine against it as she crossed her arms.

''Mr. Right,'' she muttered. *''Hah.''*

How could she have ever thought it? Bobbie wondered, her entire body trembling with rage as she yanked off her dress and flounced back to the bedroom. Her shoes and dress landed in a heap on the floor. She stood there for a moment, glowering, and then slung her briefcase on the bed and began searching feverishly for the letter of invitation. The Tanner heir's name had been mentioned at least once in that letter. She was sure of it. And if that was the case...

Well, she thought disgustedly, thirty-five might be a bit young for self-imposed, forced retirement, but maybe it was time. If she hadn't remembered a name as memorable as Reno, then she was obviously on the verge of either senility or insanity!

Spotting the blue stationery as she rifled through the papers, Bobbie yanked it out. Her eyes moved quickly from the signature up to the body of the letter. She was positive this Annette person had said something about— Yes. There it was in print, followed by a bunch of propaganda about extending an invitation to this marvelous business opportunity "in his absence and on his behalf."

Sure, Bobbie thought, staring at his full name. How stupid of her. She should have known the initials R.N. stood for Reno; it only made sense!

"Reno," she mumbled under her breath. It had to be a nickname. In fact, she decided, that was probably where he'd been during his "absence"—propped against some blackjack table in Reno, Nevada.

And to think. Only last night, she had actually decided the name was sexy. . . .

Tossing the letter aside, Bobbie snatched up her largest piece of luggage from the closet. Throwing the suitcase across the bed, she started filling it with stacks of folded clothing from the dresser drawers.

To heck with this marvelous business opportunity, she told herself. She could do without it.

And she could certainly do without a week of R. N. Tanner!

Thank goodness she had brought her own car. She could call her travel agent first thing in the morning, she decided, and then get out of here. Even the most primitive shack in the Caribbean would have to be better than this place.

"What an understatement," she muttered, dumping another stack into her suitcase. Compared to this place, Motel Hell would seem like Shangri-la!

The telephone jangled, startling her as she began tossing cosmetics into her overnight case. She stormed across the bedroom and caught the phone before the second ring.

"What?" she asked, her voice snapping into the receiver.

"Uh, ma'am?" a shaky drawl replied. "This is Wayne. You know, from room service. Um, the boss just called here. He said you'd prob'ly want some dinner, and that I should bring you whatever you want. He said—"

"You can tell your boss," she said, emphasizing the last word, and then stopped herself. Even though she was furious with his employer, there was no need to take it out on an innocent boy.

"Thank you for calling," she continued, her voice now under some degree of control. "But no. I don't believe I'll be ordering dinner tonight."

Bobbie waited while he tried to persuade her by reciting the specialties of the evening, her mind grasping only a few items from the list. She was hungry, but she would eat the bedspread before she'd accept a meal offered by Reno Tanner.

"Everything sounds delicious, Wayne, but no. Thank you anyway, though."

Bobbie hung up, a disheartened frown on her face as she sank onto the edge of the mattress. Why couldn't she be one of those fortunate people? she wondered. The kind of people who tended to *lose* their appetites when they were upset?

Her shoulders sagging, she glanced around the room and found herself shocked by its appearance. The top three dresser drawers were hanging open, ready to fall off their gliders. Her line of sight moved to the shoes and dress strewn across the floor, to the closet doors flung wide, to the messy piles of clothing that were half in, half out of the suitcase beside her.

She was normally such a levelheaded person, yet she'd just mutilated an entire bedroom. Never had she thrown her belongings around in such violent disarray. Never had she reacted to anyone with such a screaming, uncontrolled display of temper.

And never, never, she reminded herself silently, had she reacted to a man's kiss the way she'd reacted to Reno's.

What was there about that man? she wondered all of a sudden. She had never been one to react in wild extremes. Yet in the past twenty-four hours she had tasted emotional extremes that were unlike anything she'd ever experienced before.

Why, the smell of him alone was enough to... She closed her eyes for a moment and inhaled deeply. The masculine scent of him still lingered around her. Or did it? Maybe it was only her imagination.

Releasing a long, audible sigh, Bobbie shuddered as she felt the last tremors of rage leave her body. Seconds later, a pensive heaviness washed over her.

More than being angry with him for the accusations he'd made, she realized suddenly, she was angry with him for who he was. Instead of being Reno, the cowboy she'd thought she could trust, he was R. N. Tanner. Instead of being the honest, direct man she had wanted him to be, he was the irresponsible man she had assumed he would be.

He had acted exactly as she'd imagined R. N. Tanner would act, and she could never remember feeling so... So hurt and disappointed.

"Darn it," she mumbled, pressing her cheeks against her open hands. She hated to admit it, but she was just as disappointed in herself as she was in him. She'd been so proud of herself, so smug about being older and wiser. This incident only proved that her so-called sense of judgment was no better now than it had been years ago.

Bobbie caught sight of her reflection in the mirror. Glancing down at the black teddy, she frowned as she decided one of his accusations had been close to the truth. She hadn't exactly set out to seduce him, but she'd certainly been ready and willing to let Reno try to seduce her.

Casting a gloomy look at the teddy, and remembering how Reno had been suspicious of her early arrival, she realized she probably should have announced herself to someone. Considering the way she'd been dressed, and the way she'd been acting, she could see why he might think what he did. No wonder he'd threatened to...

Her mouth dropped open. Why, that man had virtually rejected her proposal—and she hadn't even submitted it to him yet!

Her back stiffened, and she grabbed her notebook from the nightstand. Flipping through the pages, she reminded herself that she had already jotted down some good ideas. Or at least the start of some good ideas.

In an attempt to think clearly, Bobbie took a series of deep, calming breaths. For the past twenty-four hours she'd been allowing her emotions free rein, and it just wasn't like her to react that way. She'd built her career—her life—around careful, logical thinking.

Why was she letting this man affect her reasoning? And run her off from a challenging job? In the past she'd had a couple of clients she hadn't especially seen eye-to-eye with, but that had never kept her from working with them.

Okay, Bobbie admitted. So she was attracted to him. So what? Now that she knew who he was, she could at least put that attraction into some sort of perspective. Or, if nothing else, she could at least ignore it.

Dropping her notebook onto the bed, she stared at the open suitcase. She couldn't contact her travel agent tomorrow, anyway. Tomorrow would be Sunday. And she'd be foolish to abandon a job of this size and stature. She had said it herself: she was a businesswoman, first and foremost.

Her mind set, Bobbie stood up and put on her dress. She would stay for the duration, and things would be just as he'd said. Strictly business.

She would simply march herself in there and let him know where she stood. If he still had doubts about her motives and intentions, she'd clear him up on those, too.

Beyond that, she would inform him that he'd be getting a proposal from her—whether he wanted one or not. In her entire life, no one had ever dismissed her from a job. And she'd be darned if she would let R. N. Tanner be the first!

Stepping into her high heels, Bobbie smoothed her dress and eyed herself in the mirror. She turned then, a look of renewed self-confidence on her face as she picked up the pale blue stationery and strutted through the parlor.

Stopping for a moment to square her shoulders and lift her chin, she realized there was more at stake here than a business deal.

She needed to prove to herself that she could resist the attraction she'd *thought* she felt for him.

Yes, she decided. If he continued to act the way he had tonight, a week with Reno Tanner would do her a world of good!

After a few days with him, she'd be able to leave for the Caribbean with no doubt in her mind about what she *wasn't* looking for in a man.

Bobbie switched off the lamp beside the door and then groped for the knob in the darkening room. Starting out the door, she raised her shoulders even higher, only to swallow a gasp as she ran into a wall.

As her eyes began to focus, she saw that the wall was blue. Dark, dark blue.

Chapter Four

After securing her footing on the wooden porch, Bobbie twisted away from the hold Reno had on her arms.

She took a step backward. "What do you want, Mr. Tanner?"

"I just want to talk to you. That argument got a little out of hand, and—"

"It most certainly did." As Bobbie waved the letter of invitation at him, she noticed a young couple passing on the walking path nearby and lowered her voice to a raspy whisper. "How was I supposed to know who you were? Your initials were mentioned exactly once in this letter. And if you had taken the time to write it yourself, neither one of us would've been in the dark from the very beginning."

Reno glanced behind him, smiling at the retreating guests before turning to her again. "Why don't we take this inside?"

Not waiting for an answer, he simply ushered her into the parlor, shut the door behind them and reached for the switch on the lamp.

"Look, Bobbie," he said, standing to his full height and keeping his eyes on hers. "I realize now that you had no idea who I was. But this afternoon, when I found out you were one of the developers, I just..." He crossed his arms over his chest. "I put a few things together and got the wrong idea, that's all. It was a stupid mistake on my part, and I'm sorry. I apologize."

"Fine. Now where's the rest?"

"The rest of what? I told you, I apologize."

"Considering your accusations, I think you owe me an explanation, don't you?"

He ran his fingers through his dark hair and started pacing the floor. "Yeah, I guess I do."

After a few seconds, he stopped and looked directly into her eyes. "I was furious when I found out who you were. The last thing in the world I wanted you to be was a real-estate developer."

Both stunned and confused by his answer, Bobbie wondered why Reno would be experiencing the same kind of reaction to her true identity that she had had to his.

"But why?" she asked quietly. "Why would you care what I do for a living?"

"Because I don't want any real-estate people here. Because I don't want to sell any..." He raised one hand. "Look, I was mad. My actions were completely irrational, I'll admit, but I was on the defensive because I thought you were trying to—"

"I know exactly what you thought," she said, her spine stiffening. "You made that perfectly clear. What I want to know is why you thought it. Is there something in my background that makes you think I'd stoop to such tactics? Something you know and I don't? Because if there is, I'd certainly like a chance to dispel any misconceptions you might have."

"I don't know anything about you, Bobbie, so there's nothing for you to dispel. I've already told you, it was stupid. I was wrong."

"But if you don't know anything about me, then why on earth would you simply assume I was trying to..."

Her eyes continued to question him. And in the ensuing moments of silence, Reno's expression changed until, finally, he appeared to be glaring at her.

"All right," he said at last. "Okay. If you must know, I jumped to the wrong conclusion because I don't hold much regard for people in your profession."

Maddened by his blunt, unreasonable statement, Bobbie had to bite her tongue to keep from taking her own turn at being on the defensive. But then she realized that it almost came as a relief, knowing Reno Tanner had some unknown prejudice against everyone in her line of work and not just her personally. She could deal with that. In fact, she decided quickly, at some time in the very near future, she would make it a point to find out why. And to change the way he felt.

For now, though, she would simply refuse to take his comment personally. And the best way to start changing his attitude about people in her line of business, she realized, was by showing him she was proud of her profession and knew how to act accordingly.

"Well," she said, "that explains it. And if it'll make you feel any better, let me assure you that I don't make a habit of mixing business with pleasure. Believe me, Mr. Tanner, if I had known who you were, I never would've let you..." Noticing the smile that suddenly touched the corners of his mouth, she raised her chin and tried to keep her tone even and unemotional. "I never would've let you save me from drowning."

Reno watched her closely for what seemed an endless amount of time. At last, though, he glanced over her shoulder.

"So," he stated, nodding toward the bedroom. "I guess this means you're leaving."

"I gave it some thought," she said, then realized it was foolish to try to sound nonchalant when the bedroom looked as it did. "But no, I'm not leaving. I came here to do a job, to submit a proposal to you, and that's exactly what I intend to do. In fact, I was on my way to tell you just that. And to assure you that in at least one area, we're in complete agreement: from now on, things will be strictly business between us, just as you said."

"Good. Apology accepted, then?"

"Yes," she answered, employing her most businesslike tone as she met the handshake he offered. "Apology accepted."

He held on to her hand for several seconds. And just as she was thinking she should do something to end the handshake, a knock sounded at the door. Startled by it, she pulled her hand back from his.

When Reno turned to answer the door, Bobbie turned the opposite way in an attempt to compose herself. Ignore him? she thought. If the erratic pounding and racing of her pulse was any indication, Reno Tanner was going to be a difficult man to ignore.

"Thanks, Wayne," she heard him say from behind her. "No. That'll be all."

When Reno closed the door, she pivoted to face him again.

"What's this?" she asked quickly. Still watching him advance toward her, she eyed the elaborately set cart, complete with fresh flowers, candles and wine.

"Well, I could be wrong, but it looks like dinner to me."

"No, thank you, Mr. Tanner. I think—"

"Is it my imagination, or do you always want things your own way?"

"Of course not. After what's happened, though, I don't think it would be approp—"

"Bobbie," he said, his voice level, "I may have acted like a first-class jerk, but if nothing else I'm a man of my word. I promised you dinner tonight, and that's what you're going to get." His words were firm. Authoritative. "Now sit down and eat. We'll call it a business meeting."

When he returned her look of stubborn indignation, she took the chair he held out for her. "Fine. I'm famished, anyway, so I might as well eat."

"Along with getting in the last word," he said, taking the seat across from her.

Refusing to argue any further, Bobbie took a bite of her salad as she watched him take charge of the wine. No matter what else she thought of Reno Tanner, she realized all of a sudden, there was one thing about him she liked very much. He seemed extremely sure of himself and not the least bit intimidated by anyone or anything.

Realizing he was studying her, she smiled pleasantly and took another bite. Seeing the piece of stationery she'd placed on the dinner cart, she picked up the invitation and scanned it, reminding herself that this was strictly business.

"You'll have to pardon me, Mr. Tanner, but there's—"

"Mr. Tanner sounds a little indifferent, don't you think?" He set down his fork. "We can be strictly business without being so formal, can't we?" With a tilt of his head, he smiled. "Considering what we've been through—what with me saving your life and all—don't you think you could at least call me Reno?"

"Well, yes. I guess so." She put the letter aside. "Is that your real name? Reno?"

"No. My real name's R. N. Tanner."

"That's all? Just the initials?"

"Yeah." After lifting his wineglass, he shrugged his shoulders. "Well actually, they stand for something."

"For what?"

"Reno, Nevada."

Bobbie's eyes widened as she thought about her earlier conjecture, about the possibility that he might be a gambler.

"According to my parents," he explained, "I was one of those late-in-life, unexpected blessings. Evidently I was conceived in Reno, when they were there on vacation one Christmas."

"Oh," she said, realizing she couldn't recall even one time when a man had shared such an intimate family story with her. And judging by the faint grin now on Reno's face, which almost looked sheepish, she wondered how seldom he shared it with anyone.

Bobbie smiled then, amused by another thought that suddenly crossed her mind. For all she knew about Reno, gambling might very well run in the family—but at least Jubal Tanner hadn't spent *all* his time at the gaming tables.

She fell silent then, concentrating on the meal and trying to ignore the way he seemed to be studying her while they ate.

Finally, looking for a subject to explore—anything to keep from simply watching Reno watching her—Bobbie glanced at the blue stationery again. "There's something I don't quite understand. If you have no desire to sell, why am I here? Why have any of us been invited?''

"Desire and necessity are two different things. I'll be needing some capital within about the next year, so I have to sell. It's that simple."

"Are you sure?" she asked, still reaching for topics of conversation. "I mean, have you considered other alternatives?"

"Like what, for instance?"

"I don't know," she answered truthfully. "But what about the guest ranch's contribution to the overall picture? The Hideaway has an outstanding reputation and, I would imagine, a more than healthy profit margin, too. Have you thought about expanding it?"

"My, my," he commented. "You are a businesswoman, aren't you?"

Bobbie straightened. "Yes, I am. Does that surprise you?"

"No, not at all. I'm just surprised you would suggest the option that was the first one I considered myself." He cleared his throat. "Yes, I gave some thought to expansion, but there were a couple of factors that caused me to rule it out pretty quickly. First of all, the idea seemed to be long on expenditures and short on capital—until somewhere way down the line, anyway."

"Maybe you ruled it out too quickly, then. Abilene's not exactly a sleepy little town, and neither is Fort Worth. Surely at least one of the banks there would jump at the chance to provide interim financing for a project of that scope."

"I'm sure they would, but I decided it was best not to give them the chance. That outstanding reputation you mentioned is the main reason I ruled it out completely. I'm convinced that the Hideaway's in demand because of the overall feel of the place. And when I broached the subject of expansion with some of our regular guests—people who've been frequenting the Hideaway for years—every one of them brought up virtually the same point. They have plenty of resort-type places to choose from, places with the same activities or more, but they come here to get away from it all. The Hideaway has a certain quality about it, and size seems to be a major factor."

"What quality?"

"A stress-free, informal atmosphere," he said. "One that's conducive to total relaxation." Smiling, he raised his wine-glass. "Hopefully you've noticed."

He was absolutely right, Bobbie realized. This morning, in the middle of the creek, she had finally started letting her own hair down, to put it mildly.

"Well," she said at last. "I guess I had noticed. Not on a conscious level, of course, but . . ."

"That's good, then. It's not supposed to flash like a neon sign. Even though we work hard to create it, it's supposed to be subtle."

"Oh, of course. Then that explains the first-names-only policy." The whole idea behind the dude ranch's philosophy was an interesting concept, and Bobbie was still piecing it together in her mind when she asked, "That's why you introduced yourself to me as just Reno, then, isn't it?"

"Yeah, basically. All the regulars know who I am, of course. But that's the general policy, so I try to go by it—especially with the newer guests. People I don't know. It's just less complicated that way."

"Less complicated?" she asked.

"Yeah. I've had a few problems in the past. A few people who sort of latched on to me, I guess you'd say, once they knew who I was. A few people who seemed to want more of my attention than I wanted to give."

Bobbie stared at him for a long moment, wondering if he was referring in particular to female-type people. If so, that would explain his remark about being deceived before, about knowing when a woman wanted him in her bed.

"Don't get me wrong," he explained. "I like that sort of thing as much as the next guy. But I have a ranch to run, so I don't have much time for it, that's all."

Bobbie prayed her eyes weren't reflecting her shock at what he was saying. She had never met a man who was this frank about—

"Well," he said, "enough of that. I'm just glad I have a manager who's more than capable of taking care of all that for me. Annette seems to love the detail and the paperwork, too— almost as much as she does the socializing part of the job."

Good grief! she thought. The man was talking about people wanting his attention for visiting, not for...

Swallowing the air that had become trapped in her lungs, Bobbie realized she had to make a better effort to keep her mind on business. A much better effort.

Reno tried to listen as Bobbie started agreeing with him, saying something about busy people having to be protective of their time. But probably since he couldn't even remember what he'd said to bring on her comments, he was having one hell of a time concentrating on what she was talking about.

How could he expect to keep his mind on business? he wondered. Instead, for some reason, he kept asking himself why the sight of her was so interesting. So exciting and inviting.

Here he was sitting across the table from an obviously savvy woman, a successful businesswoman who also happened to be decked out in a sexy scrap of a black dress that left just exactly enough to his imagination. And to top it off, for some unknown reason, she was blushing like crazy all of a sudden. He'd never seen anything like her before.

Despite the fact he didn't understand one thing about Bobbie Powell, Reno knew he wanted to know. He wanted to ask her about personal things like her love life, for God's sake, and her age. He would guess her to be somewhere around thirty, thirty-one. She was a dedicated businesswoman, though, possibly even totally dedicated. And in order for her to be so prominent in her field, he thought surely she had to be older.

Yet there was no man in her life—he was certain of that. After the way she'd responded to him this morning, in the middle of the creek, he'd bet his bottom dollar on it. She had said she'd never been married, either. And he wondered if that was simply the way she preferred things, or if maybe it was the price she had paid for her success. Which was the cause and which the effect?

"I'm sorry, Bobbie. What were you saying?"

"I was just saying that if you don't already have one, perhaps you could hire a good financial consultant, someone who could go over your assets and suggest—"

"I have another asset or two," he said, realizing it wasn't his own assets he'd been thinking about. "But nothing that's as easily liquidated as a few parcels of land."

"Yes, but sometimes it's difficult to be objective when you're looking at your own situation. Possibly an outside party could go over your entire package—personal and business assets combined—and come up with a more logical solution."

Hell, he thought. Why was he wasting his time worrying about going over Bobbie Powell's personal assets, when Bobbie Powell had her mind on the bottom line? On business and logic?

Beyond that, he was beginning to wonder why the hell she was going on and on about his alternatives. What was she trying to do, anyway? Make him think she didn't want the commission? He might not know much about the real-estate game, but he knew she couldn't have clawed her way to the top by talking clients out of multimillion-dollar deals.

Maybe this was her way of gleaning information, he decided. Well, if that was the case, he had news for her. If she hadn't done her homework, if she didn't already have a complete rundown of his assets, then he damned sure wasn't going to play right into her hands. What he did or didn't choose to liquidate was his concern, not hers. And the way he figured it, when it came to the financial problems that were now his, he'd already sacrificed enough of himself. He had to draw the line somewhere.

"I appreciate your suggestions, Bobbie. I've given a lot of thought to this, though." He pushed back from his unfinished dinner. "Logical is fine, but I've always gambled more heavily on instinct than I have on logic. And instinct tells me this is the quickest and easiest way out of my problems."

That statement, he noticed, seemed to have left her appalled. And, for a change, speechless.

"Even after the sale," he went on, "the Diamond T will still be the fifth-largest ranch in the state. And that's all that matters." True, the declaration was a bit oversimplified. But basically, Reno consoled himself once again, that's what would have mattered to his dad, too.

"Yes," Bobbie replied after another moment's hesitation. "Yes, of course." Looking even more businesslike, she glanced at the blue letterhead. "There's something else I'm puzzled about. Why are you letting each of us choose our own parcels out of the lot, instead of simply doing that yourself? It's a wonderful opportunity, of course, the kind of challenge I'm rarely offered. But I can't help wondering why you'd be willing to give us that kind of freedom with your land."

"I love every single acre of this spread," he answered truthfully. "There was no way I could single out the parcels myself, so I decided it was best for someone else to do it. And that way, too, each one of your proposals will be that much more custom-made." She didn't have to know that he'd done it far more for himself than he had for them. He'd elected to give the developers free rein over selecting their parcels, hoping in the long run for a broader range of choices for himself. Allowing the developers more freedom up front, he'd figured, would add to his own sense of freedom in the end.

"Well, I guess that's reasonable." Smiling, she glanced at the shaded areas that monopolized the miniature plat at the bottom of the letter. "And there's certainly enough to choose from, isn't there?"

"Yes, there is." He stood then, pitching the linen napkin across his plate.

"Thank you for dinner," she said quickly. "For the business meeting."

"No problem." After she accompanied him to the door, he turned to face her. "Tomorrow's Sunday, but it's the only day I have free. If you can be ready by eleven, I'll show you around the ranch." He stood there with his hand on the doorknob while she seemed to take forever deliberating his offer.

Finally, she took two backward steps. "Thank you, Reno. That's kind of you, but it's really not necessary."

"Why not? I thought you said that's why you arrived early. To get a feel for the place."

"That's true. But as you pointed out, you have a ranch to run. And I'm sure I'll continue to do fine on my own."

"I'm sure you could," he replied. "But as my granddaddy always said, no pain, no gain."

Her expression was one of sudden and complete puzzlement. And again, she seemed to be at a loss for words.

"Look, Bobbie. After some of the things I said to you earlier tonight, I realize I'm not exactly tops on your hit parade right now. And I don't blame you for not wanting to spend any more time with me than you have to—but you're a businesswoman. Right? And if you were to get a feel for how I feel about this ranch, I'd say that would give you a distinct advantage over the competition that's arriving Monday, wouldn't you?"

"Well," she said at last. "Yes. That does seem logical."

"There's that word again."

"What word?"

"Logical. Are you always so logical?"

"Yes," she said, raising her chin an extra inch in the air. "Yes, I am."

He kept his eyes on hers, and after a moment, the spark of stubborn determination seemed to change to a different look altogether. What it was now, he wasn't sure.

"I'll see you in the morning," he said then, reaching up briefly to run his knuckles along the softness of her cheek. "Sweet dreams."

With that, he turned and left.

On his way down the porch steps, Reno wondered why the hell he had done that. Oh, he knew why he'd offered her the fifty-cent tour—that was for his own benefit—but why had he acted on the sudden impulse to touch her? And why did he want to figure out that look he'd seen just now in her golden, green-flecked eyes?

But mostly, he realized as the cabin door finally clicked shut behind him, he wondered why all his instincts were telling him that she'd been sincere when she was spouting all that business about alternatives. That for some reason, she cared about how he felt when it came to his land.

Well, Reno decided, quickening his pace along the walkway. Maybe he'd figure it out tomorrow.

Chapter Five

Bobbie loosened her grip on the notebook balanced on her lap. Ever since they'd left the Hideaway a couple of hours before, Reno had been busy driving and answering her questions. And she'd been busy studying the landscape and making notations, but not too busy to see out of the corner of her eye the many odd, smiling glances he kept giving her from across the front seat of his comfortable, air-conditioned pickup truck.

Once again, Bobbie resisted the urge to look down and check to see if there was something wrong with her appearance. She had spent an inordinate amount of time in front of the closet before deciding on this teal-blue sundress, but . . . She wiggled her toes, smiling self-consciously as she realized that even her feet seemed to fascinate him. Or was it her sandals?

If only Reno knew why she'd tried to turn down his offer for this tour of the ranch. It wasn't because she was finding it difficult to spend time with him, as he had intimated before leaving her cabin the night before. On the contrary, it was because she'd been finding it difficult to spend time with him and keep her mind on business. Or on anything else that could be considered the least bit sensible or logical. In fact, she couldn't re-call even half of what she'd rattled on about over dinner.

Then, when she was getting ready for bed last night, she couldn't stop wondering about him—about three things, in particular. Why did he seem to hate real-estate people? And why did she seem to be taking that personally, even though she had promised herself she wouldn't?

Mostly, though, Bobbie had wondered how he really felt about the Diamond T. Some of the comments he'd made over dinner had seemed conflicting. If he truly loved this ranch, as he had said he did, then why would he be so quick to sell? To "gamble on instinct," of all things, instead of searching for another way out of his financial problems?

In the long run Bobbie had realized she had no answer to any of her questions. Before falling asleep, however, she had ar-rived at one important conclusion: despite the fact that Reno managed to leave her feeling totally breathless and light-headed one minute and either confused or infuriated the next, she had never enjoyed a man's company more. And because of that re-alization, she had vowed that today would be a fresh start for them.

Thankfully, Reno seemed to be in a much more amiable mood, too. She returned another of his pleasant smiles and then glanced out the passenger window as they passed a beautiful, wide, low-lying mesa, one of several she had seen on the prop-erty.

Yes, she reminded herself, today she was going to relax and enjoy herself and soak up the flavor of both Reno Tanner and the Diamond T. And by doing so, maybe she would be able to come up with a proposal that would help his ranch and, at the same time, help him see he was wrong about people in her line of work.

"Are you about ready for lunch?" Reno asked.

"Sure, that's fine. Whenever you'd like to start back."

"We still have a lot of ground to cover. If it's all right with you, I thought we'd just stop and eat at the bunkhouse dining hall."

"With the cowboys?" she asked, her eyes widening with anticipation at the thought of seeing the wranglers who actually rounded up the cattle.

"Probably not," he answered, grinning as he checked his wristwatch. "It's after one. I'm sure they're through with lunch and back out again."

"But it's Sunday afternoon. Shouldn't they be . . . gathered around playing poker or something?"

"No, I don't think so."

Judging by Reno's amused tone, Bobbie wondered if perhaps the men were in town, making their weekly visit to the equivalent of Miss Kitty's saloon. "Where are they, then?"

"Most of 'em are out cutting hay," he explained. "With all the rain this year, we've had a good crop. Several cuttings."

"Oh," she said, realizing that was far from what she'd envisioned. In the movies, real cowboys never did anything as mundane and unglamorous as cutting hay.

He pulled up in front of a cluster of modern-looking buildings, returning the wave of a young man who had just lifted the hood of a beat-up old automobile. "When the time's right for haying, it doesn't matter what day of the week it is."

Reno parked the truck and got out, putting on his straw Stetson as he walked around to her side. "Not exactly what you expected?" he asked, smiling as he helped her down from the cab.

"No," she admitted. "Not at all."

His hand at the small of her back, he guided her into the structure closest to them. The sparkling clean dining hall was deserted, and he nodded toward a closed door.

"Well, ma'am," he said, his grin teasing and his drawl exaggerated beyond the usual, "if you'd like to freshen up, I'll just mosey on into the back and rustle us up some grub."

He winked then and turned to saunter toward the kitchen, leaving her standing there on legs that seemed to have turned to putty. In the movies, she decided, real cowboys weren't nearly as virile-looking as Reno Tanner. . . .

By the time Bobbie regained her sense of equilibrium, visited the rest room and arrived in the dining area again, Reno was approaching her, two plates balanced in one large hand and two glasses of iced tea in the other.

"I hope a sandwich is okay," he said, directing her to a table close to the wide expanse of windows and taking a seat beside her. He pulled two paper napkins from between the ketchup and steak-sauce bottles.

"A sandwich sounds wonderful," she said, reaching for the napkin he offered her. Bobbie took a sip of the refreshing tea and then, finally, a bite of the thick sandwich with all the trimmings.

"Mmm," she commented. "This is some of the best roast beef I've ever eaten. Does this come from your own cows?" When he rolled his eyes toward the ceiling, she corrected herself by asking, "Your own stock?"

"Yeah. We're doing some crossbreeding, trying various combinations with the Texas longhorn." He gestured toward her sandwich. "It's lower in cholesterol, if you're concerned about that sort of thing."

"Isn't everyone?" she said with a wry frown, then added, "but I thought longhorns were virtually extinct."

"They were at one time. But now they're being built up again."

Bobbie listened with fascination as Reno explained how the longhorn—around forty million head of them, to be exact—had been responsible for the economic recovery of Texas after the Civil War, and how, only a few short years later, man in his infinite wisdom had "improved" them to the point where they were nearer extinction than the buffalo or the whooping crane. Eventually, money had been appropriated by the federal government for the purpose of preserving the breed, but only for their historical significance and heritage.

"Around the mid-1970s, though, breeders seemed to rediscover their genetic capabilities—the traits that had evolved to make them the survivors they were over a hundred years before." He listed qualities that indeed sounded impressive, even to a novice like Bobbie: longevity, hardiness, calving ease, disease and parasite resistance.

"Wait a minute," Bobbie said, holding up her hand. "All those things sound really important, but what about their horns?"

"What about their *horns*?" he asked, obviously questioning what she meant by the question itself.

"Yes, those huge horns." She held out her arms. "They have about a six-foot spread, don't they?"

"Yeah. More than that sometimes." He tilted his head. "But what is it you're wanting to know about them?"

"Are you saying those horns were evolutionary?"

"Sure," he said, his tone matter-of-fact. "Like anything else in nature: survival of the fittest, adapt or perish." When she still looked curious, he laughed and added, "You want it in official-sounding terms? Okay, then. They developed horns for protection, allowing the dominant males to propagate the breed."

"Oh, of course," she said quickly, her cheeks growing warm. He had stated it in an official manner, but there was something about sitting here alone with Reno, simply watching him while he talked about... Horny males propagating? Obviously, Reno thought of the entire process as business, but to her ear—or maybe to her way of thinking—he had managed to make it sound more sexual than official.

"Well," she said, deciding to change the topic to another area she'd found interesting. "What about this crossbreeding? You make it sound almost experimental. With modern science being what it is, I thought you'd already figured out all that."

"Not with cattle. Cattle breeding isn't nearly as predictable as the other industries."

"Like poultry, you mean?"

He glanced stealthily around the empty room, then reached over and gently pressed his index finger against her lips.

"Shh," he whispered. "That's a dirty word around here."

"Oh," she whispered back, briefly and involuntarily running her tongue across the spot he'd touched on her lips. "I'm sorry. I should have realized."

"But yes," he said in a normal tone. "Other industries like that are the reason we keep testing and experimenting. That's why we're sitting here eating these guinea-pig sandwiches, as the

hands call them. A lot of people are worried about cholesterol, so they're eating a lot more—''

"Of that other stuff?"

"You're catching on," he said with a grin. "Yes, and especially that other stuff that carries the brand names they associate with high quality. Anyway, that's what makes cattle
breeding more of a challenge now than it's ever been before:
getting Jane and John Q. Public to eat beef."

"People will never stop eating beef," she said with confidence.

"True, but that's not the point. Cattle raisers are trying to
find ways to get them to eat *more* beef. Experimenting with
things like how much fat it has to have to taste good, and how
much it can't have in order to pass dietary requirements for
cholesterol."

"And how much is that?"

"At least three to four percent, but no more than seven." He
gave her a look that said he thought she had a few screws loose
and rattling around in her head. Then he asked, "You're really
interested in hearing this kind of stuff?"

"Yes," she answered bluntly. "I had no idea there was so
much involved. So what can you do about the fat content? Get
the butchers of the world to trim more of it off?"

"They're doing more of that nowadays, anyway. But some
of us are working on ways to breed the fat out. And that leads
back to the beef from the Texas longhorn, which, as it turns
out, has less cholesterol than the other breeds." He smiled and
added teasingly, "You want an official explanation of that,
too? Stuff like F-1, or one-half brood cows, three-way cross
calves, complete products, that sort of thing?"

"No, I don't think so," she stated flatly. "I think you just
moved completely out of my league. I have no idea what any of
those things mean." She frowned. "It all sounds terribly tech-
nical and complicated. Not at all what I thought it would be. I
thought you just . . . roped 'em and branded 'em."

In an attempt to escape his beautiful, arresting blue gaze,
Bobbie looked out the window and watched the young man
who was working on his car. When she heard Reno laughing
under his breath, she turned her head. His knuckles were

braced directly beneath the cleft in his chin, and for what must be the hundredth time, Bobbie wanted to reach up and skim her fingertips along the slight, handsome indentation.

"What's so funny?"

"Oh, nothing," he answered. "It's just that you look so damned disappointed. Like all your illusions about cattle ranching have just been shattered into a million pieces."

"Well," she said, smiling hesitantly as she glanced around the room, "I guess I did have a few preconceived notions. This place, for instance, looks a lot like the cafeteria in my office building. I guess I expected long, rough tables and benches. And crusty-looking old cowhands sitting around rolling their own cigarettes or something." She pointed out the window. "And horses tied up outside. Instead, all I see is one nice-looking, clean-cut boy doing a tune-up on his car."

"If it'll make you feel any better, that clean-cut boy is my foreman's son. He's one of my best hands, actually." He nodded toward the youth. "And he is wearing jeans and cowboy boots. Does that help?"

"Yes," she said, laughing with him. "A little."

"And things look a lot different around here during roundup," he added, his baritone voice teasing. "We wear chaps and everything."

A vision floated through Bobbie's mind: Reno Tanner wielding a red-hot branding iron . . . with suede chaps tied over his long, hard legs, covering his thighs but exposing the button-fly front of his Levi's.

Her stomach did a sudden, unexpected somersault and Bobbie lifted her hand. She caught herself just in time, though; instead of blowing out a long gust of air and fanning her face, she gestured toward the young man outside. "He doesn't use that car to round up cattle, does he? Please tell me you still use horses. I'd hate to think even that's been modernized."

"Yeah, we still use horses. Along with a couple of things that are a little more modern."

"Like what?" she asked suspiciously.

"A few four-wheel-drive vehicles," he said, looking sheepish all of a sudden as he raised one shoulder. "And a helicop-

ter.'' He held up a placating hand. ''But the pilot's real crusty-
looking. Honest.''

''Well, thank goodness for that. I'd like to be left with a few
of my preconceived notions.''

He simply smiled and studied her at length.

Self-consciously, she brought her hand to the bodice of her
sundress, as if she could hide the part of her body he seemed to
be curious about. ''Is there something wrong with my dress?''

''No,'' he said quickly. ''No, it's nice. That color's good on
you. It's just that . . . Well, I guess I had a few preconceived
notions of my own. I didn't expect you to be dressed like this.''

''It's the middle of August,'' she said, laughing. ''What did
you think I'd be wearing? A tweed skirt and one of those blaz-
ers with my company crest sewn on the pocket?''

''Well, yeah. Something like that.'' His gaze slid down her
legs, all the way to her bare toes. ''I thought you'd be wearing
sensible walking shoes—'' he glanced back up at her ''—and I
guess I figured you might be a little older, that's all. How'd you
get to where you are? Being so young?''

Bobbie felt a sudden impulse to ask Reno just exactly how
young she thought she was—and to ask his own age, something
she had started wondering about over dinner the night before.

Instead, she decided to say, ''I guess it must be like one of
those genetic traits you were talking about.''

''How's that?''

''I grew up around big business,'' she explained, ''the world
of finance. My dad's a self-made man, as they say—an oilman
who started at the bottom and fought his way to the top. I'm the
eldest of his three daughters, so because of that, I assume, I was
reared more in the manner of a firstborn son.''

Bobbie smiled as she thought of her childhood days: early
mornings in her dad's study, weekends spent in his office. The
smell of fine cheroots and old leather. ''I guess it sounds rather
strange, but while other little girls were listening to fairy tales,
I was sitting on my daddy's knee paying rapt attention to tales
he always managed to make sound far more exciting to me:
stories of competitive decision-making, corporate shenanigans, that sort of thing.'' She glanced away, realizing that to
Reno, it probably did sound rather strange.

"Bobbie Powell," he said, as if he were running the name through his memory bank. "You're not Upton Powell's daughter, are you?"

"Yes," she answered with pride. "Do you know him?"

"No, but I certainly know of him. Doesn't everyone?" He tilted his head and laughed. "I'd say he's to the real Dallas kind of what Jock Ewing was to the TV show. A powerful man in quite a few circles, from what I understand."

She shrugged her shoulders. "I guess you could say that."

They went back to their sandwiches. And silence.

As they finished eating lunch Reno continued to study her, but he seemed to be watching her in a different way now. With even more curiosity. And Bobbie began to wonder if Reno Tanner was the same as so many other people she'd met. People who simply took it for granted that Upton Powell's backing was how she'd "gotten so far by such a young age." People who had no idea how hard she'd worked to get there on her own.

She had had enough of those speculative looks to last her a lifetime.

How long was it going to take, Bobbie wondered, to prove to the world that her father's power and money weren't the sum total of who she was? How much longer would she have to keep proving that?

Judging by the look on Reno's face, she decided sadly, it would be at least another week. And if that was the case, she wanted to get on with it. Starting right now. Right this minute.

"Are you ready to leave?" she asked, collecting her plate and glass as she stood.

"Sure," he said as he got to his feet. "Here. Let me take those for you. I know where everything goes back there."

"Thanks," Bobbie said quietly, intent on concealing the almost devastating sense of disappointment she felt. "I'll wait for you outside."

They left the bunkhouse complex, traveling north on the main road for a short distance, and then west, going on to unpaved roads that were far rougher than the ones they'd traveled before lunch.

After less than half an hour, Bobbie decided she would clearly go insane if she didn't get some fresh air. It was blessedly cool inside the truck's cab and unbelievably hot outside, but she had to get out nonetheless. She had to get away from that...that wonderful scent of his. Despite its lightness, it seemed to be overpowering her. Overwhelming her.

Bobbie turned around and eyed the gun rack mounted against the back windshield of his truck. If she knew how to work one of those things, she decided, staring at the two rifles, she'd use it right now to make a citizen's arrest. If it wasn't against the law for any one man to smell this good, then it certainly ought to be!

"Would you mind pulling over?" she asked abruptly, pointing to the clump of live oak trees she'd just spotted. "It's really pretty here. I'd like to get out and look around awhile."

When Reno stopped the truck, Bobbie almost jumped out. As she headed toward the trees, though, she realized he was right behind her. Her pace quickened—until she stepped on a rock and nearly lost her balance. And as soon as Reno caught her upper arm, she tried to pull away from him.

"Bobbie!" He kept his hold on her arm and spun her around to face him. "What's with you all the sudden?" He glanced downward and back up at her. "Those flimsy little sandals aren't exactly made for hiking. I was just trying to help."

Before she could say anything, he added, "You've been acting like this ever since we finished lunch. What's wrong?" His eyes widened, and he gave a short laugh. "Don't tell me you're put out just because I was *looking* at you?"

"No," she answered immediately.

"That's it, isn't it?" He gave her the most incredulous look. "I don't believe it. Just because we agreed that this was strictly business, does that mean I'm not supposed to notice you?" He took a couple of steps back from her. His hands moved to his sides, his fingers spanning the snug, faded denim riding low on his trim waist. "For God's sake, Bobbie. I'm a man. And you're a woman. And you're not exactly hard to look at, you know."

How did he manage it? she wondered. How could Reno Tanner make that simple, offhand, gently scolding declaration sound like the finest compliment a man had ever paid her?

"So what do you want to do?" he asked. "Put blinders on me? Have me arrested?"

A small laugh formed in her throat as she thought about the rifle she'd been tempted to use for that very purpose.

"No," she said at last, smiling softly as she answered his question. "No, that's fine. I won't have you arrested."

"Okay," he stated. "Good. And now, while we're still on the subject, why don't you tell me what else has been bothering you?"

"I—I don't now what you're talking about, Reno."

"Bull." His gaze seemed to be boring into hers. "I'm not wearing blinders, Bobbie. And if I'm not mistaken, you seemed to be warming right up to me when you thought I was a stable hand. But ever since you found out who I was, ever since you heard my last name was Tanner... Well, I've known a few women who reacted just the opposite, but never this way round. I don't mind telling you it's kind of refreshing, but I can't help being curious about it, too."

Bobbie stood there watching him, surprised by all that he had said and even more surprised by the array of conflicting emotions she was suddenly experiencing: relief, because she'd been wrong about what he was thinking in the dining hall only minutes before; sheer joy, simply because she was a woman and Reno had said he found her attractive; and shame, because she hadn't realized he might have had the same problems she'd had over the years—once people heard their last names and made the proper connections.

Something else was apparent, too, Bobbie decided. Her thinking last night had been at least partially correct. When he'd referred to guests who had tried to demand too much of his attention, at least some of those guests were women.

"Ever since you found out who I was," he continued, "you've been acting like it's all you can do just to tolerate my presence. So maybe you'd like to explain that to me."

"I'm sorry, Reno. It's not that." Taking a step forward, she placed her hand on his forearm. "It's just that. I felt it was important to be businesslike."

"That's fine." He covered her hand with his palm. "But we don't have to go to extremes, do we?"

"No." Time seemed to stand still as she enjoyed the warmth and closeness of him, the hard muscle of his forearm beneath her fingers, the feel of the crisp, manly sprinkling of dark hair. "No, of course not."

"Good." He let go of her hand, moving to lean against the trunk of a huge, gnarly old oak a few feet away. "What else has been bothering you, though? What is it that's got you acting leery of me about half the time?"

"I'm not leery of you, Reno."

"Maybe that's not the right word, then. Maybe I should put it another way." His eyes held hers as he said, "It's obvious you had a few preconceived notions about me. Or about R. N. Tanner, I guess I should say. Maybe if you tell me about them, I can dispel any misconceptions you might have."

It was a reasonable request, she realized, and worded exactly as she had said it to him only the night before.

"All right," she said. "It's nothing specific, really. It's just that I've never heard of a rancher who would willingly give up any of his land. I guess I just keep thinking that if it were me who'd inherited this beautiful old ranch, I'd do everything I could to—"

She stopped then, seeing the look of disbelief that was suddenly on his face.

"Are you tryin' to teach Granny how to knot?"

She simply stared back at him, her eyes questioning.

"Just an old expression," he said, sounding thoroughly exasperated with her. "One my granddad liked to use." He ran his fingers across his scalp. "I thought you were an expert in real estate. Are you trying to tell a cattleman how to run a ranch?"

"Of course not. But you said you love this place, and . . ."

"And what?" he asked. "Just exactly what are you getting at?"

"Well, if you truly love this ranch, and if there are other assets you could liquidate, it doesn't seem logical to me that you would choose to take the quickest and easiest way out."

Great! Reno thought. Just what he needed: a real-estate tycoon, a therapist and a financial genius, all wrapped up in one gorgeous little package.

Well, he decided angrily, he'd had just about enough of Bobbie Powell's easy answers and advice. In fact, he'd had all he could stand. "That's what I really hate, you know it? That casual, logical, analytical attitude you seem to have about all this." He glared at her as he added, "Land is nothing more than a commodity to you people. A short-term commodity, at that. Something you can buy and tear up and sell again, just so you can make a fast buck."

"That's not true!"

"Isn't it?" he shot back at her. "All right, then. Tell me. Have you got any idea what it takes to run a spread this size—any size—day in and day out? Year in and year out?" His fingertips jabbed his chest. "Do you have any idea of the piece of *yourself* that goes into a place like this?"

"No, I don't, but—"

"No, you don't," he said, interrupting her. "In the last couple of months, I've tied up every personal cent I have just to get this ranch back on its feet. When I said I had a couple of other assets I could liquidate, Bobbie, I was talking about personal assets. And I'll be damned if I'll sacrifice everything that means anything to me just because I've had to bail this place out of the fix my brother got it into, so why don't you just take your casual, logical advice and—"

"Your brother?" she asked in a whisper, looking shocked. "You have a brother?"

"Yes, I have a brother. And it's obvious you don't know anything about me—so don't stand there telling me I don't love this ranch, because I do." He reached up, kneading the tension in his tight jawline. "And I'll do anything within reason to save the bulk of it. Which is exactly why you're here."

Reno straightened to his full height, taking a couple of deep, ragged breaths. He turned on his boot heel, his tone even and steady as he said, "Let me know when you're ready to leave."

By the time she got to the truck and took the passenger seat, Reno had had a few minutes to cool down. His burst of anger had nothing to do with her, he knew. Because of his recent worries, both financial and personal, he had no patience anymore. Not for anyone or anything. He had asked her a question and then promptly chewed her head off for answering it.

His door was still open, but she shut the door on her side and turned to face him.

"Look, Bobbie," he said immediately, "I'm sorry for losing my temper. That was ridiculous and uncalled for."

"No, I think I deserved it." Her voice was quiet, and there was a look of genuine remorse on her face. "You were right. I did have preconceived notions about you. I had heard that the ranch was in trouble, and I simply assumed it was your fault. That was ridiculous and uncalled for, too, I know, but I'd like to think I would've used better judgment if the timing hadn't been what it was."

"The timing?"

"Yes. The invitation to come to the Diamond T crossed my desk on what you might call... an unusual day. A day when I wasn't thinking too clearly." Her frown was one of self-recrimination. "Nevertheless, I shouldn't have drawn conclusions about someone I didn't even know. Something that's none of my business."

"Still," he said, flexing his hand around the steering wheel, "I had no right to say what I did just now. No matter what I think of real-estate developers as a whole, I shouldn't have..." He lifted one shoulder. "I guess I owe you another explanation, don't I?"

"No, you don't have to explain. I know exactly what you think, and I guess maybe if I were in your situation, I might think the same thing." Her words were slow and deliberate, as if she were choosing them carefully. "It's obvious we've both had our share of preconceived notions, Reno. Maybe we should both try to set them aside now. Maybe we should just let our actions speak for themselves. I can't possibly know how you feel about your ranch, but... Well, maybe what you said is true of some developers, but I'd like a chance to show you we're not all the same."

"That seems fair," he commented at last. "And maybe I'll have a chance to prove that I normally have a lot more patience than what I've shown you so far. I've lost my temper with you twice now, but I'd like to think I wouldn't have—if the timing hadn't been what it was."

"You, too?"

"Yeah," he said, with a short, mirthless laugh. "I wouldn't have blurted out that business about Cal—my brother—if I hadn't been chewing on this for such a long time. Trying to come up with a solution."

For some reason, possibly because of his uncharacteristic behavior of late, he felt that Bobbie was due at least some measure of an explanation. "Cal's had some resentments toward me for as long as I can remember. So after Dad died, I intentionally stayed away for a couple of years, taking care of some of my own business concerns, thinking that Cal needed to prove himself, and that running this place would give him the chance to do just that. And truthfully, the ranch's problems weren't all his fault: the fluctuating oil market, too much rain one year and too little the next, on top of a few bad investments and a couple of problems he had with some of the personnel." He took in a long breath of air and pushed it out. "I don't make a habit of dragging my brother's name through the mud, Bobbie, so I hope I can count on your sense of discretion."

She smiled then and said, "Discretion's my middle name."

"Is it?" he asked, smiling in return. "Hmm. Roberta Discretion. That's almost as odd as Reno Nevada."

"Well, all right. Actually my middle name is Louise. Does that sound a little better?"

"Much better."

"And as far as trying to give you advice about running your ranch..." She glanced down at her folded hands. "Believe it or not, I don't normally make casual suggestions about areas of life where I'm totally out of my element, so—" her eyes met his again "—as my Grandma Louise would've said, from now on, I'll tend to my own geraniums."

"Ah," he commented, grinning as he turned the key and started the ignition. "That must be the infamous Grandma

Louise who lived on a farm and let you help with the milking.''

"It is. And that's why it was ridiculous of me to assume it was you who... I can't believe I gave no thought to the outside factors that affect any farm or ranch. Ordinary things like rain, for heaven's sake.''

"Understandable. Most people don't have to think too much about rain, except to decide whether or not to take an umbrella to work with them.''

"I never even worry about taking an umbrella.''

"You don't?'' Reno asked. His mind drew a vision: walking with Bobbie in the rain, the wind whipping through her dark, wavy, silky-looking hair.

"No,'' she said, then lifted her shoulders. "I just always keep one in the car.''

Did she ever do anything on impulse? he wondered. Maybe not, but there was definitely an impulsive, illogical side to her. He hadn't seen it, but in the middle of the creek, he'd at least sensed it.

"I've become too citified, I guess. Gotten too far away from nature.'' Her eyes took on a dreamy, faraway look. "My grandparents died when I was quite young, but I can still remember how much I loved spending time on their farm. I was their very first grandchild, and rank apparently had its privileges, because at times I was invited to spend whole weeks alone with them. And now I remember how important the weather was to my grandpa. In fact, that was the first thing he'd talk about when he came into the house in the evenings. I'd be in the kitchen with Grandma Louise—I always called her that because my mother's name is Louise, too.''

Reno listened as she inhaled deeply, as if she could actually smell the aroma of biscuits and apple pies baking in her grandmother's kitchen.

"Anyway, Grandpa would always put his arms around Grandma Louise and give her this wonderfully affectionate kiss on the cheek. She had immigrated from England with her parents nearly fifty years before, but she was still very straitlaced, very British, and she would always slap Grandpa's hands and tell him he shouldn't do that in front of the little one.''

Bobbie laughed softly then, and Reno remained silent, thinking that her grandparents sounded very much like his own.

She touched her lips and glanced upward. "Then Grandpa would lean over and hug me real tight before he sat down at the kitchen table and started giving his weather forecast for the next twenty-four hours. And even though his prediction always seemed to end up being right, I can never recall a time when that shocked me." She tilted her head and laughed again. "A child's trusting nature, I guess."

When—and why—had she lost that trusting nature? he wondered, watching as she suddenly cleared her throat, erased the smile from her lips and began leafing through the pages in her notebook.

He reached forward, adjusting the fan on the air conditioner, and Bobbie momentarily glanced his way and drew in another deep breath. She must be unbelievably sensitive to smells, he realized, recalling how she had done that in the dining hall, too, while she was talking about the way her dad had raised her.

"Well," she said, looking self-conscious as she lifted the notebook and turned it toward him. "I guess I should get back to tending my own geraniums."

It was strange, he decided as he turned the steering wheel and pulled out onto the road once again. No matter what they were talking about, Bobbie always managed to change the subject back to business.

Remembering what she'd said about being trained by Upton Powell, Reno wondered if perhaps this was her routine with all her clients. Perhaps she got personal enough to gain their trust, but it was actually all business. And gaining a new client was the bottom line.

For the time being, it would be best to keep that possibility in mind. To proceed with caution since this was strictly business.

And when it came to business, Reno told himself, as soon as he got back to his office, he was going to make it a point to find out what he didn't know about Roberta Louise Powell.

* * *

Bobbie leaned forward, reaching for another Caribbean brochure from the stack on the coffee table, and then tucked her bare feet under her sundress. After flipping through the leaflet she tossed it onto the sofa cushion beside her, where it landed in a heap with the others she'd scanned in the last hour.

How could she expect to decide on a vacation spot when she couldn't even decide whether she ought to get up and get ready for bed? And when she did, was she in the mood for a quick shower or a long, hot soak in the tub?

She reached for the rest of the stack, fanning it in her hands. Somehow none of the islands seemed as appealing as they had when she'd picked up the brochures a couple of days ago. In fact, the only thing that did seem appealing now was trying to figure out Reno Tanner. Ever since she'd decided she genuinely liked the man and had been dead wrong about him—ever since she'd gotten carried away and told him that story about her grandparents—Reno had been unbelievably quiet and pensive. He'd been polite enough, she knew, yet he had offered nothing more than concise answers to her questions about the Diamond T.

After their tour was over, she had hoped Reno would invite her to join him for dinner or a drink. Or even to his office to discuss the ranch, for heaven's sake. Instead, though, he had simply walked her to her cabin, standing on the porch only long enough to smile and say good-night.

Bobbie had gone to the main dining room a bit later, where she'd met a lovely, lively group of people at her assigned table, but— Hearing the knock that sounded on her door, she stood and answered it.

"Hi, Reno," she said, not trying to conceal her smile as she held the door open wide. "Come in."

"Thanks," he said, closing the door behind him as she started clearing the pile of travel brochures off the sofa. "That's okay, Bobbie. I have some paperwork to take care of tonight, so I won't stay but a few minutes." He picked up one of the leaflets she placed on the coffee table. "Going somewhere?"

"Yes," she answered, still intent on making the sofa look presentable. All right, Bobbie admitted inwardly, she wasn't trying to make the sofa look presentable. She was trying to make it look inviting. "I decided a few days ago that I needed to get away for a while. I was thinking about going to the Caribbean. I just . . . haven't decided exactly where. And when."

He exchanged the brochure for one she was holding in her clutches. After glancing at the travel agent's stamped address, he handed it back to her. "I guess this explains the bad timing, huh?"

"Well, yes. Sort of." Bobbie lifted a shoulder. "But that's okay. I've got someone watching over things for me at the office. I can still take a vacation after I leave here."

He simply nodded his head.

"I'll get right to the point," he finally commented, the expression on his face now deadly serious. "I just wanted to say I've been wrong about you. About all six of you, maybe."

"All six of me?" she asked, trying to lighten the atmosphere by laughing and glancing behind her, over one shoulder and then the other.

"Okay," he said, grinning briefly as he made the admission. "About real-estate developers in general. Some of what you said today made me start thinking I might be wrong. So I've been in my office, studying the bios I should've read a long time ago. And I have to say I'm especially impressed with yours, Bobbie."

Bobbie took a seat, smiling softly. Reno had just explained his earlier behavior, the behavior she'd been so puzzled about, and as she continued to watch him, Bobbie decided she had never known a man who could appear this strong and powerful and sure of himself while he told a woman he'd been wrong about her. About anything.

"I've seen your credits," he added, "the awards you've gotten for coordinating your projects to suit the environment, for enhancing the land rather than changing it or taking away from it. It's obvious you're not into bulldozers and . . ." He cleared his throat. "What I'm trying to say is, I've realized it's not real-estate people I hate. I hate what your presence here means to me, that's all."

When her eyes widened, he said, "What I mean is, I hate the fact that it's come down to this. That I have to sell, whether I want to or not. It probably doesn't sound very logical to you, Bobbie, but what really irks me—'' he ran his fingers through his dark hair ''—is this feeling of being cornered. I guess I'm just not accustomed to it.''

"That sounds perfectly logical to me," she said quickly. "I— I've never liked that feeling, either.''

He watched her closely, as if he were weighing her comment.

"I'm glad you explained this to me, Reno. I realize now how difficult it is for you, having to sell, but maybe I'll be able to come up with a proposal that will make it...less painful for you somehow.''

"I hope so." He stood there for another few seconds before he added, "Well, thanks for listening.''

"You're welcome." Bobbie rose from the sofa, dropping the handful of brochures onto the coffee table and joining him in front of the doorway. He paused, glancing from her eyes to her hand, which was now on the doorknob, and back into her eyes again. "Was...was there something else you wanted to say, Reno?''

"Yeah," he answered, "there is something else.''

"What is it?" She let go of the knob and pivoted, facing him squarely and studying the odd expression in his dark blue eyes. "Please. Go ahead.''

"I was just thinking it's kind of nice—'' his words were slow and deliberate ''—both of us having our preconceived notions out of the way." He leaned close, bracing his forearm against the door behind her. "And now that we have all that straightened out...''

"Yes?" Her spine brushed lightly against the door as she took a tiny step backward.

"I've been thinking—'' he moved even closer ''—that maybe I was wrong, insisting that things be strictly business between us.''

"You have?''

"Yes, I have," he answered quietly, a faint smile touching the corners of his mouth. "It's like what happened today, for instance, when we were in the dining hall. I've been trying to think about business, of course . . . but there's a certain part of my mind that keeps wanting to find that place on your neck."

"What place?" she asked, her voice sounding breathless as Reno lifted his free hand. He reached out, his thumb tracing a leisurely, provocative path down the column of her throat.

"That sensitive spot I found yesterday morning," he murmured in answer, "when we were in the middle of the creek." His fingers grazed the back of her neck, and when he stopped the movement of his thumb, she felt its gentle pressure along the side of her throat . . . just below her pulse. "Right about here, I think it is."

Bobbie swallowed hard. And when his thumb brushed her skin again, sliding a mere fraction of an inch to the side, she jumped.

"Yeah," he whispered, "that must be it. Right there."

Feeling the tremor that rushed through her body, Bobbie realized he was absolutely right. And at the same time, she realized she was virtually gasping for air. Her pulse was throbbing, pounding, as Reno stroked the spot he'd been talking about. She had never even known she had one area of flesh that was more sensitive than another, much less where it was.

"I know you don't make a habit of combining business with pleasure, but is there some reason we can't bend the rules? Just this once?"

"Well," she whispered, her gaze never leaving his, "I—I don't know if that's such a good idea, Reno. The other developers are arriving tomorrow morning, and . . ."

"And you're worried about appearances?" His warm, tender touch still held her captive. "That's understandable, but I don't think you need to be concerned about that."

"You don't? I mean, why not?"

"Because I'm not suggesting we flaunt anything." His eyes suddenly glimmered with a rakish spark of mischief. "I can be discreet. And discretion's your middle name, remember?"

"Well, yes. But it wouldn't do for anyone to get the idea that—"

"That I'm giving you preferential treatment?" he asked, finishing the statement for her. "That's not what I had in mind. I wouldn't want that, and neither would you." He shook his head. "No. What I'm suggesting is that we keep them totally separate. We can do that, can't we?"

"Well," she murmured, realizing that once again, she seemed to be having a difficult time forming complete sentences.

"I wouldn't want you to feel cornered," he said as he tilted his head and leaned closer, his voice hushed, his breath a hot, lazy caress against her temple, her earlobe. "So why don't you sleep on it?" In what seemed to be slow motion, he lifted his head again. "You can give me an answer tomorrow, after you see how discreet . . . how businesslike I can be at the opening meeting."

"All right," Bobbie whispered, her gaze fixed on the ruggedly handsome hint of a five o'clock shadow. She reached up then, her thumb briefly grazing the cleft in his chin, her palm moving upward along the sandpapery roughness of his jawline.

That scent, she realized, wasn't something out of a bottle—not completely, anyway. It was the scent of him. And it was nothing short of breathtaking. Heart-stopping.

He took her hand then, bringing it to his lips, kissing her fingers before he said, "Good night, Miss Powell. Sweet dreams."

Dear Lord, Bobbie thought moments later, staring out the window and watching Reno saunter toward the main building. How had he gotten out of her cabin? She couldn't remember stepping away from the door, so maybe he'd had to push her aside—or climb out the window.

All she knew for certain, at the moment, was that he had left her burning inside. Aching for more of his touch. For more of *him*.

Perhaps Reno's attitude about life was something to think about, she decided all of a sudden. Instead of using logic, perhaps it was better to gamble on instinct. Other men had courted her on a personal level with designs that ended up being strictly business—but Reno Tanner wasn't other men. Maybe this time her instincts had been right all along. Maybe Reno *could* be Mr. Right.

She knew little about him, but more than anything, she wanted to find out. And how was she to know for sure if she didn't pursue the answers? If she didn't explore the possibilities?

Her memory, she realized, could still feel the touch of his lips. Lifting her hand, she stared at her fingertips and then pressed them against her mouth.

As she watched his tall, muscular form disappear completely, Bobbie made up her mind about two things. Tonight, right now, she was definitely in the mood for a long, hot, leisurely soak in the tub. And tomorrow, when Reno asked for her answer, she was going to give him a yes. An absolute, unequivocal yes.

Chapter Six

Bobbie put on her earrings and smoothed the lines of her oyster-white linen dress. It was tailored enough for the initial meeting, she knew, yet casual enough for the Hideaway's informal atmosphere.

Checking her wristwatch for the hundredth time, Bobbie saw that she was ready with twenty minutes to spare. But for once in her life she didn't want to arrive early for a meeting, mainly because she didn't want to appear as eager as she actually felt. Beyond that, Reno had left her with a delicious sense of anticipation—a single-minded train of thought she'd been nurturing ever since the night before—and she planned to keep on enjoying every minute of it.

Yes, she told herself, slipping into her high heels and turning away from the mirror. She had to admit she liked the idea of Reno waiting until after the meeting for her answer. She liked the feeling of being unmistakably pursued, especially without the feeling of being pushed at the same time.

Glancing at her watch again, she left the bedroom. Thankfully, she didn't need to arrive early, anyway. Annette had hosted a get-acquainted luncheon only a couple of hours before, so all the introductions were out of the way—with the exception of Reno himself. And Bobbie had actually been relieved when she saw that he wasn't in attendance. It had given her a chance to meet Annette and the other developers, and if Reno had been there, she knew she would have been a nervous wreck.

After realizing she wouldn't be able to concentrate on anything constructive for the next few minutes, Bobbie decided to use the remaining time she had to assure herself that things were going well in Dallas. Picking up the telephone in the parlor, she placed her call to Judith Cavanaugh.

"Hi, Roberta," her friend said, and Bobbie smiled as she realized she hadn't thought of herself as Roberta lately.

"I was hoping you'd call today," Judith added.

"Why? Is there a problem?"

"Heavens, no," the woman answered, sounding both sincere and amused. "On the contrary. Everything's going beautifully—very routine—so enjoy yourself and don't hurry back. I owe you three or four weeks, and this is a great time to repay you."

"Thanks, Judith," she said. "I may just take you up on that."

"Good," her friend replied. "Oh. You remember when you asked me on the phone the other day if I knew anything about the Tanner heir? The son? Well, I've been asking around for you. Discreetly, of course."

Grinning as she thought about Reno's use of the same word, Bobbie tried to concentrate on what Judith was saying.

"And evidently there are two sons. I haven't been able to turn up anything on one of them, but a friend of mine gave me a juicy little tidbit about the other one."

Bobbie listened to the information Judith had garnered from a woman who, with her husband, frequented the horse-racing circuit and "had seen him everywhere in the last couple of years." Bobbie frowned as she thought of Cal Tanner at the racetrack throwing good money after bad. Reno had been extremely kind, not to mention discreet, in calling his brother's shenanigans "a couple of bad investments."

"And I do mean everywhere," her friend added. "Santa Anita, Pimlico, you name it. Wherever they went, Reno Tanner was—"

"Wait a minute, Judith. I think you must have your facts switched. Or your brothers switched, I guess I should say. Your friend must have been talking about Cal Tanner, not Reno."

"No, Cal's the much older one, from what I hear—the one I'm still trying to find out about. And I'm sure she said Reno, because I remember thinking, 'Wow, what a sexy name.'" Judith gave a short laugh before she paused. "Roberta? Are you there?"

"Yes," she said, struggling to keep her voice calm. "Yes, I'm here." Her fist tightened as she pushed the receiver against her ear and ignored the rap on her cabin door.

"Well, anyway..." Judith's voice took on a conspiratorial tone. "Here's where it gets interesting." The knock sounded again, heavier this time. "It seems that this Reno Tanner owns a racehorse, and not just—"

"Judith?" she interrupted, knowing she had heard all she wanted to hear, all she needed to hear. "There's someone pounding on my door, and I really must get to my meeting. Thanks so much for the information, though. You'll never know how helpful it's been."

And how timely! she thought, hanging up the phone and pivoting toward the door. Her friend had just saved her from making an absolute fool of herself over a man who had let his family's ranch go to ruin while he was out gallivanting across the country. Playing the ponies!

"Morning, ma'am," the gangly, red-haired teenager said as Bobbie yanked the door open.

"Good morning, Wayne." Pasting a smile on her face, she kept her voice cool even though she was seething inside.

Wayne stepped into the parlor, carrying an expensive-looking crystal vase that he handled with great care. The vase held at least two dozen yellow roses, and there was no doubt in Bobbie's mind who had sent them.

She stared at the flowers, and despite the glorious, intoxicating fragrance that filled the room, her anger seemed to reach a full boil.

Correction, she decided quickly. Full blown! If Reno Tanner thought a devious maneuver like this was going to cinch his little proposition, he had another think coming.

Wayne held up the vase. "Where would you like me to put these?"

Her mind still stewing over the boy's employer, Bobbie turned her head and sucked in a long, deep breath of rose-scented air before she muttered, "Don't even ask."

"Ma'am?" he inquired.

"Oh, nothing, Wayne." She forced another smile and reached for her wallet. "Just put them on the coffee table, will you please?"

Once again, the young man tried to refuse the tip she extended. But this time Bobbie insisted, her trembling fingers pushing a ten-dollar bill into his hand. After all, she reasoned with herself as Wayne thanked her profusely and left the cabin, the unsuspecting teenager deserved to be paid handsomely for playing messenger boy for a deceitful, conniving boss.

The nerve of that man! she thought, shoving her wallet back into her bag. While making his brother sound nothing more than young and irresponsible, Reno had made himself sound nothing less than a saint, telling her he'd stayed away from the ranch intentionally—out of brotherly love. Saying he'd used the couple of years away to take care of some of his own business concerns. Just exactly how many of his business concerns tromped around on four hooves and sported a feedbag? she wondered, snatching the envelope from its nesting place in the greenery and baby's breath.

"Oh!" she muttered disgustedly, tossing the sealed envelope onto the coffee table and grabbing her clutch bag.

There was no way she was going to muddy up her thinking by looking at whatever sweet, persuasive, devious words were inside that envelope, Bobbie told herself as she turned on her heel and headed for the door. She wanted to get through this meeting with only one vision in her mind: Reno Tanner jetting from track to track, scurrying to beat little old ladies to the two-dollar window at Pimlico.

Bobbie slammed the door and locked it, her shoulders sagging as the real issue suddenly crossed her mind.

Was she doomed forever to be attracted to Mr. Wrong?

Dropping onto the porch glider, Bobbie put her head in her hands. What was wrong with her, anyway? Ever since she had met Reno Tanner, she'd been acting so silly, so foolish. Why had she been convinced he was different? Probably, she decided with sadness, because she so desperately wanted him to be different.

He wasn't, though. He had suggested they get personal, but not until *after* he'd read her bio. After he'd studied her professional credentials. Period.

After losing his temper he had made it a point to apologize properly. And hoping to cement that apology, he had sidled up to her and suggested more than business. Nevertheless, it had been strictly business. For the sake of his ranch.

Maybe she would have seen it, too, she thought disgustedly, if she hadn't been so captivated by everything about him. Or if any of the few experiences she'd had with men in the past had been anything but bad experiences.

But she might as well face it. She had no idea how to deal with men in general, much less with a man as devastating and appealing as Reno Tanner.

Well, Bobbie decided resolutely, squaring her shoulders and taking another deep breath. As soon as this darned meeting was out of the way, she was going to give some serious thought to that very issue. Come hell or high water, she *was* going to have a decent personal relationship with a man. She *was* going to find her Mr. Right—at some point in the very near future.

And that future, she told herself with renewed determination, would not include the likes of Reno Tanner. He could pursue all he wanted, stoop as low as he wanted, but she refused to pay him even the least little bit of attention. Since she had no idea how else to handle it, she would just ignore him.

And, she thought, the corner of her mouth lifting in a derisive frown as she stood up from the glider, she would ignore the smell of him, too. When she had to be around him, she would simply make it a point not to breathe very much. Or not at all! She would sooner die than let that man know she was interested in him for anything other than business.

She was here on business. And for that reason alone, she would be halfway civil to the man. But if nothing else, before she left this godforsaken place, she would show Reno Tanner she wasn't quite the fool he'd taken her for.

Reno slowed his pickup, realizing the woman he'd just spotted was Bobbie. He parked near the swimming pool and sat there for a while simply watching her, his mouth curved in a smile.

Obviously she had chosen not to go with Annette and the other developers on their afternoon trek around the ranch. Instead, she was stretched out on a chaise longue and appeared to be asleep, which was probably a good thing.

He chuckled under his breath. After what he'd done at that damned meeting, he knew there would be hell to pay. But maybe with a nap plus the couple of hours he'd had to spend in the breeding barn, she had had a chance to cool down some by now.

Hell, he thought, it had just been an innocent little wink. But even though he was sure no one had seen it but Bobbie, he still should have known better. That businesslike manner of hers was really something, and from the minute they'd met, he'd been confused by those conflicting looks she kept giving him. One minute those gorgeous hazel eyes seemed to say, "Take me, I'm yours." And the next minute they'd flash him a message that clearly said, "How dare you, sir!"

And the look she'd given him after that wink, he decided, was definitely of the how-dare-you variety. He'd even seen her spine stiffen. Then, as soon as the brief meeting was adjourned, she'd gotten out of there like someone had lit a fire under her. She hadn't even waited around to visit informally, as the other developers had done, or to take one of the plats that had been set out for them.

Well, he told himself, still smiling as he tossed his hat on the seat and got out of the truck. Her feathers had been ruffled, but he'd see what he could do about that. In fact, if he had to be honest with himself, he'd have to admit he actually liked the fact that she was riled. If calming her down now was going to be anything at all like the time she'd gotten herself tossed in the creek, it would undoubtedly prove interesting.

He walked the short distance to the grassy area on the far edge of the pool area and saw that Bobbie was indeed asleep. Most of the guests were inside, he knew, out of the intense midafternoon heat. Except for a couple of people sunning themselves on the opposite side of the pool, they were alone.

Reno raised the back of the chaise next to hers and then stretched out on it, crossing his ankles and leaning back against the cushion of his hands. He turned his face so that he could watch her. Awake or asleep, she was one easy woman to look at.

His gaze moved down then, traveling the length of her, past the gentle rise and fall of her breasts under her summery-looking blouse, past the open magazine that formed a steeple over her narrow waist, past the snug, white fabric of her shorts. It was the first time he'd seen her legs, and they looked every bit as good as he'd known they would. Her thighs had that extra ounce or two of flesh on them, the way a woman's legs were meant to be. Firm enough, smooth and long and sleek—yet they had a certain softness, so that when a man pulled her against him, she felt good. Just right, in fact.

Bobbie shifted positions then, a long, languid, purring sound escaping her throat as she rolled toward him.

Watching the soft, innocent smile that touched her lips, Reno found himself wondering exactly how it would feel to have her curled up next to him in the middle of the night. Or to carry her inside on a hot, lazy afternoon just like this one and make love with her on cool, crisp sheets. Or to kiss her, first thing in the morning, with her soft warmth pressing against the length of his body.

No doubt about it, he told himself. Waking up next to Bobbie Powell would be one hell of a way to start the day....

She drew her legs up, sighing again, and Reno smothered a groan. Rubbing the smile off his face, he realized his thinking was a little premature. The first thing he had to worry about was getting back in her good graces.

Reaching out, he managed to grab her magazine before it fell to the grass between them. He creased the spine, saving her place before setting it on the other side of his lounge chair.

The title of the article caught his attention, and he picked the magazine up again and started reading. Amazing, he thought, leaning back and trying to suppress a laugh as he scanned the bold captions within the article. It was amazing that some writer could actually peddle this kind of—

"What's so funny?" he heard Bobbie ask.

Smiling, he glanced at her. She was still mad, all right. He could tell by the dry tone of her voice. By the level stare she was shooting his way, even though her eyes weren't fully open yet. This, he told himself, was going to take some fancy broken-field running. Still grinning, he decided maybe he could tease his way out of it.

"It's this article," he answered. "You women don't really take this stuff seriously, do you?"

"What stuff?" Bobbie asked. She sat up, rubbing her eyes and then squinting at him suspiciously.

"Articles like this one, 'Looking for Mr. Right—the right way.'" He thumped the page. "This is garbage. If a woman's looking for a man—"

"And what if I am?" she asked quickly. "Not that it's any of your concern, of course, but what if I am? Is that a problem?"

"A problem?" he asked, quirking his eyebrow as he gave her a puzzled glance. "No. No problem at all." Boy, he thought, talk about the direct approach. If there was one thing he could determine about Bobbie Powell, it was that she was certainly full of surprises. "Looking to get married, are you?"

"No, Reno," she stated flatly, a sudden spark in her eyes as she jacked up her chin. "I thought I'd just sit around for another thirty-five years. Maybe by then I'll become a lonely, bitter, desperate old woman, which is what I really want."

Thirty-five, huh? Reno thought. Interesting.

He watched as Bobbie raised the back of her chaise, bringing it to the same level as his. And when he saw the color flooding her cheeks, he finally realized why she had reacted so strangely to his teasing: she'd been on the defensive.

Yeah, he decided, that had to be it. She was plain old embarrassed, thinking he'd concluded she might have designs on him just because he'd found out she was looking at some arbitrary write-up in a women's magazine.

"Well, sarcasm aside," he said, grinning at her, "as I was saying, if some woman—some hypothetical woman—was looking for a man, this wouldn't be the way to go about it."

"Why not?" she asked, her voice taking on that slightly higher pitch he'd learned to recognize. "I scanned the article. It all sounded perfectly logical to me."

"It might sound logical, but that doesn't mean it makes any sense." He ran his index finger down a printed column and asked, "Steps one through ten? Hell, Bobbie. According to this, you might as well just shake hands and then swap resumes and financial statements."

"Maybe that's not such a bad idea." She lifted that proud, regal-looking chin even higher in the air and added, "What's wrong with following the safe route?"

"And what's wrong with taking a few risks?" There was no doubt about it, he thought. She really was damned cute when she was riled.

"And what about those of us who aren't gamblers? By nature?"

"Well," he said, wondering if she was being defensive or facetious or downright serious. "If you don't go by instinct at least once in a while, maybe you ought to give some thought to what you might be missing." He tilted his head and smiled. "As my granddaddy always said, no guts, no glory."

"Your granddaddy was a mighty talkative old cuss," she commented dryly. "Did he have something to say about everything?"

"Yeah," he answered, chuckling as he propped his boot on the chaise and brought up one knee. "I reckon he did. And you're a mighty sarcastic little thing, aren't you?"

She pointed at the magazine he held against his raised thigh. "And what makes you such an expert on this particular subject?" she asked, apparently intent on overriding his question with one of her own. "Why is it you seem to have far more insight than the author, who's probably a Ph.D. or something?''

"That's the problem right there. The author's a female. I never said I was an expert, but I am a man. And that's why I know this article needs a man's slant. A man's point of view." He gestured toward the boxed-in portion of one page. "Take this, for instance—this sidebar about finding Mr. Right through the personals. These examples of promising ads are unbelievable."

"Why?"

"Because you can't take these ads at face value." More determined than ever to nudge her out of her mood, he lifted his eyebrows. "This may come as a shock to you, Bobbie, but there are a few men in this world who tend to stretch the truth. Some of them exaggerate and some of them twist things around. And some of them even lie."

"No!"

"Yes," he said, laughing at the feigned look of shock on her face. "And if you're a man, you know how to read between the lines." He scanned the first sample ad. "Take the lead-in to this one, for example. 'I know who I am, what I want, where I'm going. My time's my own; I do things my way.'" He looked her straight in the eye. "Now what does that tell you?"

"Simple," she answered at last, staring right back at him. "It tells me, here's a mature, stable, sensible man who knows himself well, who's successful in his chosen profession. His life is already fulfilling; he's simply looking for some nice woman who'll enhance it."

"Wrong. All it tells you is one thing. The guy's bossy. Probably downright domineering." He tilted the magazine, reading silently for a few seconds before he said, "Oh, and this one. This is really a jewel: 'I have no fear of closeness with the opposite sex. Looking for a strong woman who'll share my love of hearth and home.'"

"What's wrong with that?" she asked, as if she were totally disgusted with him. "If you ask me, it sounds rather refreshing. A man who isn't afraid of intimacy. A man who's secure in his masculinity and wants a warm, loving home life."

"No," he stated flatly. "You see what I mean? A woman sees the word hearth and automatically equates it with warmth—and love—but that's not what this guy wants at all."

"Oh? What *does* this guy want, then?"

She sounded especially defensive about this particular ad, Reno decided. Nevertheless, he was determined to lighten the atmosphere. She couldn't stay peeved with him forever.

"Okay," he said, smiling as his hand moved back to the sample advertisement. "This baloney about closeness with the opposite sex just means he's used to having a woman around the house. At forty, maybe fifty years old, he's probably lived with Mama all his life."

"Then why would he be looking for a strong woman?"

"Translation: a woman with a strong back. Poor old Mom probably went to her greater reward a couple of weeks ago, so the guy's looking for a quick replacement. Someone to pick up his dirty socks. Scrub the floors, cook his meals."

Aha, he thought. She'd been chewing on the insides of her cheeks; he was almost sure of it. She was unbelievable, though—on the verge of laughter, but too damned stubborn to give in to it.

He held up the magazine. "You mark my words, Bobbie. This guy's not looking for Mrs. Right; he's looking for a maid."

She turned her head, staring straight ahead, and finally released a long, exasperated sigh. "How tall are you, anyway? Without your boot heels?"

"Six three," he answered, puzzled by the change of topic. "Why?"

"Funny," she muttered under her breath. "I didn't think they could stack it that high."

"Hey," he said playfully, cupping her chin and turning her face toward his. "Be careful now. If you don't watch out, you're liable to give me a little smile."

She simply lifted her eyes skyward and kept them there.

"Aw, come on now, Bobbie. You're mad as a wet hen; I know that. But cut me a little slack here, will ya, darlin'?"

"I'll thank you not to call me that again," she said, pulling back from his hand. "I am not your *darlin'*, and—"

"Bobbie!" he reprimanded her teasingly. "It was just an innocent little wink. No one saw me. I swear."

She crossed her arms over her breasts and glared at him. Then she nodded in the direction of the article they'd just discussed. "So you're saying women—being the poor, defenseless, gullible creatures we are—can't possibly see through these devious men of the world. Is that right?"

"No, of course not. I'm just saying that if you're a man, you know how these guys' minds work."

"I'll bet," she said wryly. "Tell me," she finally added, "does it itch?"

"Does what itch?"

"In the summertime—when you shed your skin?"

"Bobbie," he said evenly, "why don't we lighten up a bit, huh?" He let out a sigh then and finally, slowly, grinned at her. "I'm trying my best to get on your good side, but I'm beginning to wonder if you have one."

"Maybe not, but I'll tell you what you've got. You've got a lot of nerve!"

"Because I winked at you?" he asked incredulously. "When no one else was even watching?"

"No." She shot him a look of stubborn indignation. "I couldn't care less about your . . . your lascivious winks."

"Well, *what*, then?"

"You want to know what?" she asked, her tone venomous. "I'll tell you what! I've had just about all I can stand." Bobbie snatched the magazine out of his hand and waved it in front of his face. "You, cowboy, are such a cad! How dare you talk about men who misrepresent themselves to unsuspecting women?"

"What the hell are you talking about?" he asked, watching in awe and confusion as she jammed the magazine into her tote. She grabbed the oversize bag and jumped up, all in one swift motion, and sashayed away from him at breakneck speed.

He caught up with her as she flounced past his truck.

"Wait just a minute here," he said firmly, spinning her around to face him. "I asked you a question. What the hell are you talking about?"

She started shouting at him, and after hearing partial references to a bit of everything—his brother, his ranch, the time he'd spent away from the ranch, and even something about Pimlico and little old ladies and the roses he'd sent her this morning—Reno finally caught on to what Bobbie was ranting about.

"What are you doing?" she asked, still furious, as he opened the door of the cab and planted her firmly on the passenger seat. "Where are you taking me?"

"You'll see," he said, buckling her seat belt, "in a couple of minutes. Do you think you can shut up that long?"

"No!" she yelled.

Ignoring her scowl and a stream of violent protests, he patted her thigh and then slammed the door, rounded the truck and got behind the wheel. They rode in stony silence, with Bobbie staring out the window while Reno glanced her way from time to time, shaking his head and collecting the last shreds of his patience. He had to keep reminding himself this really didn't have anything to do with him. It had to do with her suspicious nature. Apparently, Upton Powell had taught his firstborn daughter not to trust anyone.

Nearing his destination, he turned off the main road and headed toward a thick grove of native pecan trees.

"Where are you taking me?" she asked again.

"My brother's house," he said, steering the truck around the huge grove and then pointing to the massive, plantation-style home that had been hidden from view. "It used to be the main house. I grew up here.

"Cal's been gone for a couple of months, though," he explained as he parked the truck in front of the old carriage house, "so don't worry. There's no one here right now." When he reached behind him, he saw her shrinking back from him, hugging the door handle. "And you can get that crazed look out of your eyes. I just brought you out here to show you something."

He reached behind him again, and that's when he realized what had gotten her nervous. "Good God, Bobbie." Laughing out loud, he lifted the binocular strap from the hook at the bottom of his gun rack. "I didn't haul you out here to shoot you." He put on his hat, went around to her side and helped her down. "Oh, I'll admit you're trying my patience, but under normal circumstances, old cattlemen tend to have an abundance of that."

Reno took her arm, and as he guided her toward the wide veranda that skirted the entire front of the house, she gave him what could only be termed a dirty look and said, "That's not all you old cattlemen have an abundance of."

"Keep tryin', honey. You may push me past my limit yet." With a toss of his head, he indicated the truck. "And if that happens, I'll just go back and get the gun."

"And if you call me honey just one more time," she insisted, almost stumbling as he coaxed her up the stairs and onto the veranda, "*I'll* go back and get the gun."

"Yeah," he said, tossing the binocular case onto the nearby glider swing. "Sure."

Standing behind her, Reno pinned her legs against the porch rail. He focused the binoculars and then put them in front of her eyes.

"I can do it myself," she said, twisting the field glasses out of his grasp. "What am I supposed to be looking for?"

"A racehorse."

"Which one?" she asked. "What color?"

"About the same color as your hair," he answered, laughing as she reached up and swatted his hand away from her soft chestnut waves.

"The one that looks pregnant?"

"No," he said, directing the field glasses away from the brood mares she'd spotted. "Definitely not that one." Rolling his eyes, he smiled as he placed his hands on her shoulders. "I thought you spent some time on a farm. Haven't you ever heard the term 'in foal'?"

"Of course," she said huffily, still moving the binoculars around. "I knew that. But it's not a term that just rolls right off my tongue, you know. Women...think differently, as you so kindly pointed out a few minutes ago." She adjusted the focus. "All right, I see it. What about it?" Bobbie shrugged her shoulders, and as he slid his hands closer to her neck, she cleared her throat. "It's just a stupid horse."

"It's a Thoroughbred, and it's a he."

"So?"

"So, you called him a stupid horse. Would you care to know what I call him?"

"Not especially. But I assume you're not going to be happy until you tell me."

"Right. He's named after the Diamond T, and after my parents, Jubal and Lee Tanner."

"Translation?" she asked, her tone nasal as she copied the word he'd used out by the pool. And still she refused to look at him.

"Diamond Jubalee," he answered. "Does that ring a bell?"

She turned around slowly, her eyes now wide with disbelief. "The . . . the horse that—" For only the second or third time since he'd met her, she seemed to be at a loss for exactly the right words. "The horse that—"

"The stupid horse that took two legs of the Triple Crown last spring," he said, finishing the question for her. "Yeah. That's the one."

"I—I had no idea."

"I didn't think so."

"Then that's . . . That's one of the other assets you were talking about?" Tilting her head, she gazed up at him with the most puzzled look in her eyes. "Well, what's your problem, then? If you need money, why don't you just sell that horse?"

"Don't even suggest it," he said, his jaw stretched tight. "We're talking about a magnificent Thoroughbred here, Bobbie—a horse that happens to mean a hell of a lot to me—and I don't intend to do anything of the sort."

"Well, I can't imagine why not! Surely you could make all kinds of money if you did."

Reno had to remind himself that Bobbie had no idea how strongly he felt about Jubalee, that, like so many other people, she would automatically assume that this particular type of horse would be nothing more than a business investment. A money-making possession.

She turned and peered through the field glasses again. "And what's he doing here, anyway? If he's so great, so magnificent, shouldn't he be out racing somewhere? Winning bundles?''

"Gigantic purses?''

"Yes,'' she stated emphatically, as if she were an expert in all facets of horse racing. "Exactly. Instead of frolicking in some pasture, why isn't he out running real races?''

He couldn't help laughing at that one. "Because I don't allow him to run real races anymore. He has to play in his own backyard now or not at all.''

She turned around and gave him another befuddled look.

"Because right after he won the Belmont last year, I took him out.''

"Why, for heaven's sake?''

"Instinct, Bobbie. I gambled on that being the right thing to do. I took him out while he was at his prime and still on top— and before there was a chance of anything happening to him.'' She still didn't seem to understand. "Accidents, injuries, things like that. Obviously, you don't know what all's involved.''

"No, I don't. But . . . but what good is he doing you if he doesn't even have a chance to win any more races?''

He turned her around and stuck the field glasses in front of her eyes again. "You see those brood mares? As soon as I see a couple of normal, healthy foals on the ground . . . Well, as soon as those pregnant horses have their babies, Diamond Jubalee is going to start keeping company with a whole lot of lady horses. And that's when he'll get his own stud farm and start bringing in the really big bucks.''

Reno moved closer, his chest against her back, his breath stirring her hair as he rubbed the tight cords along her neck. "And that, honey, is why I've been 'hanging around every racetrack in the country.' Sort of acting as his procurement officer for the future. Does it all make more sense to you now?''

"Oh,'' she replied softly, almost timidly. After placing the binoculars on the railing, she glanced out at Jubalee. "Of course. I should have thought about that. For some reason, though, it just never entered my mind. I picture racehorses running, not . . .''

"That's understandable,'' Reno said with a quiet laugh. "You may have spent a little of your childhood on your grandparents' farm," he offered, "but being the very strait-laced, very British lady she was, Grandma Louise probably made it a point to keep you in the house at all the appropriate times."

She bowed her head, her face in her hands as she whispered, "Oh, Reno, I'm so sorry." Then, to his surprise, he felt her body tremble, and without any further warning, she began to cry. "I—I'm afraid I'm just not any good at this."

"Come on now, Bobbie," he murmured, his arms circling her, his mouth nuzzling the back of her hair. "That's not true at all. You're a city girl; I don't expect you to know everything there is to know about country life and horses and—"

"No," she moaned, trying to choke back her sobs. "No, that's not what I'm talking about."

He turned her around and lifted her face, searching those beautiful, expressive green and gold eyes, watching the tears roll down her cheeks.

"I'm making such a mess of things," she said, a note of desperation in her soft-spoken, tremulous words. "I don't think I know how to do this! I don't think it's possible for me to combine business and . . ."

"And pleasure?" he asked, smiling down into her tear-filled eyes.

"Yes," she whispered plaintively, looking away and finally back at him. "I've been working so hard at being a business-woman for so long now—" she flattened her palm against her chest "—that I'm afraid there's no other kind of woman here anymore."

"Take it from me, Bobbie. You're worrying about noth-ing." His hands moved to her face, his thumbs grazing her cheeks as he tried to wipe away her tears. "Under that beauti-ful, businesslike exterior lies a very real woman."

"But you don't even know me," she said, her voice even more plaintive. "How can you say that? Why?"

"Because I'm a man, honey, and you need a man's slant on that sort of thing." Her eyes were questioning his. "Bobbie, a man doesn't pull a woman into his arms—" still smiling faintly, he raised his eyebrows "—and save her from drowning with-out getting some indication of the woman she really is. Without getting some clear-cut message about the kind of woman who's waiting for him beneath the surface.

"So just take it from me, darlin'." He covered her hand with his own, and through her fingers, he felt the strong, erratic beat of her heart. "There's another woman in there. You probably just haven't been letting her out to play often enough, that's all. But we can work on that together, can't we?"

"Well." Her fingers moved nervously beneath his. "I'm not sure. Maybe so, but . . ." She looked away. "But first I have to apologize for the horrible things I said to you a few minutes ago." She glanced up at him again, an expression of total remorse in her eyes. "And I owe you an explanation, too."

"Apology accepted. And you don't have to explain."

"Why not?"

"Because I know exactly what you thought. You thought I was a cad—a black-hearted cad who was ready to take advantage of a sweet, unsuspecting, gullible creature like you." He laughed quietly as he saw the slight but obvious look that came across her face. "Now that's more like it. I knew I could get you to give me a little smile."

"I didn't even say thank-you for the roses," she whispered at last. "They just sort of . . . arrived at the wrong time. But thank you, Reno. They're beautiful."

"You're welcome. I'm glad you liked them."

"I—I didn't even open the envelope and read the card. I hope it hasn't been thrown away."

"You want me to tell you what it said? Just in case?"

He watched as Bobbie smiled softly, radiantly, and nodded.

"It wasn't much. Just something like, 'I'm hoping for a yes.'" She was such a contrasting mixture of thoughts and emotions, he decided. So cautious and guarded and serious at times, so completely transparent and open and innocent at others. "And now that you know I'm not some black-hearted cad, now that I've shown you almost twenty-four hours of my usual patience, how about giving me an answer?"

He tilted his head and grinned slyly at her. "I'll warn you, though. If it's not a yes, I can make your life miserable. At the dinner table tonight, right in front of all those other developers, I'll give you one of my most lascivious winks. And then I'll say, 'Pass the salt, will ya, darlin'?' "

"You wouldn't!" She gave him that how-dare-you look of hers—this one with a stern, playful smile that was impossible to resist. "That's blackmail, cowboy."

"I know," he murmured. His hand moved around her neck, pulling her toward him.

"Yes," she whispered, her mouth mere inches from his. "My answer is yes."

"Good," he said, "that's all I wanted to hear."

On a low moan of pleasure, she parted her lips.

Easy, Reno told himself. This woman needed a slow hand. A light, steady, easy touch.

His fingers tangled in the silky, cool softness of her hair as he cupped the back of her head, tilting her face to bring it even closer to his. God, but she smelled good. Better than any woman had a right to smell. Like honeysuckle in the middle of a hot summer night. Like warmth itself.

A long, low whistle cut through the quiet. "Dammit," Reno muttered under his breath, letting go of her just before she stepped back.

"What is it?" she asked breathlessly, still facing him as she reached up to straighten the collar of her blouse.

"Oh, nothing. I'm being summoned, that's all." His gaze on the pulse shuddering rapidly near the base of her throat, he nodded toward the distance. "It's Hollis, Jubalee's trainer."

She turned her head, glancing over her shoulder toward the small, wiry man who was now motioning in their direction. As Reno lifted his arm, acknowledging Hollis's beckoning signal, Bobbie swallowed and said, "He . . . looks like he could be a jockey."

"He used to be. He rode quarter horses years ago." Reno sighed and gave a short, exasperated sound of amusement as he ran his hand along his face. "He says he gave it up 'cause he got a little too big, but I'm wondering now if it actually had something to do with his lousy sense of timing."

He took her hand in his. "You want to go with me? It probably won't take but a minute."

"Sure," Bobbie said quickly, realizing that—no matter how embarrassed she felt about breaking down and crying like she had, no matter how red and swollen her eyes might be right now—she wanted to know more about Reno Tanner. About everyone and everything in his life.

She bounded down the veranda steps, keeping up with his long-legged strides. Not wanting him to let go of her, she tugged on his hand, pulling him in the direction of his truck so that she could get her sunglasses.

Only moments ago she had ached for him to kiss her, just as she had the night before. But for now, having her hand in his seemed just as good. Well, she thought as she opened the passenger door, almost as good.

Realizing she would have to dig in her tote for the glasses, Bobbie decided she had no choice but to let go of him. His arm came around her then, and he gingerly lifted the magazine from her bag.

After the initial meeting had let out, she had made a quick stop in the lobby drugstore—and that's when the front-cover teaser for that stupid article had caught her eye. Thankfully, though, Reno hadn't seemed to guess she'd been deadly serious when she bought the darned thing. Deciding it was best to play along with the razzing he'd already given her about it, she turned and gave him the nastiest look she could manage. "That wasn't funny, you know."

"It wasn't?"

"Well, all right," she admitted, going back to her chore while she tried to school her sudden grin. "It might've been funny—maybe—if the timing hadn't been what it was."

"I guess I'll have to work on that."

"Maybe so." She kept rummaging through the tote bag, knowing she ought to give up the search, what with Reno standing so close behind her. "I know I've got sunglasses. Somewhere in here."

"Boy, howdy," she heard him murmur under his breath. "This guy's nothing but a pervert. Listen to this, Bobbie: 'Sexually open-minded man wants totally uninhibited woman. Must have fine set of—'"

"What?" she asked, her mouth dropping open as she twirled around. "Let me see that." She noticed the look on his face then. "Why, you liar," she said, laughing as she gave him a slug on the arm. "There's no such thing in there! You made that up."

"What can I say?" he asked, lifting his shoulders. "I was just working on my timing, that's all."

"Well, keep working on it, cowboy." She yanked the magazine out of his hand and shoved it into her tote. "I'm sure I'll find my sunglasses if I keep digging. Meanwhile, why don't you just guide me in the right direction?"

"Sure," he said, taking her arm. "I like the sound of that."

"You're impossible," she muttered, growing more flustered by the moment as she went back to her seemingly hopeless task.

Finally, before they reached the fence line where Hollis was waiting, she found the dark glasses and slipped them on just before Reno made the proper introductions.

"Nice to meet you, Miss Bobbie," the fiftyish man said with a wide, natural grin. After a gentlemanly tilt of his beat-up old hat, along with a warm handshake, he turned to Reno. "Sorry to bother ya, boss, but it seems like the breedin' barn has an APB out on you. Sounds like two or three different problems over there." The man turned to Bobbie then, a twinkle in his eye as he said, "But I'll be glad to keep your lady friend company for a minute or two—if you wanta just call from my office."

"Why, thank you, Hollis," Reno said, his tone indulgent. "That's mighty nice of you to offer."

"No problem, boss. No problem at all."

Hollis didn't even watch as Reno left them, but after a moment, Bobbie realized the twinkle in his eyes had been totally friendly and not the least bit lecherous. Hollis suddenly seemed bashful—almost to the point of being uncomfortable.

"Tell me, Hollis," she said quickly. "Why is it so beautiful here? I mean, why does this particular spot look so different from the rest of the ranch?" She lifted her hand, making a wide sweep of the entire area. "It's almost lush here. Why is that?"

"That's because of the underground springs, ma'am. The ones that feed Comanche Creek here." He pointed toward the main house on his left. "That's the first bend: the little bridge you just crossed on your way over here." His arm moved to the right then. "And there's the second one. And over yonder—just past that old, run-down shack you can hardly see from here—that's another one."

"That's amazing. And it's all one creek?"

"Yes, ma'am," he said with pride, as if he owned it.

"And what about the two huge, long mesas off in the distance over there? Those aren't on the Diamond T, are they?"

"Oh, no, ma'am. That's right on the outskirts of Santa Anna." He nodded in the direction of the twin peaks. "Santa Anna Mountain, or mountains, as some folks call 'em. Years ago, they used to drive cattle right through that gap."

Longhorns, Bobbie guessed correctly. However, after another of her questions, Hollis had to set her straight on the fact that the mountains and the town had not been named after the obvious person, but instead after a Comanche war leader named Santana who once lived nearby. Accordingly to Hollis, the best information available was that the old Comanche chief must have borrowed the spelling of his name after learning that Santa Anna was the president and emperor of Mexico, where the Comanches had made numerous raiding trips.

Reno approached them just then, announcing that he had received a rundown of the problems at the breeding barn and that, unfortunately, he needed to leave right away.

Realizing that dropping her off at the Hideaway might take time Reno could ill afford, Bobbie assured him she would be fine on her own. "If Hollis doesn't mind," she added, "I'd like to stay awhile and get someone to pick me up later." Trying to look smug, she lifted one palm. "I'll just call the Hideaway and casually drop the boss's name when I'm making my request. That'll work, don't you imagine?"

"No need, Miss Bobbie," the older man piped up, grinning from ear to ear. "I'll be glad to tote you back when you're ready."

After they both thanked Hollis, Reno took her arm and pulled her aside. "It looks like I'll be busy for the rest of the day, Bobbie. Tomorrow, too, I'm afraid."

"That's okay," she assured him. "I understand. After all, you have a ranch to run. And I have work to do, too." She smiled as his hand slid down the length of her arm, as she felt the pressure of his fingers on hers. "When it comes to the history and geography of this area, Hollis seems to be a walking encyclopedia. I have a couple of ideas for my proposal, so maybe he'll mention something that can help me develop one of them for you."

"Good," Reno commented, his lips brushing her forehead with a light, brief kiss before he said goodbye.

Bobbie leaned against the fence as she and Hollis continued their conversation. She glanced toward the main house, keeping an eye on Reno as he quickly retrieved his binoculars and headed for the truck. And when he backed out and drove across the bridge, she returned his wave.

Still smiling, Bobbie realized his masculine scent couldn't possibly be lingering in the great, wide expanse of outdoors surrounding her. There was only one answer to the phenomenon. Somehow, in only a few days' time, she had managed to memorize the scent of Reno Tanner.

Chapter Seven

After greeting all the developers and asking them if they had enjoyed their lunch, Reno walked around the table and stood beside Bobbie's chair.

Glancing pointedly at her name tag, he said, "Bobbie! On that question you had about the plat, I've got a few minutes right now. Why don't you come on up to my office and we'll get it out of the way?"

"Why...certainly." She stood, straightening the lines of her dark designer jeans before picking up her shoulder bag. "Of course."

As they walked away from the group, she could feel his fingers through the lightweight silk fabric at the small of her back, then at her elbow.

"That's odd," she said once they crossed the lobby, a knowing grin on her face as Reno guided her past some offices and through a door marked Private. "I don't remember having a question about the plat."

"You didn't." He lifted his brows, a devilish gleam in his dark blue eyes. "But if you'd like to dream one up real quick,

I'll be more than happy to answer it for you." He pressed some numbers on a keypad next to an elevator, and after the doors opened and closed, he turned to her and said, "I called you a couple of times yesterday from the breeding barn, but you were never in. Did you decide to go out with Annette and the others?"

"No," she stated, her tone coy. "I've already had a private tour, you see. So Wayne's mom packed me a lunch and a thermos of lemonade, and I went to Cal's house and sat out on the veranda all day."

"A real lady of leisure, huh?"

"Not totally," she said, still smiling. "Actually, I curled up on one end of the porch swing and got some work done. I hope that's all right, my camping out there all day."

"Sure. No problem." The elevator stopped, and he led her a short distance down the hall and through the first doorway on the left.

His office was unbelievable, and Bobbie simply walked around in a circle, taking it all in. The first thing to catch her eye was the headgear of a Texas longhorn mounted on the wall, running at least six feet across. Then she spotted a wrought-iron plaque of the ranch's brand with what appeared to be the original branding iron hanging from one side of it and a dress Stetson from the other. And then, finally, she noticed all kinds of memorabilia that pertained to Diamond Jubalee: photos, loving cups, a silky flag with the Diamond T brand emblazoned on it. After reaching out to run her fingers along one of the gold trophies, she decided against it and drew her hand back.

"It's okay," he said from behind her. "It's not a museum. You can touch anything you like in here."

Anything? she wondered, turning to smile at him as he closed the door behind him.

"Anything at all," Reno said, as if he had read her mind. He crossed the room and propped himself on one edge of the huge old desk that monopolized the entire corner she was now standing near.

Feeling the warmth in her face, Bobbie set her handbag on a credenza. Her eyes scanned the rows of simply framed certificates on the wall: memberships to various cattle-breeding associations, all very official looking with their shiny seals, and finally, his college diploma.

"You graduated in—" She leaned closer, making sure of the year. "Oh," she said dejectedly. "That must make you . . ."

He reached for her, turning her around and pulling her between his thighs as he remained where he was.

"Yeah," he answered with a rakish grin. "Thirty-four. But that's okay. I've always considered maturity a fine quality in a woman."

His hands moved around her waist, pulling her closer still as his voice lowered to a husky, velvety whisper. "And don't worry. I'm being discreet, remember?" With his head, he gestured in the general direction of the developers he had just pulled her away from in the dining room. "You'll never hear the words robbing the cradle pass through these lips."

He winked then, and Bobbie felt her knees go weak. It wouldn't have mattered if he were twenty or sixty, she decided all of a sudden. Reno Tanner made her feel anything but over the hill. On the contrary. At this very moment, standing so close to him, feeling the heat of his body through the denim covering his hard thighs, she felt like a giddy schoolgirl whose heart was threatening to stop beating.

"Is that why you brought me up here?" she asked breathlessly, playfully. "To flaunt the fact that you're a tiny bit younger than I am?"

"No. I brought you up here to talk you into playing hooky for the rest of the day." Slowly, gently, he moved his thumb up the length of her arm. "So how 'bout it?"

The offer was tempting. Unbelievably tempting. But just thinking about Reno over the past couple of days had been enough to keep her distracted. And he was counting on her help. For that reason alone, she needed to keep business at the front of her mind.

"I—I don't think so, Reno. Friday's only two days away, and I really should work on my proposal. Annette's already agreed to let me use one of the typewriters in the office, and—"

"Look, Bobbie, I don't expect a written proposal in such a short amount of time. I was simply planning to talk to each of you before you leave and then have you submit a formal proposal later.''

''But I'd feel much better if I could give you something in writing.'' Her hand moved to her breastbone, as if that might help her catch her breath.

''Then I'll have a typewriter set up in your cabin. You can work on it tomorrow, can't you?'' He glanced downward and, just as he had on the veranda the day before, covered her hand with his own. ''Why don't you let her out to play? Just for a while? You've been working almost the whole time you've been here, and so have I.''

Her tongue touched the corner of her mouth. ''Well . . .''

''You won't be sorry. I promise.''

Without thinking, Bobbie lifted her free hand, skimming her fingertip over the slight indentation in his chin. ''Well, all right. If you're sure it's no trouble. The typewriter, I mean.''

''I'm sure.'' Still clasping her hand, he led her through a door at the far end of the office. ''Come on, then. I have a full day planned for us.''

They walked through a very small kitchen and into a very large sitting room, its walls lined with what appeared to be old family photos, all in black and white. He let go of her and started unsnapping the cuffs of his shirt, and Bobbie's eyes widened when she saw that the next room in the string of adjoining doors led to a bedroom. A very masculine-looking bedroom.

''Hey,'' he said, laughing softly. ''Don't look so startled, Bobbie. I'm just changing my shirt.'' He reached up and touched her arm. ''I'm taking you to town, honey, not to bed.''

''Of course,'' she heard herself agreeing quickly. ''I knew that.''

Reno tilted his head. ''Not that the thought isn't tempting, mind you, but I have this rule. I never sleep with a woman before the first date.'' He lifted his shoulders. ''It's old-fashioned, I guess, but that's the kind of cad I am.''

She laughed nervously. ''I like old-fashioned cads.''

''Good. Now why don't you make yourself at home. I'll be ready in a minute.''

In what seemed a natural act, her eyes followed Reno as he sauntered into the bedroom. Finally realizing that he wasn't planning to shut the door, Bobbie forced herself to deny the urge to stand and stare at him while he changed his clothes. Instead, she crossed the living room and studied the rows of photographs.

"This must be Granddaddy in his younger days," she called to him, "the man standing beside the old wagon loaded with hay. You look just like him."

"That's Granddaddy," he said, returning to stand beside her.

"Who are all these other people?" she asked, trying to concentrate on the photos rather than gawking at Reno. He looked incredibly tall and handsome, dressed in dark Levi's, a crisp white shirt with long sleeves, and a dove gray summer-weight sports coat with a lineny-looking texture.

"That's my parents," he said with a nod, and Bobbie's gaze moved back to the pictures. "And look there—next to my mother. Remember Lady Lee?"

"Oh, my goodness. It's—"

"Yeah. The proverbial old gray mare was my mother's favorite horse. I must admit, I'm kinda glad you wouldn't listen to me that morning, but she's a great little mare. You'll have to ride her someday."

"I will." Bobbie smiled as she thought back to that morning. It didn't seem possible that it had been only four days ago.

"And this is me and Cal."

"How old were you there?"

"I was about five, I guess. So he must've been around fourteen or fifteen."

It was a wonderful picture, taken during roundup. Even at such a young age, Reno looked as if he belonged on horseback. Cal, however, looked less than thrilled.

Instead of telling Reno how cute he'd been as a preschooler and then asking more questions about his relationship with his brother, both of which Bobbie would have loved to do, she moved on to the next picture. Judging by its poor quality, it was one of the oldest photos. "Who are all these children? Did you run a summer camp here at one time?"

"No, these were kids from the orphanage in Abilene. See this woman standing in the middle of them?" He pointed to the only grown-up in the picture. "That's my grandmother. She had a real soft spot for these kids, since she was an orphan herself."

"Really?"

"Yeah. You've heard of the orphan trains, haven't you?"

"I think so," she said, then realized how she remembered it. "Yes! I saw a movie about that on television; it was based on a factual event." It was sometime around the turn of the century, as Bobbie recalled. The train had transported a bunch of homeless kids from the streets of several cities back East, stopping in almost every town throughout the farm belt in order to find homes for them. "You mean, your grandmother was actually on that train?"

"She was on one of them," he said. "There were quite a few trains over quite a few years' time. And most of the kids were adopted by people who really wanted them, but my grandmother was one of the unfortunate few, I guess you'd say, one of the kids who was taken in by people who just wanted cheap labor to help with the cooking or the farming. When she was only fifteen, she ended up running away from the couple who had adopted her. And after she and Granddad were married, they never had a lot of ready cash, but they had wide-open spaces and plenty of food to put on the table, so they started inviting these kids out to the ranch a couple of times a year." He tilted his head and smiled teasingly. "As my talkative old granddaddy used to say, every city kid ought'a at least know what it's all about: ropin' and ridin' and feelin' free."

Bobbie stared at the pictures in that particular grouping, noticing there were other photographs that were much the same, taken with various children over various years. She had to clear her throat of the lump that had suddenly formed there.

"I think I would've liked your talkative old granddaddy," she whispered. "And your grandmother, too."

Reno simply rolled his gorgeous blue eyes. "Women," he muttered disgustedly.

"What's that supposed to mean?" she said with a laugh.

"I tell you one simple little story, and you start getting sappy on me."

"Me?" she said with innocence. "No, not me."

Just then, she spotted a picture that had to be Reno in his early twenties, his arm wrapped protectively around a woman who appeared to be a few years younger.

"That's Faye," he said, answering Bobbie's unspoken question. "We were only married for about a year. That picture was taken a few months before we were divorced."

There was no negative emotion in his tone, she noticed. No bitterness. If anything, it was simply matter-of-fact.

Reno moved to the telephone, and while he placed a call to confirm an appointment of some sort, Bobbie's eyes went back to the photo. The woman Reno had once been married to wasn't at all what Bobbie would have expected. What had she expected, though? she wondered. She wasn't sure. Faye had been a pretty woman, in her own way, but perhaps Bobbie had expected someone more glamorous.

She studied the young couple in the picture. And as she glanced from Reno to Faye, as she studied the pose, Bobbie sensed an absence of...something. They looked as if they were close friends, she finally decided, rather than passionate young lovers.

Just then, Bobbie spotted another photograph of the same woman, one in which she was several years older. She was standing beside an old school bus filled with kids, and both the bus and Faye's T-shirt carried the name of a church-affiliated orphanage. Apparently, after their divorce, the woman had taken a job there. Or possibly she had been a volunteer.

Curious about both the ex-wife and the marriage itself, Bobbie decided that when the proper time arose, she would steer the conversation in that direction. Reno obviously wasn't upset by it, or the pictures would have been removed.

Reno hung up the receiver and glanced at his wristwatch. "My lawyer's office," he explained. "He's expecting me in about an hour. It won't take but a few minutes, though, and after that, the rest of the day is ours."

"That sounds wonderful," she said. "In fact, I really need to look at some maps. If there's a public library nearby, maybe you could just drop me off on your way there."

"Sure," he said, guiding her through the kitchen and into the office, where he grabbed his dove-gray hat and she retrieved her shoulder bag.

"Just a minute, Reno." Bobbie stopped short before they left the office. "We really shouldn't be seen leaving together. What if—"

"Oh, right," he said, a mockingly shrewd frown on his face. "Hold on."

After making a quick trip to his bedroom, he returned with a straw Stetson that he plunked on her head. The hat covered her eyes, resting on the bridge of her nose, and she pushed it back and gave him a feigned look of exasperation. "I'm serious, now."

"I know," he said, his finger brushing her nose. He took her elbow then, leading her to the elevator at the opposite end of the hall. "We'll go out the back way. I'm parked out there anyway, so I'll go first and get the engine started." Once in the elevator he backed her into the corner, his hands grasping the rails beside her hips. "I'll pull the truck around and pick you up at the door. You've seen *Bonnie and Clyde*, haven't you?"

"Reno!" She pressed her hands against his hard chest, putting up what she hoped appeared to be a halfway decent fight as she lifted her gaze to his. "That would be a little conspicuous, don't you think? Me, making a flying leap for the running board?"

"I don't know why." He glanced downward, his gaze raking her body as the elevator doors glided open. "You've got the legs for it. I think you can carry it off."

"Thanks," Bobbie said, laughing as she tried to regain her sense of composure. "But taking the back exit is good enough." She glanced around the parking area before stepping out into the bright sunlight. "I just don't want any-one—"

"Getting the wrong idea. I know." He helped her into the truck and was behind the wheel in no time. "We'll take the roundabout way." He steered the truck westward, onto a narrow, unpaved road instead of the main one. "If Annette's taking everyone out, she won't use this route. It'll be fine." Keeping an eye on his driving, he flashed a grin in her direction. "But keep the hat on. Just in case."

The road took a bend to the south. After adjusting the straw hat, Bobbie pointed to the buildings on the right, a group of rock structures that looked too large to be cabins. "I've been meaning to ask someone. What are those buildings?"

"Conference facilities. A lot of our regular guests like to hold their business meetings here. They like the relaxed atmosphere, the recreational possibilities, that sort of thing."

"Ah," she said, realizing the concept fit right in with the idea that had been forming in her own mind over the last couple of days. "Interesting."

The maps she wanted to check today, she assured herself, would be the deciding factor. After that, she'd be able to get her proposal down on paper. And as anxious as she was for Reno's opinion of it, she was even more anxious to get it out of the way. No matter how appealing Reno made it, she simply wasn't accustomed to combining business with pleasure. Not successfully, anyway.

A few minutes later, Bobbie noticed they were traveling eastward, toward Cal's house. "We are taking the roundabout way, aren't we?" she asked, glancing at the grove of native pecans they were approaching. Tired of adjusting the huge straw hat, she gave up and hung it on the bottom of the gun rack. "It's a shame for that beautiful old house to be standing there empty. Will your brother be back soon?"

"I have no idea. He took off several months ago, and I haven't heard a word from him since."

"Where did he go?"

"I don't know that, either. We weren't exactly on the best of terms when he left." He shook his head and frowned. "As much as he resented Dad leaving me Diamond Jubalee, he seemed to resent it even more when I used Jubalee's winnings to bail the ranch out of trouble." He lifted his shoulders. "I guess I'm still trying to figure out what Cal wants from me. My dad and I were always close. There's not much I could've done to change that, even if I'd wanted to."

"I'm sorry, Reno. I guess I don't know what this must feel like for you. I don't have a brother, and my sisters and I have always gotten along."

"Always?" he asked, laughing.

"Well, almost always," she said, smiling in return. "Except for the usual little scrapes about who took whose sweater and—"

"And who took whose boyfriend?"

"No," she said with a laugh. "We all went to private girls' schools, so..." She glanced away. There was no sense in telling the man everything about the protected environment she'd grown up in. "Well, I don't see my youngest sister very often, but I'm just a year older than Alix. She and I have always been very close."

"Does she live in Dallas, too?"

"No, not anymore. She moved to Bandera a few years ago."

"From Dallas to Bandera? That's quite a switch. What brought that on?" He raised the fingers of one hand from the steering wheel. "Wait a minute. Don't tell me. Mr. Right, right?"

"Right. She and her two children were staying at a friend's ranch near Bandera one summer. Alix was divorced, trying to get back into her career as an artist, and this man just sort of walked into her life. They ended up getting married and buying the ranch where they met. They love it there."

"He's a rancher?"

"No," she said, laughing. "Not really. It's a small place— nothing at all like this. He's a veterinarian."

"What about Alix's kids? Do they like this guy?"

"Oh, yes. They're just as much in love with the man as she is." How odd, she thought, that Reno would seem concerned about her niece and nephew. To him, they were nothing more than two faceless, nameless children. "Before Joe came into their lives, Kim and Mike had a father of sorts, but Wilton was certainly never what you'd call a real daddy, like Joe has been to them. Right after he and Alix were married, he took steps to adopt them, so it's been wonderful for them. And they're especially happy now."

"Why's that?"

"Well," she answered with a smile, "as you and my veterinarian brother-in-law would probably say, Alix is due to foal next month. So Kim and Mike are busy arguing over whether the new baby will be a boy or a girl."

"That's great, then." His facial expression changed from a smile to a frown. "Uh-oh," he said quickly, swerving off the road and hitting the brakes. "Duck down."

"What? Who—" Before she knew what was happening, Reno's forearm came around her neck and he pulled her toward him, burying her face against his broad, hard shoulder. "Oh, no!" she whispered. "Who saw us?"

"No one," he said, lifting her chin and smiling down at her. "Just practicing. I figured we could use a drill."

"Why, you . . ."

In what seemed like slow motion, Bobbie watched as his lips came down on hers, smothering her laughter and her idle protests, and she felt herself melting against Reno's heat. His strength. Her hands moved to the tempting V at the top of his shirt, her fingers skimming the dark, crisp hair on his chest.

She reveled in the gentle pressure of his fingers at the back of her neck, brushing through the hair at her nape. And when he parted her lips with his tongue, she welcomed its moist warmth, meeting it with her own as he explored the recesses of her mouth. All she could think about was him . . . and the fact that this was what she'd been yearning for, that this was what had been missing. To be with Reno like this, to be in his arms.

He raised his head, his own breathing as labored as hers.

"You are a cad," she whispered.

"I know," he murmured, his baritone a low, languid caress.

He reached up, his fingers rearranging one or two wisps of her hair—as if that would fix Bobbie right up again. It might take care of her outward appearance, but obviously the man had no idea of the effect he had on her insides.

"Well," he said then, sounding regretful. "I guess we'd better get going, huh?"

In no time at all he was around to the passenger side. And by then, Bobbie had realized that his truck was taking up a parking space at the airstrip. "I thought you said we were going to town."

"I did." He stood there with the door open. "*Cow*town."

"We're flying into Forth Worth? Just for the day?"

"Why not? It's less than an hour, ground to ground."

That didn't seem possible, Bobbie decided. At the busy airport located directly between Dallas and Forth Worth, landing time alone would have to be almost that lengthy, not to mention how crowded things were once you touched ground. "But just driving from the airport, with all that traffic . . . Isn't that a lot of hassle?"

"Not at all. We'll be landing near the stockyards. At a little private airport where I keep a car."

"Oh," she stated, finally climbing down from the truck. "That's different then. That sounds like fun."

"See? Didn't I promise you you wouldn't be sorry?" He gave her a tough, scolding look and took her arm. "Now stop arguing with me, woman, and let's go. I have an appointment to get out of the way—so we can really start having fun."

Reno sat in the car for a minute, realizing he could still detect Bobbie's light, flowery scent even though he'd dropped her off at the library a good ten minutes ago.

"Fun," he said aloud, a smile on his face. Yeah, trying to coax Bobbie Powell into having a little fun was the most fun Reno had had in ages. In fact, he could think of nothing he'd like better than to skip this damned appointment and just get on with the rest of the day.

His expression changed to a frown, and he checked his watch. He was right on time. Unfortunately.

After another moment's hesitation, Reno locked the car and walked inside the stately old building. Even though Quint Meadors was his long-time friend as well as his attorney, these trips to Fort Worth had gotten to be about as much fun as reporting to the dentist for a root canal. Okay, he admitted silently as he passed the empty reception desk. Maybe a little less fun.

When he opened the door to the inner office, Quint held up a welcoming hand and kept on with his telephone conversation.

Within a couple of seconds, it became apparent who was on the other end of the line. Reno took a seat on the opposite side of the big desk, and Quint gave him a pantomimed gesture that said, "Still no luck."

No luck, Reno decided, pretty well summed up his family situation nowadays. For quite some time now, actually. For a man who'd been raised to hold family high on his list of priorities, it was a pathetic state of affairs when he was forced to deal with his one and only brother by way of a middleman. Two middlemen, he corrected himself. Cal's attorney plus his own.

"Then check with him again," Quint was saying now. "My client is interested in hearing from his brother for only one reason, and it's not legal. Legally, he's got all he needs. Cal's aware of that, and so are you." Thumbing through the file before him, Quint fished out the power of attorney—already signed—that Cal's attorney had drawn up before he'd left. This time, the face Quint made said, "I'm definitely dealing with a screwball here."

"No," he went on, "what Reno wants now is simply to mend some personal fences. He's not even asking for an address or a phone number. All he wants is for Cal to give him a call; it's not an unreasonable request, by any means." He paused for a moment. "Yeah. Let me know, will you?"

Quint hung up and said, "Why don't we just give up on this angle? Hire a private detective?"

"No," Reno stated emphatically. "Cal's forty-four years old now, and if he wants to hide out somewhere for a while, I figure that's his business. I just want to let him know that if he wants to talk, I'm willing. Or that if he gets some of this figured out for himself, I'm ready to put the past behind us and get on with things as they stand now. The decision's got to be his at this point."

"Okay," Quint agreed grudgingly, rocking back in his swivel chair. "We'll go on to the next subject then. I do have some good news for you, for a change."

"What?" he asked immediately. Even though he'd been doing a decent job of shoving it to the back of his mind, there was only one area in his family and legal life where Quint knew that Reno was still holding out hope for good news. "What? Are you saying it's been approved?"

"Not yet, but—"

"Then why the hell are you bringing it up?"

"Calm down, Reno. I'm bringing it up because it's looking good. Real good. But you're going to have to be patient for just a little while longer. Private adoption is never easy—and certainly not in this case. I warned you of that in the beginning."

"Which is exactly why I don't want to discuss it in the interim. They're either going to approve it or they're not. Susan's either going to be mine or she's not. There's no gray area here, Quint. If there was, maybe I'd feel a little better about the whole thing. But as it stands—" He pushed his fingers through his hair. "Well, I just don't want to count my chickens before they hatch, that's all."

"Sit down," Quint said.

"Why?" Reno asked bluntly, figuring he could damned well pace if it suited him.

"Because you're wearing a hole in my carpet. And because when an old cattleman starts making references to his chickens, I figure it's time I set his mind at ease."

"Tell me it's been approved, then. That'll set my mind at ease." What bothered him most, he realized, was that it was a little girl's mind that needed to be eased. It was one thing for this poky group of people to keep him waiting and worrying, but to Reno's way of thinking, it was downright criminal to ask a seven-year-old kid how she felt about having him for a daddy—and then to keep *her* waiting and worrying all this time. That was what had been driving him crazy: convincing himself that there was nothing pending, just so he could be in the right frame of mind to convince Susan of the same thing.

"Sit down," his friend repeated, "and I'll tell you how good it sounds right now. As of today." When Reno finally complied with his request, Quint said, "Faye called this morning. She says it's looking real good. You're liable to hear something positive any day now."

"Yeah, sure. And the way I see it, almost anything could go wrong between now and then. They could look at this new financial situation I'm in and decide that's a problem. They could—"

"Oh, please," Quint interrupted sarcastically. "Don't give me that bull, because I know your financial situation better than anyone. You have a little problem right now with cash flow, but it's not like you're so broke you can't pay attention. We both know that even if you came close to going under, with what you own, you could have one hell of a little garage sale. Believe me, they're not gonna let something like that hold up the final papers."

"You never know," he argued.

"Listen. I'll tell you why I'm willing to talk so positively myself at this point. Now that it's down to the final stages, now that you've already made it through the initial digging into background and character and all that, I figure you've got one important, extra factor going for you. Faye's pulling harder than anyone for this adoption to go through. She's right in there fighting for you, and it certainly doesn't hurt that she's got some clout with these people. Personally, I don't think you can miss at this point." Quint laughed then. "Face it, buddy, how many guys can say they've got their ex-wives in their camp?"

"Correction," Reno said flatly. "One ex-wife in my camp."

Quint lifted his shoulders. "I look at it this way. One out of two's a far better average than most of my other clients have got."

"Speaking of which, I guess you've got those checks ready for me to sign?

"Oh, yeah." Quint opened a file and slid it across the desk top. "Same time every month, just like clockwork."

Reno pulled his chair up to the edge of the desk, located a pen and started flipping through the stack. "What's this?" he asked, studying the invoice and statement behind the first check. "An eight-dollar charge to the corner drugstore? What's Glendelle doing with the allowance I give her? If she doesn't have enough cash in her purse to pay for a damned tube of lipstick—"

Sifting through some of the other bills, he noticed that Glendelle had torn off the top of one particular statement and sent it with no itemization of the charges. "Let me use your phone for a minute, will you, Quint?"

Within a matter of seconds he placed the call to American Express, giving them the required information for an authorized rundown of the individual charges for the month of July. After jotting down two important items, he hung up the phone.

"Airline tickets," he said. "Well, she didn't fly to Las Vegas and Mexico City to get away from the snow back home in Fort Worth, that's for sure. I'd say we're talking more along the lines of blackjack and jai alai. I'd say she's back at it again, wouldn't you?"

"I'd say I don't want to say—until I'm officially invited to say it."

"What does that mean?"

"That means that as both your friend and your lawyer, I got tired of fighting you on the subject of Glendelle Phillips Tanner a long time ago."

"Okay," Reno admitted. "You're right. So why don't we say that as of today—as my lawyer—you're officially invited to say?"

"In that case, I'd say you're probably right. I saw her at the theater last week, and you know that diamond pendant her folks gave her at her coming-out party? The one she wears all the time?"

Reno rolled his eyes and asked, "The one she could use to signal passing ships?"

"Yeah. Well, until the other night, I'd never seen her without it on. Not once. So when it was noticeably missing, I couldn't help wondering if maybe she'd finally broken down and hocked the damned thing." Quint leaned back and added, "So in answer to your question: yes, I'd say you're right. I'd say there's no doubt she's gambling again. Probably worse than ever."

Reno nodded toward the stack of statements and checks. "Do you happen to have a total on these?"

"Sure do."

He glanced at the bottom line of the calculator tape Quint slid across the desk to him. Seeing the exorbitant figure—well over twice the amount Reno knew it took to cover every one of

Glendelle's monthly expenses, even considering the extravagant life-style she'd always been accustomed to—he released a long, weary sigh. It wasn't the amount that bothered him. It was the scheming and the lies; it was the number of times she had schemed and lied in the three years they'd been married and the three years since. Even more than that, it was the empty promises she'd made over and over again.

"You know, Quint, I used to have this vast storehouse of..." He glanced into the air. "Lately, I've been noticing I just don't have much patience at all anymore." His eyes moved to the American Express bill. "And maybe it's got something to do with crap like this. Maybe it's because I've had enough of my own problems to worry about lately, without adding Glendelle's calculating little tricks to the lot." He glanced at his friend. "Maybe it's because I've talked to her till I'm blue in the face. So do me a favor, will you? Void these checks. All of them." He pushed the file toward Quint. "Bundle up the rest of this stuff and send it back to Glendelle with a cover letter. I don't care how you word it, but basically, just tell her she's seen the last of my good side. Tell her my patience has run out—and so has her allowance."

"I'll be glad to, and congratulations."

"On what?"

"I'd say that woman's been an albatross around your neck for long enough now, wouldn't you?"

Reno laughed bitterly. "Is that a reference to poultry?"

"No. It's a reference to that sense of guilt you've been carrying around for too many years now. You've been more than generous with her. Against my advice and better judgment, you handed her one hell of a divorce settlement, and—"

"I can't help feeling guilty about it, Quint. If I hadn't been the one to take Glendelle to the racetrack for the first time—if I hadn't been the one to hand her the money for that first bet—then maybe I'd feel differently." Still frowning, he added, "But that's the way it went."

"Come on, Reno. That was nothing but an innocent gesture. It's the kind of thing a man does for a woman when he's courting her." Quint gave him a pointed look. "She's the one who let it become a problem. And all along, she's the one who's been letting it get worse. God knows you've put up with enough of her broken promises to get help."

"Well." He ran a hand across his clenched jaw. "I'll deal with the guilt. You deal with her this time, huh?" He gestured toward the file. "When she calls—which she will the minute she gets this stuff—just let her know my decision's firm. I offered to give her an allowance for a few years to help her get back on her feet and make something of herself, not to line the pockets of some casino operator in Las Vegas."

He glanced at his wristwatch and stood, pushing his chair back. "Let me know as soon as you hear something about the adoption, will you? But not until you have something definite for me."

"Sure," Quint answered, then asked, "You staying in town for a while?"

"Yeah. Why?"

"Why don't you meet me in about an hour? What do you say, buddy? A couple of old bachelors on the town, celebrating your big decision? I'll bet we could get ourselves lined up with a couple of—"

"Thanks anyway, Quint, but it looks like you'll just have to fend for yourself tonight. This old bachelor's already got plans. With someone pretty special." He glanced at his watch again and lifted his eyebrows. "In fact, I'm on my way to the library. I promised I'd pick her up right about now."

Reno turned to leave. And before he shut the door, he heard the unmistakably puzzled tone in Quint's voice as he asked, "A librarian? Since when do you have a thing for librarians?"

It was true, Reno thought as he stood there quietly, watching Bobbie from several yards behind the table where she was working diligently. She really was something special. He'd decided on the way over here that that was exactly how he felt about her.

He'd decided something else, too, and that was what his next strategy needed to be. Had to be. No matter what else Reno had in mind, for the time being, he needed to move slowly.

Yeah, he reminded himself. He'd keep things light. And then, just as soon as Bobbie started relaxing a little, he would simply ask a few questions—however many questions were necessary in order to find out why she was still so skittish.

He was sure now that it wasn't because of him, personally, or even because of Upton Powell and the way Bobbie had been reared. No. This attitude of hers had something to do with another man entirely, and Reno was convinced that once he knew more about the past, he'd know exactly how to handle things in the present.

Moving closer, he peered over Bobbie's shoulder to see what she was working on so intently. It was a photocopy she'd evidently made of a map. Using a compass, she was busy drawing another circle. Each one of the already existing circles, he noticed, had the same center point: the small town of Santa Anna.

He watched her trade the compass for a ruler, measuring and then double-checking the map's scale. Finally she made a notation on a separate sheet of paper. Obviously, she was figuring mileage from the Diamond T to various cities: the major cities of Texas as well as the entire Southwest. On the plain white paper, she'd used columns to break it down, and he read some of the entries.

less than 200	less than 300	less than 450
Ft. Worth/ Dallas	Amarillo	El Paso
Lubbock	Houston	Monterrey, MX
Midland/ Odessa	Okla. City	Tulsa, OK
San Anto- nio/Austin		

Unbelievable, he thought, glancing at the separate, individual notations she'd made for the distances to New Orleans, Mexico City and various other places.

"Hi there," he whispered at last, touching her shoulder.

With a start, she said, "Oh. Hi there, yourself."

He pulled out the chair beside her, turning it around and straddling it. Reaching forward, he used the pad of his index finger to touch the center of the eyeglasses that were perched on the very tip of her nose. "You should wear those all the time," he said. "I like girls who wear glasses."

"I only use them for close work," she answered with a smile, her voice still quiet as she removed the half-glasses and put them away. "And besides that, I'm not a girl anymore, remember?"

"Okay, then," he conceded. "If it'll make you feel any better, I'll put it a different way. I like old broads who wear glasses."

"Oh, thanks," she said, laughing softly as she began to close books and gather her papers.

"I don't believe you," he said, holding up the chart she'd made. "All this time and precision for nothing."

"It's not for nothing," she answered immediately. "It's for you. For my proposal for you."

"That's not what I'm talking about," he explained. "Hell, Bobbie, if you had just asked, I could've written this out for you in about a minute and a half. I have a plane, remember?"

"I know," she said sheepishly. "But I didn't want to ask."

"Why not?"

"Because I didn't want you to ask me why I was asking. I don't have my idea completely ready for you just yet."

"Then I won't ask you about it until you do," he assured her. It was more obvious now than ever. This woman didn't like to feel pushed on any subject—whether it be personal or business. "Are you about ready for dinner?"

"I'm starving." She glanced down at her jeans. "But I guess I'm not exactly dressed for dinner, am I?"

"You worry too much about appearances," he said with a grin. "You look great. Especially for what I've got in mind."

"I do, huh? What's it going to be, then? Pizza? Hamburgers and shakes?"

"Nah," he said, trying to look arrogant, "I thought I'd save McDonald's for the next time we step out on the town. This being our first date and all, I thought I should try to impress you. I figured I'd just pull out all the stops and take you to this great little joint that has the best chicken-fried steak in the world."

"Oh, my. The best in the whole wide world? That does sound impressive." She gave him a dreamy look. "You really know how to sweep an old broad off her feet."

"I know." He tilted his head. "So how 'bout it, old girl? What do you say we get this stuff put away and get out of here? We'll just mosey on down the road and strap on the old feed bag."

"You old cattlemen do have an abundance of it, don't you?"

"I guess you're talking about charm," he said. "Yeah, I reckon we do."

"Keep working on it, cowboy." Her smiling eyes shifted away from him. "Oh, look. There's a poor, unsuspecting woman you can practice on right now." Bobbie pointed to the librarian who'd just walked out of their section. "Not that I need a break from all that charm, of course, but why don't you shovel a little of it on someone else for a while?" She passed him the ruler and compass. "While I start putting books away, why don't you return these and thank her for lending them to me?"

"You want me to thank her properly, then?"

"By all means," Bobbie answered, laughing at the smug, smart-alecky look on his face. Her gaze lowered to take in the rest of him. How could it be? she wondered. How could Reno Tanner make such a simple posture look so unbelievably sexy? Surely she had noticed men straddling chairs at some point in the past, but right now, for the life of her, she couldn't remember when.

She watched as he unfolded his tall, long-legged frame and stood, pushing the chair back into place. And when he spotted the atlas she was closing, his expression changed to one of seriousness.

"I'm sure glad you wanted to spend some time here," he said. "From what I've heard, someone published a book just recently about one of my ancestors. I'll ask the librarian; maybe they'll have a copy of it."

"Oh, I hope so," she replied excitedly. "I'd love to see it, too."

He walked away then, apparently intent on his mission, and Bobbie turned to the shelf directly behind her to start putting away the reference materials she'd used.

As she found the correct slots for the last two books, Bobbie heard Reno calling her name from what sounded like several aisles away.

"Come here," he was adding, his voice hushed. "You're not gonna believe this. They do have a copy."

"Really?" Searching for and finally locating the row he'd been calling her from, she headed for the middle of it. "Where?"

"Right here." Just before she reached where he was standing, he pointed to the top shelf. "Look. *The Life and Times of Cletus Tanner*."

"Where? I still don't see it." She raised up on her toes, straining to see the general area he was indicating. "Well, Reno, this doesn't even look like the right section for—"

His short, quiet, devilish sound of amusement interrupted her, and when she turned around, Bobbie found herself so close to him she could feel his breath on her face.

"Cletus Tanner, my foot!" she muttered, barely managing to smother a laugh. "You really are full of it, you know that?"

"And you really are a gullible little creature," he whispered, "you know that?"

"Well, if I am, it's only because you're such a good liar."

"Well, if I am," he repeated, his voice low and husky, "it's only when it suits my purposes."

His arms moved outward, and he braced his hands against the shelves and moved even closer—until Bobbie's entire back was pressed against the stacks.

Her fingers traveled up his chest, and she made a halfhearted, futile effort to push him away. "Reno!" she whispered, "someone's going to catch us."

"So? What are they gonna do? Kick us out?"

"Yes," she said sharply, trying to sound cross.

He lifted one shoulder. "Big deal. We're leaving anyway."

"That's beside the point," she said, laughing. "They might—"

"What? Confiscate our library cards? I don't have one. Do you?"

"Well, no. Not for this library, but—"

"But what?" he asked, smiling as he added, "you worry too much."

"I know."

"And you argue too much, too."

"I know."

"So stop arguing with me, will you, woman?"

"I will."

"Yes, but when?"

"Now," she murmured. "Right now."

"You're sure?"

"Yes!" she whispered frantically, lifting herself up, bringing her mouth to within inches of his. "Yes, I'm sure."

Dear Lord, she thought. Right now, there was only one thing she knew for sure. Charm couldn't be the right word. It was much more than that. But whatever it was, Reno Tanner did have an abundance of it. He had far more than any one man's share.

Beyond that, whatever it was, he was clearly driving her insane with it!

She was aching for him. No, she was dying for him. She wanted to scream something utterly stupid and trite, something like, "Just shut up and kiss me, you fool!" She wanted to throw her arms around him and pull him closer than he already was—which probably wasn't even physically possible.

Slowly, ever so slowly, his mouth lowered. Almost to her lips. Almost . . .

"Good," he whispered at last. "That's all I wanted to hear."

Chapter Eight

Bobbie let out a slow, pleasurable sigh. "Well, cowboy, there's one thing you weren't lying about. That was *definitely* the best I've ever had."

"See? Didn't I promise you it would be?"

"Yes, you certainly did." She pushed back her empty plate and glanced around the busy, crowded little café. "I guess I just never realized how good chicken-fried steak could be. But now I know, and I'm duly impressed."

"Good," Reno said, shifting positions. The small, corner booth obviously wasn't designed for his build. He turned, stretching out his legs and propping one elbow on the edge of the table.

As it had all during dinner, Bobbie's mind again drifted back to the scene that had taken place—to the scene that had almost taken place—nearly two hours before. What would she have done, she wondered, if Reno had done exactly what she had yearned for him to do? If he had actually kissed her, instead of simply taking her by the hand and leading her out of the library, what else would she have begged him for besides the kiss she had wanted so badly?

The closest answer she'd been able to come up with was a vision—an unbelievably vivid one—where she was ripping off every stitch of Reno's clothing, along with her own, and then begging him to take her. Right there on the floor of that particular branch of the Fort Worth public library!

Dear Lord, she thought. It was best to keep trying to erase that picture from her mind. Especially when Reno was now glancing her way with curiosity, making her wonder if he really was trying to read her mind.

"Why are you looking at me like that?" She gestured toward the empty plate in front of her. "Does it surprise you that I really know how to strap on the old feed bag?"

"No," he said with a laugh. "What surprises me is that a woman like you has never been married. I'm curious, that's all. I keep wondering why."

How could she answer a question like that? Instead, she rolled her eyes dramatically and pushed out a long, labored gust of air. "I thought I told you that the other day."

"When was that?"

"Out by the pool, remember? When I let it slip that I was an old broad. That I was getting a little long in the tooth."

"Yeah, but you were being sarcastic then, and I'm being serious. So why haven't you ever gotten married?"

After several moments of silence, Bobbie finally shrugged her shoulders. "My work has kept me too busy, I guess. It's taken an unbelievable amount of time and effort to get established in this crazy business I'm in." That was true, she decided. Her work had indeed kept her busy. "Speaking of which, you haven't told me what you think of the other developers."

"I haven't thought much about them. I'm reserving judgment till Friday, when I hear what they have to say."

"But surely you've given some kind of thought to them."

"No." He lifted one hand. "Well, some, I guess. Nothing specific, though. Just sort of a first impression of each one."

"Like what?"

"You want the truth?"

"Of course."

"All right, then. Here goes." He leaned back, resting his laced fingers over his lean stomach. "The redheaded woman from San Antonio always has this blank stare on her face—like the lights are on but there's no one at home."

Bobbie couldn't help laughing at that one, especially since she knew there was a reason for that blank stare. Vivian Kingford was nothing less than mesmerized by Reno's presence. Bobbie knew that for a fact.

"Okay," she said at last, still smiling. "Who's next? What about Rex Edwards?"

"Which one's that?"

"You're impossible, Reno! You don't even know their names, do you?"

"I know your name," he stated flatly, as if that made up for everything else.

"And what's that? Old girl?" She tried to look offended. "No, I don't think I want to hear your impression of me."

The waitress showed up then to clear their plates and refill their glasses of iced tea. When the woman asked if they'd like dessert, Bobbie answered yes, but that definitely she would have to wait a while to make room for it.

Ignoring Reno's look of amazement that she could manage dessert on top of everything else, she said, "Now. What's your impression of Rex? He's the older gentleman from Houston."

"You must be talking about the guy with the wild, curly gray hair, huh?" After she nodded in agreement, he frowned briefly and said, "I keep thinking he needs to have something done with that hair. He always looks like he just grabbed ahold of the business end of a snake."

Bobbie shook her head, pretending to be disgusted with him. Then she said, "Come on, now. I'm serious. Surely you've thought more about them than what they—"

"You're doing it again, you know."

"Doing what again?"

"Changing the subject on me. I don't want to talk about the other developers. I want to talk about you." His eyes never left hers. "Whenever I start getting the least bit close to you, you either make some sarcastic little remark—which I kind of enjoy, actually—or you change the subject to business. Why do you do that?"

"I—I didn't know I was doing that."

"Well, you do."

"If I do," she said after some careful thought, "I guess it's because I feel comfortable talking about business. I've been lucky in business."

"That doesn't wash."

"Why not?" she asked, her voice taking on a defensive tone.

"Because something tells me that when it comes to business, Upton Powell didn't train his firstborn to sit back and wait on lucky breaks. I'd be willing to bet you've made your own luck."

"All right," she admitted, deciding she might as well give Reno an honest answer. Obviously, he wasn't willing to settle for anything less. "Maybe luck isn't quite the right word, then. Let's say I'm comfortable talking about business because I've been successful in business. With men, on the other hand, I haven't had very much success. Or luck, or whatever you care to call it."

"Well, I'd say you weren't exactly one of a kind in that respect. I haven't had the best of luck with women, either, but—"

"Ah," she said, anxious to find out more about Reno's ex-wife. "You must be talking about Faye. About your divorce."

He simply lifted his broad shoulders.

"Was it something simple?" Bobbie asked, reminding herself to give him a casual smile and keep it light. "You were too young? Your granddaddy didn't approve?"

"You're really intent on changing the subject, aren't you?"

"No," she answered. "I'm just curious, that's all. I saw another picture of Faye, and I was wondering if she worked at the same orphanage your grandmother was involved with."

Reno tilted his head and grinned. "Okay, then. I'll make you a deal. I'll tell you about Faye, and then you tell me about you."

"Okay," she said, returning his grin. "It's a deal."

"Good. I'll make this quick, then. Faye's a counselor at the orphanage—has been for years—but she also grew up there.

That's how we met, when we were both kids and her whole group came out to the ranch on a regular basis. I was a couple of years older than she was, and she always liked to tag along after me.'' He leaned back, his shoulders against the wall beside the booth. ''She had a stutter back then. A very slight one, but some of the kids liked to pick on her and I sort of . . . stood up for her, I guess you'd call it.''

Reno lifted his glass, taking a long drink of iced tea before adding, ''We got married right after she graduated from high school. So, yes, I guess you could say we were too young. Or not worldly or wise enough, or whatever the right word might be. We cared a lot about each other, but before we got married, I guess neither one of us realized there was a big difference between passion and compassion.''

He rested his big palm over the top of the glass. ''For as long as I'd known her, Faye had had this dream of having a real family. A home of her own. Looking back on it now, I guess I wanted to give her the kind of stability I'd known all my life but that I thought she'd been denied.''

Reno lifted one shoulder. ''Anyway, that year we were together, we were both going to the same college, both struggling to understand ourselves and grow up. And somehow, we managed to realize we just weren't meant to be married. Not to each other, anyway. We're still real good friends, though.''

''That's nice,'' Bobbie said, meaning that and so much more. The story had tugged at her heart. How many young men would care that much about someone else's problems and needs and yearnings? Not many at all, she decided quickly. ''Did Faye ever marry again?''

''Yeah, several years later. She has four kids now and seems really happy.''

''That's wonderful.''

Reno nodded his head. ''Now,'' he stated bluntly, ''I want to talk about you, remember?''

Their waitress breezed by again, checking on their iced-tea situation. The dinner crowd had started thinning out, and Bobbie noticed that the woman's pace was slower, her smile brighter.

"And now that we're down to basics," Reno commented after the waitress moved on to her next station, "discussing individuals and not just the opposite sex in general, what about that man you mentioned when we were out riding the other day? The one you almost married?"

"What about him?"

"Well, for one, what's his name? And just exactly how does that 'almost' business work?"

"Harrison Wainwright," she replied, "and it's fairly simple, actually. I was sort of . . . left at the altar."

"Sort of?"

"Well, it's a long story. I doubt that—"

"No problem," he interrupted, smiling as he turned the face of his watch toward her. "We have plenty of time, don't we?"

She took a sip of tea. It had happened ages ago, Bobbie reminded herself. And she no longer felt anything for Harrison. "The wedding was planned down to the last detail, and about a week before the big day, I walked into his office." Bobbie realized she needed to back up a bit. "Harrison and I both worked for the same property-development firm at the time.

"Anyway, I'd gone in to ask if he wanted to have lunch with me. But he was facing the window, talking on the phone. And before I could let him know I was there, I heard him say something like, 'Just give me another couple of weeks. I'll have the money for you by then.' I couldn't imagine what he was talking about, but after I slipped quietly out of his office, I couldn't stop thinking about it. There was something in his tone that worried me, and it didn't make sense. If it was a small amount of money, why would he put off repaying it? And if it was a lot, how would he be able to come up with it in a couple of weeks?"

"Maybe he was due to come into some money. Something he hadn't told you about for some reason."

"Maybe. But the only thing I could think of was that Harrison knew I had a trust fund coming to me. I couldn't recall ever mentioning exactly when it was to become mine, and we had never discussed dollar amounts, of course, but... Well, he had wanted the wedding to be on my twenty-fifth birthday, and I'd thought that was really sweet. Kind of romantic and sentimental. But after hearing what he said on the phone that day,

I started wondering if it was more than a romantic gesture. I was ashamed of myself for even suspecting such a thing, but after wrestling with it for a couple of days, I knew I couldn't walk down the aisle with him. Not when I had that kind of doubt in my mind.''

"So it was you who called off the wedding?"

"Oh, no," she said with a laugh. "It was going to be a huge, lavish affair with about half of Dallas invited, and I couldn't simply call it off. Not when it was only five days away, and certainly not when I had nothing to base it on but a niggling suspicion."

She shook her head . "No, I didn't call off the wedding. But I knew I had to find out what was going on. I also knew that if what I suspected was true, it would be useless to just come right out and ask him. So I came up with a little test. And sure enough, he failed."

"How?"

"Well . . . the day after the test, he started getting cold feet, as he so eloquently put it."

"Yeah, but what kind of a test was it?"

"For heaven's sake, Reno. It's too ridiculous even to repeat."

"No. I want to hear it." His tone was emphatic. "Maybe the guy really did start getting cold feet. Men have a different way of looking at things, remember? Maybe your test didn't take that into account."

"You don't give up, do you?" When Reno slowly shook his head and grinned, Bobbie said, "All right, fine. Since you insist. It sounds kind of stupid now, but it was the best I could come up with at the time. I went in to his office and told him I was a little short until payday. And then I asked him for a loan—some piddly amount, as I recall, something like two or three hundred dollars. It was a bald-faced lie, of course, but I told him my American Express payment was due and—"

"American Express, huh?" he asked with a short laugh.

"Yes," she said, laughing in return as she shrugged her shoulders. "Well, why not? As the say in their ads, Membership has its privileges."

"That it does," he agreed. "So you asked him for a loan. And what'd he do? Turn you down?"

"I didn't give him a chance to answer one way or another. I just rattled on with something about my father refusing to give me the money. I said I'd even asked if I could borrow it against my trust fund, and that Daddy had just glared at me and said, 'Absolutely not, young lady.'"

She stopped then, irritated that Reno was trying his best not to snicker. "I told you it was a ridiculous story. I never should've—"

"No, honey," he said quickly, laughing good-naturedly as he held up a placating hand. "It's not that. It was that low, gruff imitation you did. Something tells me that's not exactly how your dad talks."

When she lifted her eyes and tilted her head in a silent act of admission, he said, "Okay, I won't laugh again—I swear. And I won't interrupt anymore, either. So you told this Harrison guy a little white lie about needing money and that you'd asked your dad for a loan against your trust fund." He winked. "Now go ahead from there, because I wanta hear that Upton Powell voice just one more time."

"All right," Bobbie said with laugh, "but just once. I told this Harrison guy that Daddy said, 'Absolutely not, young lady! You know how I feel about that. Not one penny till your thirtieth birthday!' Well, that was another lie, since I was due to receive it on my twenty-fifth birthday, but..." She lifted her shoulders. "But it worked. The shocked expression on Harrison's face told me everything I needed to know, so I got up to leave his office, saying something like, 'Never mind. I really shouldn't be asking you for a loan. I'll figure out something.' And he didn't offer any protests."

"Maybe the guy was strapped for cash."

"I don't believe this," she stated disgustedly. "I may be gullible, Reno, but I'm not stupid! And what about you? I thought you could see right through all these devious men of the world." She stared at him in sudden exasperation. "Obviously, you need a woman's slant on this. It wasn't the loan that did it. That wasn't even the issue! The issue was, less than twenty-four hours later, four days before the wedding, he decided he wasn't ready for marriage.

"Translation," Bobbie added slowly, with a pointed note of sarcasm, "he didn't intend to wait five years for something he'd planned to get within the next few days."

"Easy, darlin'. Don't get excited. All I'm saying is that maybe the guy really did care for you. It seems to me that—"

"Do you men always stick together?" she asked, her tone reflecting both anger and impatience. "Why are you siding with him?"

"I'm not siding with him. I'm just saying maybe there were things you didn't know."

"Maybe not, but what I do know is that the man hasn't changed one bit. Even now, he's still the same—"

"You still keep tabs on him?"

"No! Absolutely not. But we're in the same line of work. The same city. Unfortunately I can't help but hear things about him. And see him at times."

"So is this Harrison guy the reason you've worked so hard at being a businesswoman?"

"Meaning?"

"Meaning, could it be that you've been trying to prove something to him? That you can be more successful than he is?"

"Of course not," she answered immediately. "That's ludicrous."

"Well, then," he added, pausing for a few more seconds, "could it be that you still care for him?"

"Absolutely not! That's even more ludicrous."

"Is it? Because it seems to me that I see a spark in your eyes when you talk about him."

"If you see a spark in my eyes, Reno, it's for a completely different reason than the proverbial torch carrying you have in mind. It's for one reason only, in fact. I hold nothing but disdain for that man—and for his entire life-style. That was ten years ago, and let's just say he hasn't let any grass grow under his feet since then. He's now on Bride Number Three!"

"Well," Reno said, lifting his shoulders and deliberating for several moments. "I'm not trying to defend the man's actions, that's for sure. I don't know anything about him and you do, but why does it bother you that he's been divorced a couple of times? What I mean is, you seem to be sure he wasn't sincere in your own case—and I see your reasoning—but if you don't keep close tabs on him anymore, how can you be absolutely sure he hasn't cared about these other women? His past and present wives?"

It was a logical question, Bobbie decided. Actually, it had been a series of questions, but the way he'd asked them had made her realize she'd gotten irritated with him for just trying to be reasonable throughout their entire conversation about Harrison Wainwright.

She smiled, letting him know she had set aside her irrational anger. "Trust me on this one, Reno. Suffice it to say, I didn't have to hide behind a curtain in Harrison's bedroom to know exactly how he felt about each of his wives. Each time he took another bride down the aisle, he took another step up the corporate and-or financial ladder." She rolled her eyes. "Another giant step each time, to be precise."

"Oh," he said with a laugh. "I guess that does tend to give a pretty clear message about him."

Just then, their waitress approached the table. "You about ready for that dessert, hon?"

"Yes," Bobbie answered, glad for the interruption. "I can't make up my mind, though. How's the pecan pie?"

"Oh, hon," the woman said confidingly, then lowered her voice. "Warm? With a little vanilla ice cream on top? Let me tell ya—that stuff's better than sex."

Bobbie's mouth was open, but she didn't know exactly how to respond.

"Well," Reno stated, his eyes on Bobbie's as he reached up and tried to wipe the grin off his face before addressing the waitress. "That sounds like something we shouldn't pass up."

"Two slices, then?"

"Sure."

The woman scribbled the order on her pad and walked away.

Amused by the sudden rise of color in Bobbie's cheeks, Reno watched her as she glanced over her shoulder and then told him she'd be right back.

As his gaze followed her path toward the ladies' room, Reno decided his questioning had sounded casual enough. Beyond that, Bobbie's answers had told him exactly what he needed to know.

That was why she'd been so upset when she thought Reno wasn't taking his inheritance seriously. She obviously didn't treat her own inheritance lightly, and she had a fixation about people who did.

Along with that, he realized, she might also have a problem with people who took marriage lightly. And if that was the case, if she'd been judging all men by that one jerk's actions, Reno damned sure wasn't going to put his foot in his mouth by trying to explain his own situation with Glendelle. It was far too complicated to go into at this early stage of the game. First he needed to keep proving to Bobbie that she could trust him. He needed to give her time to realize he wasn't anything like Harrison Wainwright.

Yeah, Reno thought with a smile, Bobbie Powell just hadn't been letting herself have any real, honest-to-goodness fun. She'd been taking life too seriously—just as he'd been doing lately.

As soon as they were through here, though, he decided, he planned to do something about that. He was going to take Bobbie to a dark, cozy little dance hall nearby. An intimate little place where, for a few hours, he'd have a legitimate excuse to snuggle up to her....

By the time Bobbie returned from her trip to the ladies' room, dessert had been delivered. After they each took a bite, Reno gestured toward the pie. "What do you think?"

"Well" she answered, sounding almost hesitant as she lifted a shoulder, "it's okay, I guess, but . . ."

"I know." Leaning forward, he shielded one side of his face. With a tilt of his head, he indicated their waitress across the room. "I wouldn't tell her this, of course," he murmured secretively, "but I think maybe she's been sleepin' with the wrong man."

Bobbie shook her head as she rolled her gorgeous hazel eyes. And this time, her blush was accompanied by soft, throaty laughter and a beautifully chastising smile.

Yeah, Reno told himself as he laughed along with her, this Harrison Wainwright fella had been a lot more than an irresponsible opportunist. The guy had been an absolute fool.

Chapter Nine

Annette ushered Bobbie down the hallway and into Reno's sitting room. "I'd like to thank you, dear. It certainly was kind of you to offer to take the last appointment of the six."

"No problem at all." Trying to appear nonchalant, Bobbie adjusted the bottom edge of the short-sleeved, ivory cotton sweater she wore over matching tailored slacks. "With my being the only one here with my own vehicle, I decided there was no sense in holding up the plane, especially with everyone trying to get back home on a Friday afternoon."

"Yes, and for that reason alone, I'm sure the other developers appreciated your thoughtful gesture."

Thoughtfulness had been only part of it. Bobbie still wasn't sure whether she'd done it for personal reasons—to be alone with Reno—or out of good business sense. As the last of the six, she knew she would be better able to judge his reaction to her idea.

Annette guided her into the small kitchen. "Feel free to help yourself to anything you can find in here." After indicating the fresh-smelling pot of coffee, as well as a cream pitcher and an assortment of cold drinks in the refrigerator, Annette nodded toward the closed door that led to Reno's office. "I'm sure Reno and Vivian will be through any minute now."

Not if Vivian has anything to say about it, Bobbie told herself, amused by the thought. "Thank you, Annette. I'm sure I'll be fine."

"Oh, by the way," the tiny woman commented, pointing to the file folder Bobbie was carrying and then directing her back into the sitting room. "If you'd like to go over your paperwork while you're waiting, feel free to spread things out in here."

Annette moved toward the doorway to the hall. "I don't know about you, Bobbie," she added, a confiding smile on her face as she momentarily glanced back, "but once in a while, I need to take a few minutes to collect my muddled thoughts."

"Yes," Bobbie told her with a laugh. "Me, too. Maybe I'll do just that."

"Then make yourself at home."

"Thanks, Annette," she said before the woman turned to leave. "I will."

Muddled, Bobbie decided, was far too mild a word for the thoughts she'd been having for the last day and a half, ever since her "first date" with Reno, which had left her feeling more starry-eyed than her true first date however many years ago.

While Reno was holding her in his arms that night, while they were dancing, she had decided it almost seemed as if he were making love to her. And if it felt that wonderful just to dance with him, then how would it feel to actually make love with him? She couldn't seem to stop wondering about that. And for some reason, she also kept thinking about their waitress's remark.

Bobbie had had some pecan pie in her life. Not a lot, by any means, but some. Yet merely dancing with Reno Tanner, she'd decided, was far better than any or all of the actual pie she'd had in her entire life. As soon as she'd had that realization, Reno's teasing comment about their waitress's life had entered her mind: "Maybe she's been sleeping with the wrong man."

And since that obviously had been the case in Bobbie's life, she wondered if Reno Tanner might be the *right* man.

Maybe if she knew for sure—without a doubt—that he was interested in her, in the same ways that she was interested in him. Maybe if he would just . . .

That was what had her so puzzled. She just didn't know for sure. In the library, she had thought he wanted to kiss her every bit as much as she wanted to be kissed, but that he had stopped himself because they were in a public place. And the dancing had only affirmed her thinking.

Her *thinking*? she repeated inwardly, smiling at the absurdity of the word itself. It hadn't taken any thinking at all. He'd held her so close, in fact, that she knew without a doubt that at least physically, Reno had been just as affected by their closeness as she'd been.

Then, later that night when they were flying back to the ranch, he had glanced down at the six-seater's instrument panel and made a remark about something being wrong with the gas gauge—teasing her with a pilot's version of the old running out of gas on a dark, lonely road routine. But nothing had happened after they had actually landed. Oh, he had walked her to her cabin door, and after saying something about seeing her on Friday, he had kissed her good-night. But it hadn't been the kiss she'd expected. He had acted as if he were holding back, and it was clearly driving her insane wondering and worrying about it.

And, she reprimanded herself for the hundredth time, she had to stop thinking about it.

Bobbie glanced around her, realizing how much this large, grand, ultramasculine room suited him. In fact, she decided, that was probably why she hadn't actually noticed it when she was first here the other day. This sitting room had been nothing more than a perfect, unobtrusive backdrop. With the exception of the photos on the wall, she had seen only Reno.

Now, though, she noticed that the room contained several massive pieces of gorgeous, well-tended oak, one of them a huge, antique gun cabinet. There were newer furnishings, too, all just as massive, including a sofa and two chairs of fine, rich, dark green leather. But Bobbie thought that beneath the pleasing aroma of leather, she could detect the faint scent of Reno, too, which she found even more pleasing.

After taking another deep breath and letting it out, Bobbie realized she was feeling a sense of impatience. Maybe, she decided all of a sudden, because this room didn't seem quite right without him in it.

She turned and went into the kitchen, standing there for several moments, trying to decide between a cup of coffee and a soft drink and finally realizing all she wanted was a drink of water. After filling a glass from the tap, she heard the sound of a door opening and closing. Then she heard Reno's and Vivian's retreating voices as he apparently walked her to the elevator.

Within moments, Reno joined Bobbie in the kitchen. This room, she decided as she glanced up and returned his smile, seemed much, much tinier with him in it.

"Hi there," he said.

"Hi there, yourself." She set down the glass. "Ready for our meeting?"

"Sure," he said, still smiling. "How about you, though? Is there anything you'd like before we get started?"

Yes, she wanted to answer. *I'd like for you to touch me. More than that, I'd like for you to take me into your arms and tell me exactly how you feel about me, and then I'd like—*

"A cup of coffee?" he asked, amending his question. "Or maybe some lunch?"

She hid her disappointment and said, "I've eaten, thank you. But what about you?"

"Oh, yeah," he assured her. "I managed to fit in a couple of guinea-pig sandwiches. Between rounds, so to speak."

Seeing the expression on Reno's face when he nodded toward his office, Bobbie couldn't help laughing. "Was it that bad?"

"No, not exactly," he answered, "but I hope to hell you've got a mighty good idea for me."

"Why's that?"

He leaned back against the kitchen counter, bracing the heels of his palms against its edge. "I wouldn't say this to anyone but you, of course. But truthfully, no one else has had even one idea I liked." He pushed away from the counter. "Do you mind if we have our talk somewhere besides my office?"

"That's fine," she answered, and when he led her into the sitting room, she decided she'd been right. Somehow, the combination of this room and his presence was soothing. "Tired of being in the office all morning, huh?"

"It's not that." He gestured for her to take a seat, and Bobbie was grateful that the oversize leather chair was so comfortable. It seemed even more calming to her jittery nerves.

"Actually," he explained with another nod toward his office, "I think I need to let it air out awhile." Reno moved to the sofa. After taking a seat, he turned his body toward her and then stretched his long legs out in front of him. "The way I figure it, a couple of months oughta do the trick."

"Cigarettes?" Bobbie asked, surprised, since she couldn't recall even one of the developers being a smoker.

"No. I could handle that." He made the strangest face. "It's that Vivian What's-her-name's perfume. Boy, that's powerful stuff. She must've had an accident or something—spilled the whole bottle on herself just before she came up here."

Accident, my foot, Bobbie thought, curbing a smile.

"Maybe so," she said, putting her fingers to her lips to keep from laughing. Poor, unsuspecting man. He obviously had no idea that Vivian What's-her-name had been trying to impress him. And Bobbie Powell wasn't about to give him a woman's point of view on the subject.

She cleared her throat then. "Thank you for the typewriter, by the way. It really spurred me into action."

"Did it?"

"Absolutely. It was delivered to my cabin around ten yesterday morning, and I managed to catch my secretary before she went to lunch. I gave her a raise. Effective immediately."

Bobbie returned his sudden grin, knowing she had only told him half the story. True, she had discovered that her typing skills were more than a bit rusty. But yesterday, with the way her mind kept dwelling on Reno, she had seemed to have trouble with almost everything. Brushing her teeth, for instance. In fact, Bobbie had decided yesterday morning that the toothpaste manufacturers ought to put instructions on the back of every tube. And not long after that—soon after draining the last drops from a once-full bottle of correction fluid—she had decided that Heather deserved a raise.

Lifting the file from her lap, Bobbie added, "I'm afraid all I managed to get done was a rough list of what will be included in my proposal."

"That's fine. Why don't you just tell me about it? I'd like that better, anyway, at this point."

"Good." His behavior today, she decided, was confusing her even more. For once, Bobbie felt ready to push business to the back of her mind. And for once, Reno seemed anxious to discuss only business.

"Well," she said at last, "I have a feeling you're going to like this idea—mainly because you gave me the beginnings of it over our combination dinner and business meeting last Saturday night, when we were discussing the guest ranch." After realizing that she had automatically employed a more formal posture, Bobbie made an effort to relax, to ease her spine against the back of the chair. "What I have in mind is simply an extension of the Hideaway's philosophy. Taking it to loftier heights, you might say."

Bobbie's enthusiasm began to surface as she told Reno about what she had in mind: a secondary-residence retreat, a place where high-powered executives could enjoy sun and fun while getting away from the stresses of life in the fast lane. Hideaway Springs—the name she had tentatively given it—would also include a golf course, a country club, conference facilities, a hotel and possibly even condos, if they were needed. When executives had meetings to conduct, they would have the luxury of bringing the meetings to them instead of vice versa.

"Total relaxation is the key phrase," she added, "just as it is here at the Hideaway. And in keeping with that theme, location would be one of the biggest enticements in an all-out advertising campaign. Because you're only a few miles from the geographical center of Texas, your location couldn't be better for something like this. You're accessible to top executives in all the major cities. And thanks to the airstrip that already exists on the ranch, the residents of Hideaway Springs would have the choice of commuting by plane—if not private, then commercially into Abilene—or even by car.

"You saw my chart at the library the other day. There's a long list of major cities that are only a short distance from here, so the no-hassle aspect, the ease of transportation, would be dynamite for busy people who need to get away but who don't normally have time for the getting there part. This would be for people who want a place where they can feel relaxed and at home. In this case, they *would* be at home. Their second home."

Reno was simply staring at her, and Bobbie realized that ever since she'd started her spiel, he hadn't said a word.

Feeling awkward, she opened the file folder and checked her notes. "Oh," she commented quickly, filling the silence. "And for their guests, too, the ease of transportation would be fantastic. It would be especially appealing for the owners' on-site conferences and meetings. And as far as that goes, the conference privileges wouldn't necessarily have to be restricted to owners. That could be given some thought before a final decision."

Bobbie studied his expression. His silence was definitely beginning to grate on her already frazzled nerve endings.

"Well," she said at last. "What do you think?"

After another few nerve-racking moments, he finally said, "I like it, Bobbie. I like it a lot." His sudden smile began to broaden. "It seems like a great concept. I think it could work."

Before she could reply, Reno said, "Where? I mean, what parcels have you chosen?"

"That's what really makes it perfect," she answered, her tone reflecting her excitement. "It's almost next door to the airstrip, with a paved road already existing between the airstrip and the site itself. Starting just west of Cal's house—just west of the first bend in the creek."

He looked almost stunned. "Comanche Creek?"

"Yes."

"But Bobbie..." He stared at her in a quizzical fashion. "Surely you realize I can't agree with that."

"Why not? I thought you liked the idea."

"I like the idea just fine. It's the parcels I can't go along with. Those parcels aren't even being offered."

"You're kidding."

"No, I'm not kidding." He stood and took her hand. "Come here. I'll show you."

Once in his office, he pointed out the area on the plat that was already spread across the top of his desk.

Realizing the ridiculous mistake she had made, Bobbie sank onto the chair. As she continued to stare at the shaded areas on the plat—the areas that began west of the third bend in Comanche Creek and not the first one, as she had thought—Reno went around and took a seat in the large swivel chair behind his desk.

This was all her own fault, she realized. If she had taken a plat after the initial meeting, as she should have, she wouldn't have made this kind of an error. And there was no excuse for it . . . except that she had been so angry with Reno that day, so emotional, that she simply hadn't been thinking straight. But she could hardly explain that to him now.

"I'm sorry, Reno. I—" She glanced up and then down again, trying to avoid his gaze. "When you suggested that I dream up a question about the plat the other day, I guess I should have. It's just that, well, I thought I was familiar enough with the ranch, and I was going by the little photocopy at the bottom of the letter. I simply assumed that . . ." She fished the letter out of her folder, trying to hide her embarrassment as she quickly pointed out how she had misinterpreted the boundary line.

"But," she added, keeping her tone optimistic, "when you compare these few parcels to the entire scope of the ranch, it's not really that much land. And since you like my idea, can you at least think about changing your mind? And making the parcels available?"

"No, I can't, Bobbie. I told you before—I'm building a stud farm on that property."

"You said you were planning a stud farm . . . but I didn't realize you meant right there. On that very spot." Again, Bobbie realized that her recent emotional state had kept her from asking the proper professional questions. She had never made this kind of an error before, and she was mortified. Instead of dwelling on that, though, she tried to come up with a reasonable solution. "But you haven't broken ground yet. You could build barns somewhere else, couldn't you?"

"Sure," he answered bluntly. "If I wanted to, I guess I could build barns just about anywhere. Probably even on the moon if I waited a few years."

"Meaning?" she asked hesitantly.

"Meaning, I guess I could, but I won't."

"Why not?"

He smiled as he said, "Because we're not just talking about barns here, Bobbie. A stud farm needs to look a certain way."

"I don't know much about this sort of thing, but..." She cleared her throat. "Well, can't Diamond Jubalee perform his services almost anywhere?"

His mouth kicked up in a wry grin. "Anywhere within reason, I'd say."

"In that case, I don't see the problem. I did some reading about this at the library the other day, so I realize that with Thoroughbreds, because of strict rules or guidelines or whatever, this sort of thing can't be done artificially. It has to be..." She thought the term had been a "live mount," but no matter how clinical and official it might sound to him, she certainly wasn't going to say it out loud. Not to Reno Tanner.

"Well," she continued, "I realize their mating has to be done the natural way, so to speak. And granted, Jubalee's visiting mares will be high-class ladies, but they don't have to have candlelight and Dom Perignon, do they?"

Reno laughed and shook his head. "I like that."

"What?" she said, grinning back at him. "My sarcastic little remark?"

"I like that, too, but what I really meant was, I like the fact that you did some reading about Thoroughbreds the other day."

She lifted a shoulder. "What can I say? I was interested in finding out more about Jubalee."

"Good," he said, still smiling. "Now. In answer to your sarcastic little remark about candlelight and Dom Perignon, I don't think you understood my meaning when I said a stud farm has to look a certain way. I'm glad you did some research, but for this particular conversation, it seems to be throwing you onto the wrong track." He leaned forward, his elbows against the desk top. "We're talking about the right atmosphere for people, Bobbie, not for horseflesh. The clientele who'll be frequenting this place are accustomed to the finest Kentucky farms. They'll be paying a pretty penny, and they'll expect a certain kind of atmosphere in return. It's an important part of the package."

"But you haven't started construction yet, and you have the rest of the ranch to choose from. Surely you can find another place to build your stud farm. There are plenty of nice, scenic areas around the ranch."

"That's right, but what it all boils down to is that I've got my mind set on this one for the stud farm." He leaned back again, the swivel chair tilting with his weight. "So you'll just have to find another group of parcels."

"But I can't," she insisted, "because it's that land that makes the idea work. It's the underground springs, the creek, the view of Santa Anna Mountain from that precise spot, the—" Realizing her voice was steadily rising in pitch, she fought to regain her normal tone. "For numerous reasons, that area is perfect. All my plans have been laid out around it."

"Your plans will have to be changed, then."

"Look, Reno, I think you're being unreasonable. You're turning down my idea without giving it another moment's thought. Won't you even think about it?"

"I'm not turning down your idea, Bobbie. Find another group of parcels and I'll be all for it."

"But what I'm suggesting is a place where people will spend their all-too-precious leisure hours. What you're talking about is a place people will see for a very short period of time—and they're paying big bucks for Diamond Jubalee's services, not for a pretty view. I'm talking about the cake and you're talking about the icing. It simply doesn't compare."

"Maybe not to you, but it does to me. I have my reasons, and I don't have to argue them with you."

"No, you don't," Bobbie said evenly, watching as Reno continued to hold her attention with his suddenly level stare. For some reason, the look he was giving her made Bobbie realize how increasingly nervous she had become over the past few minutes.

No, over the past few days, she corrected herself. Her insides felt like a time bomb ready to detonate.

And as far as arguing was concerned, Bobbie thought angrily, she didn't want to argue with *him*, either.

"You're right," she said, trying to keep her voice calm as she rose from the chair. "I'm sorry."

Fighting to control the raw, confusing emotions that were suddenly causing her to shake—inside and out—Bobbie turned on her heel and left his office.

Thirty minutes later, Reno found Bobbie where he thought she'd be. After checking her cabin, he had gone directly to the main house and parked behind the Jeep in the drive.

Joining Bobbie on the veranda, he noted the heavy look of sadness in her eyes as he took a seat at the opposite end of the glider swing. He propped his arm across the back, his fingers skimming her shoulder.

She sighed deeply before saying, "I had no right to argue with you, Reno. It's just that I felt so stupid about the mistake I made." She glanced down at the file folder that was between them. "I feel like an absolute fool."

"It was an honest mistake, Bobbie. And actually, I'm just as much to blame as you are. I knew you hadn't taken a copy of the plat; I should've made sure you had one." With his knuckles, he pushed her hair back from the side of her face. "I didn't come out here for an apology, though. I came out here to explain my reasons."

"You don't have to do that."

"No. But I want to." He pushed out a long breath of air. "Look, Bobbie. I've known my share of flighty women, and I don't mind telling you I find that logical nature of yours downright appealing. As far as business is concerned, I have a feeling it'll serve me well."

She glanced his way, a faint smile touching the corners of her mouth. But the look of remorse was still in her eyes.

Or was it sadness? he wondered, clearing his throat before he added, "I realize my reasons aren't totally logical, but for years my dad had this dream of building a stud farm.'' He turned his head, nodding toward Diamond Jubalee in the distance. ''Right there. In that exact spot. There's always been this myth about the old Kentucky bloodlines, and more than anything else, he wanted to make a statement to the racing world. He wanted to prove that a Thoroughbred like Jubalee—Texas born and Texas bred—could shake up their little empire.

''Unfortunately,'' Reno went on, ''he never got to see Jubalee race in the Triple Crown. But he loved that horse. And so do I. I can't explain that, Bobbie, except to say that you start feeling . . . I don't know. Like you would about your own kid, I guess. Maybe that sounds crazy, but—''

''No,'' Bobbie said, laughing quietly, her voice hushed as she added, ''that doesn't sound crazy to me. After spending the last few days out here, I think I can almost understand it.'' She looked up at Reno and smiled. ''There's something really wonderful about watching him run. I don't quite understand how it makes me feel, but there's something about all that speed and power and beauty that just . . .'' Looking timid all of a sudden, she glanced down at her folded hands and then back up at him before he spoke.

''Then maybe you'll understand it when I say there's more than logic involved here. When I listen to my head, I know I have to replace Jubalee's winnings. Because if I don't build the stud farm, if I don't take advantage of his monetary potential, then that would be foolish. For me and for the future of this ranch.'' He touched his chest. ''But when I listen to what's in here, I realize that somehow, my dad's dream has become mine. I realize that beyond this being a legacy to him, it's a legacy to how he felt about Jubalee. To how I feel about Jubalee . . . and how I felt about my dad.''

He watched as she swallowed hard. As her eyes misted.

''Yes, Reno,'' she murmured at last. ''I can understand that.''

They sat there in silence for several moments, until Bobbie took a deep, lengthy breath and finally released it.

''Why don't you stay awhile, Bobbie?'' The way things stood at the moment, he realized that restricting his appeal to her business side might be for the best. "Maybe you can come up with another site for your proposal."

"I just don't think I can do that, Reno. I'm convinced that it's this land that makes the proposal work." Instead of sounding proud of herself and her proposal, she sounded dejected. "And maybe it's wrong of me to feel this way, but I don't think I can bring myself to suggest something to you that I know is second-rate."

"All right, then. Why don't you stay awhile and try to come up with another idea? A completely different proposal?"

He covered her fingers, grazing the back of her hand with his thumb. "I know you want to go to the Caribbean, but maybe you could spend a few more days here first. As of checkout time tomorrow, we close down for a week of renovations. It's kind of different around here, but I think you'll like it." Susan would be arriving tomorrow for a week's visit, and Reno knew that along with simply not wanting Bobbie to leave, he wanted her to meet Susan. "At least give it a chance, Bobbie. Give me a chance."

When she didn't answer him, Reno glanced down at the open file folder between them on the swing. After picking up a sketch and pretending to study it, he pointed to one of the details she'd drawn. "What's this?" he asked, keeping his tone light. "This thing that looks like an artist's palette?"

Her expression was still forlorn as she glanced at it. "That's a golf course."

"Ah," he said, holding the sketch up to within a few inches of his eyes and squinting. "Of course. I should've known that. I can see the eighteen tiny little holes now. And the eighteen tiny little flags."

"Please don't tease me, Reno. Not now."

"Okay," he said, reminding himself that she didn't want to be pushed, either. "I know you need some time to think this over." He jotted the numbers 0919 in the margin and tried to give her the sketch, but she didn't take it from his hand. "This is the combination to my elevator. Why don't you come up tonight after you've made your decision. We'll spend some time alone together, and you can give me an answer."

"But don't you see, Reno?" There was a note of pleading in her voice. A note of desperation. "Time isn't what I need. Time alone with you isn't going to help. It'll just make matters worse."

"Why?"

"Why?" she repeated, her tone quiet but incredulous. "Because I can't take any more of your teasing, that's why."

"Come on now, darlin'." He gestured toward the drawing he still held, toward the golf course he'd tried to tease her about. "I know my timing's a little off sometimes, but it's not that bad, is it?"

Her mood seemed to change all of a sudden, without warning. Bobbie snatched the sketch out of his hand and jumped up from the swing.

"For heaven's sake, Reno! I'm not talking about this." Already at the opposite end of the veranda, she held up the sketch and glared at him. "I'm talking about the *library*, you big dumb jerk! I'm talking about the way you brought me home and just barely kissed me good-night, like I was some old acquaintance you hadn't seen for a while!"

He stared at her, thoroughly amazed. "You mean you're mad at me because I haven't been—"

"No!" she screamed. "It's not you I'm mad at, Reno. It's *me*. I'm upset because I don't have the slightest idea what I'm doing anymore! I'm mad because it's my own fault, choosing parcels that weren't even being offered. I'm mad because *I* don't scream and yell—but here I am screaming and yelling. And calling you a big dumb jerk!"

"For God's sake, Bobbie. You think I'm offended by something as minor as that?"

"Oh!" she muttered disgustedly, as if she hadn't heard a word he'd said. "Don't you see?" Running her fingers through her hair, she began to pace back and forth, from the front of the house to the railing. "I'm mad because all my life, I've been able to rely on my sense of logic. But then I get around *you* for a while and it seems to just—" she waved the paper through the air "—fly right out the window! I get just one *whiff* of you, and I can't even think straight anymore."

She stopped pacing and stood perfectly still, her body rigid as she glared at him again. "There! I've said it. Are you happy now?"

He stood, smiling as he closed the distance between them.

"Yeah," he whispered, pulling her against the length of his body. "I'm happy now."

His fingers combed through the soft, silky hair at her nape, tugging gently to tilt her head back. And when his mouth lowered to hers, Reno kissed her the way he'd been wanting to kiss her for days now. For as long as he could remember.

He tasted the warm sweetness of her mouth, felt the urgency of her tongue as it met each thrust of his. Dear God, he thought, had he wanted this woman forever? Or did it only seem that way?

Bobbie's arms were around him now, her fingers in his hair as she held him even closer. His hand moved quickly, almost roughly, to the side of her breast, the heel of his palm massaging one tight, hard nipple.

Reno moved his hand then, cupping the full, warm weight of her. Her fingers were suddenly clasping his, pressing him harder against the throbbing, heaving ripeness of her breast, and when he felt more than heard the low, guttural moan of pleasure that escaped her lips, he realized where they were, what he was dying to do, what he knew he couldn't do here.

Not for the first time, and not with a woman like this woman.

He knew now that she wanted to be pushed, maybe for the first time in her life. But did she know that?

He didn't think so.

No, he decided. Bobbie Powell's logical mind would need time to adjust to that fact. If he did what he was aching to do— right here and right now—she would hate him for it.

He wanted her touch, her scent. Her taste and texture and everything else she had to give. He wanted to be inside her, to feel her body moving with his. He wanted to give her everything he had to give . . . and he wanted to feel her smooth, hot flesh and see her beautiful eyes when she took it.

He wanted her in his bed, he realized, and he wanted Bobbie to know for sure that she wanted him.

"Bobbie?" he murmured. "What about you? Are you happy now?"

"Yes," she whispered, still clinging to him, still breathing in ragged gasps. "Oh, yes."

"Good." His mouth brushed her lips one more time, and then he forced himself to pull back, to finally let go of her. "I'll see you tonight, then."

Noticing her soft, wide-eyed, wondrous smile, Reno winked at her as he tried to convince himself he was calm and in control. Then, without another word, he patted her backside and turned around, sauntering down the steps and toward his truck. Before he drove away, though, he made it a point to catch another glimpse of her.

Clutching the newel post on the railing, Bobbie was standing in the same spot where he'd left her. And from what Reno could tell, she was simply gaping at him and trying to catch her breath.

Chapter Ten

An hour later, Bobbie tossed her brochures into the waste-basket and turned, smiling as she left her cabin and headed for the main building.

Obviously, all Reno had been waiting for was for Bobbie to let him know what she wanted. And now, finally, she knew exactly what she wanted, and it wasn't a trip to the Caribbean. It was time alone with Reno Tanner—and she wasn't about to waste any time in letting him know. In fact, she hadn't even taken the few extra minutes it would have required to change into something besides her slacks and cotton sweater.

Reno's actions over the past few days seemed so clear now. Even while he was letting her know he was interested, he had approached her with caution. With gentlemanly care. And it was no wonder, she had decided earlier this afternoon. While she stood there on Cal's veranda watching Reno drive away, she had suddenly realized what kind of messages she'd been giving him. She'd been acting frightened, and she liked the fact that he'd been sensitive to that. That he hadn't tried to rush her.

Bobbie glanced at her wristwatch on her way across the lobby. It was only four o'clock, but she hoped that wouldn't matter. She hoped, if Reno was in his office, he'd be glad to hear her decision a few hours earlier than he'd expected. Punching the four numbers she'd memorized before leaving her cabin, Bobbie stepped into the private elevator.

Within moments she was in the hallway on the second floor. Country and western music was playing on a stereo system that seemed to float everywhere, and she stopped and smiled as she recognized the song as one they had danced to only two nights before. The beat was just slow enough to be perfect, and the words asked, "Does Fort Worth Ever Cross Your Mind?" Still smiling, Bobbie answered the question as it pertained to her own situation: Forth Worth would never cross her mind again without her thinking of Reno Tanner and the way she'd felt when he held her in his arms that night....

A few steps before she reached the open doorway to his office, Bobbie heard the deep, sexy baritone of his voice: "Yeah. I love you, too, Susan. I'll see you tomorrow, sugar. I can't wait."

Stunned by what Reno was saying—into the phone, apparently—Bobbie stopped dead in her tracks. Those hadn't been meaningless words; she could tell by the tone of his voice that he really did love this woman. This...this Susan Whoever-she-was.

Dear Lord, Bobbie thought. Thank God she'd heard him before she had a chance to make an absolute fool of herself. Correction: before she had a chance to make an even bigger fool of herself! Her hand flew up to cover a gasp as she realized what she'd done only an hour before. She had virtually thrown herself at a man who hadn't been rushing her because he hadn't wanted to rush her. Because he already had a woman in his life.

Another thought came to her then, a thought that was far more horrifying and painful. Perhaps she had issued an open invitation to a man who'd been laying on all that "charm" for one reason: as far as business was concerned, he had a feeling her logical mind would serve him well. He had made the statement himself, and God knows it wouldn't be the first time a man had—

Hearing the sound of the telephone being hung up, Bobbie forced her hand away from her mouth. Well, she told herself adamantly, as of right this minute, for the first time in days, she would use some of that logic! She had been indulging in all kinds of foolishness, but she would simply put a stop to it.

Squaring her shoulders, Bobbie took the two steps necessary to reach the doorway to his office. Reno was leaning back in his swivel chair, smiling in a sweet, dreamy, *moony* sort of way she'd never seen before. Nevertheless, he seemed to notice her presence immediately.

"Oh. Hi, Bobbie. Come on in, honey."

Honey, she thought, fury welling up inside her. Did he toss those endearments around as easily as he did all that innate charm? Honey, darlin', sugar? Whatever suited his fancy at the time?

"I won't stay but a minute," she answered, clearing her throat, giving herself a moment as she tried to control both the sound of her voice and the trembling she felt inside. "I just thought I'd let you know I won't be staying. I really need this vacation, and—"

"Just a couple of days?" he asked, interrupting her. "After that, if you still want to leave, I'll fly you to the Caribbean myself. How does that sound?"

"No. But thank you, anyway." Again she cleared her throat. "If I stayed," she added quickly, gesturing toward the phone, "I'm afraid I'd just be in the way."

"Oh," Reno stated, realizing she must have heard part of his telephone conversation. "You mean because of Susan? No, honey. You won't be in the way. In fact, I'm anxious for you to meet her. Get to know her."

"I don't think that'll be necessary," she said, the words slow and even, her eyes suddenly shooting daggers at him.

"Well," he commented, careful not to let himself smile as he realized what she must be thinking. She was jealous, and Reno had to admit he liked it. He liked it a lot. In fact, coupled with what she'd admitted to him on the veranda about an hour ago—not to mention the physical response he'd gotten from her afterward—this was just the kind of message he'd been waiting for. "How about staying just one more night, then?"

Bobbie simply glared at him. Green fire, Reno thought as he kept his eyes on hers. How appropriate.

"Fine," she said at last, crossing her arms in front of her and jacking her chin even higher in the air. "You want another proposal from me? Fine. I'll work on it all night, if I have to, but I'll definitely come up with something for you before I leave tomorrow."

"I have a better idea," he said, still trying to squelch a grin. "If you're gonna be up all night, anyway, why don't we just work on it together?"

Bobbie gave him one of those how-dare-you looks, and before he could say anything to clear up the issue at hand, she spun around and sashayed out of his office.

Yeah, he decided, a broad smile coming across his face as he tilted his chair back again. She was really riled, but that might work out just fine. He'd let her chew on that jealousy business for a couple of minutes, and then he'd go out there to her cabin and make it a point to calm her down. It shouldn't be too difficult, he realized, to make Bobbie see she'd heard just enough of his half of that telephone conversation to—

Just then, another realization crossed Reno's mind. And as he brought the chair upright, his smile abruptly changed to a frown.

A knock sounded on Bobbie's cabin door. Temporarily abandoning her task, she moved swiftly into the parlor and frowned in the direction of the untouched dinner that had been delivered over an hour before. Wayne would be wanting to take away the cart. And this time, Bobbie decided as she flung open the door, she might just tell him exactly where his boss could—

Reno stood on the porch, his feet planted firmly apart as he simply studied her for what seemed an endless amount of time. Then he glanced past her shoulder, nodding toward the bedroom. "What are you doing?"

He had his nerve, Bobbie thought, standing there looking thoroughly disgusted with *her*. "What does it look like I'm doing? I'm packing."

"I thought you agreed to stay till tomorrow."

"I did, but I've decided against it." She turned and headed for the bedroom, reminding herself of what he really wanted from her. "Don't worry, though. You'll get your precious proposal. I'll mail it to you."

"That's not what I'm concerned about," he said, following behind her. "I wanted you to stay long enough to meet Susan."

"No thanks." Bobbie watched him lean against the door-jamb and cross his arms in front of his chest. At the same time, she felt a tight band of pain squeezing around her own chest cavity. This horrible, overwhelming feeling of jealousy was ridiculous, she knew. And the fact that the emotion was totally foreign to her only seemed to be making it that much more unbearable. "I—I don't think that's a good idea."

"Why not?" he asked, his face showing no expression, his voice low and deep and completely void of emotion. "Up in my office, you didn't give me a chance to tell you anything about her."

"Thanks anyway, but I don't believe I care to—"

"You didn't give me a chance to tell you the good news," he interrupted. "I'm going to be a daddy soon."

Dear God, she thought. This Susan was carrying his child!

A fresh sense of horror lashed at everything inside her as she simply stared at him. Surely this feeling was indeed shock, Bobbie told herself, and not envy.

"I'm thrilled for you, Reno," she finally managed to say. "Absolutely thrilled. Tell me, are you planning to tie the knot before the blessed event?"

"No," he stated bluntly. "Marriage isn't a part of the deal."

"Well." She turned to shut the last of her suitcases, refusing to let herself cry. "How very liberated of her. Of both of you." How could it be? she wondered. Only a few hours ago, she had realized she was falling in love with this man.

"Here," he commented from behind her. "Let me show you her picture."

"No!" she said frantically, struggling against what felt like a knife stabbing at her heart. Twisting and tearing. "Please. Please don't do that."

"All right," he agreed at last. "If that's the way you want it."

"Yes," she murmured. "That's the way I want it."

"So you're off to the Caribbean then." Again Reno settled his shoulder against the door frame. "What's your hurry?"

Dammit! her mind screamed. How could he sound so calm, so absolutely unfeeling, when she felt like she was dying inside?

No, she decided all of a sudden. She wasn't going to let him do this to her.

"All right," Bobbie said, her voice a level, raspy whisper as she turned to glare at him. "If you must know, I'm looking for Mr. Right."

"So," he stated, his eyebrows lifted. "You're really serious about that, are you?"

"Yes, Reno," she said bitterly. "I'm really serious about that. As you so kindly pointed out, I'm not getting any younger."

"And you think the Caribbean's the place to look?"

"Well, I'm sure as hell not going to find him here!"

"You're not going to find him anywhere, Bobbie, unless you change your attitude."

"*My* attitude?" she asked, her voice rising right along with her anger.

"Yes," he replied, his tone firm. "Your attitude. That attitude that says every man is guilty until he's proven innocent."

"That's not true!"

"It is true," he said emphatically. "I'm not him, Bobbie."

"Him who?" she screamed.

"Don't play dumb, honey. It doesn't suit you. You overhear something Harrison says on the phone, and then you overhear something I say on the phone, and you automatically equate me with him."

"I never—"

"Hell, you didn't even give me as much consideration as you gave him. You didn't even put me to some arbitrary test."

"And why should I?" she yelled, enraged that he would throw this in her face after she had shared it with him in confidence.

"Because," he said, lowering his voice, "I would've passed your damned test." He crossed the bedroom, yanking a photo out of his billfold and forcing it into her trembling hands. "Because this is Susan."

"But—" Dazed, Bobbie stared at the three figures in the picture, at the strawberry-blond girl who was standing beside Diamond Jubalee and looking up at Reno with a glorious, innocent, adoring smile on her face. "But she's only—"

"Yes, Bobbie. She's a child. She's a sweet little girl who just happened to steal my heart a couple of years ago." He held the photo in front of her eyes again. "She's seven years old. And as soon as she gets here tomorrow, I'll be able to tell her the news I got from my lawyer just this afternoon. The papers are going through, so within a matter of days she'll officially be my daughter."

"You mean you're—you're adopting her?"

Reno nodded, and tears of both shame and relief spilled down Bobbie's cheeks.

Confusion suddenly flooded her mind. "Then why did you let me..." Seeing the angry expression that was still in his dark blue eyes, she grew even more puzzled. "I don't understand," she said, her voice quiet and pleading. "Why did you let me suffer? Why didn't you just tell me she was a child?"

"Because you didn't ask." He lifted his hand, pointing toward the main building. "I've been sitting up there for more than two hours, waiting for you to come to your senses, hoping you'd realize without my telling you that I'm not Harrison. That I'm not some bastard who wants to rip your heart out and stomp all over it!"

"That's not what I was thinking, Reno. Honestly!" Before finishing the statement, she realized he didn't even seem to hear her.

"You know, Bobbie, I can be patient to a point. But you've really pushed me past my limit this time, so maybe you'd better just shut up for a minute—until I've said exactly what I came here to say."

She sank to the edge of the bed, knowing he meant to do exactly that.

"This doesn't have anything to do with me," he added. "It has to do with you. I've never done anything to lead you to believe you can't trust me. What you refuse to trust is your own instincts." He gave a short, bitter laugh before he walked toward the doorway and then turned to face her again. "This Harrison character taught you well, didn't he? After what he did to you, you decided if you risk nothing, you lose nothing. And maybe that's true, but I'll tell you something else. You also don't stand a chance of gaining anything."

"What is this?" she asked, not knowing why she was crying all of a sudden, but simply knowing that somehow, in some way, she had to retaliate. "Is this the old no guts, no glory lecture your granddaddy used to give you?"

"No!" he yelled. "This is me talking—and it's not a lecture. I'm trying to tell you how I feel, so for one minute, why don't you stop trying to figure out the logic behind it and just listen to what I'm saying?" He pushed his fingers through his hair. "Dammit, Bobbie. That logical mind of yours does appeal to me, but it also drives me crazy, especially when it comes to the personal."

He started pacing the floor in front of her. "Believe it or not, honey, some situations don't call for guidelines and logic and weighing things to the nth degree. Some things just happen. Sometimes you just have to throw caution to the wind and *let* them happen." Stopping short, he looked her straight in the eye. "I've done everything I know to try to get close to you. And all you've been doing is holding back. Telling me no."

"Is that what this is, then?" she asked quietly, her voice quivering. "An ultimatum? About . . ."

"What?" he asked, sounding incredulous. "About sex? About making love?" He shook his head and then raked his fingers across his scalp. "You're really something, you know that? Is that all you think I'm after?"

Turning toward her again, he gave her an exasperated frown.

"Fine," he said. "All right, I'll admit it. Yeah, that's part of it. I don't think I've made any secret of the fact that I want you. In fact, I'll even admit that when I first met you, that was a major part of it. I was intrigued by you. I had a lot of problems on my mind, and I thought you'd make one hell of a nice diversion."

He rolled his eyes before muttering, "And don't look so shocked, Bobbie. We're big kids now, remember? I'm a man and you're a woman. A beautiful, desirable woman."

Her mouth dropped open, but he went on talking.

"But if you think that's all it is, you're wrong. That's not my style, quite frankly, and from the minute I met you, I could tell it wasn't yours, either."

His fingers spanning the denim below his waist, Reno appeared to be disgusted with her as he shook his head. "No, honey. This isn't about sex. It's about making love and everything else that goes along with it. This is about you and me and now. And not what's happened in the past—for either one of us."

He lifted his hand into the air and asked, "You want to talk about lousy experiences with the opposite sex? I could tell you some horror stories. I've been around the dance floor a few times myself, you know, with the wrong partners, but that doesn't mean I'm not ready to learn a few new steps." He crossed the room then, stopping in front of her. "Just because I've been with the wrong women in the past, just because I've been hurt a few times, that doesn't mean I'm ready to give up on life and love and a family." Reaching beside her, he picked up the photo that had fallen on the bed. "That's what this little girl's all about."

"Reno," she whispered through her tears, "I'm so sorry. I didn't—"

"For God's sake, Bobbie, I don't want you to be sorry! I want you to let yourself want me—the way I want you. I want you to decide whether or not you're ever going to start trusting me for who I am." He leveled her a harsh glare. "This is about you making up your mind about what you want. And it's not an ultimatum, because I'm giving you two very clear choices. When it comes to me, honey, you either fish or cut bait."

The look in his eyes softened for only a moment, and for the first time, Bobbie caught a glimpse of the pain Reno had been suffering in the past few hours.

"You know exactly how I feel now," he said, his voice almost calm all of a sudden. "And now that you know, I'm not chasing after you anymore. You decide what you want, Bobbie. And then you let me know—one way or the other."

Reno headed for the parlor. After opening the door, he stood there with his hand on the knob and added a firm, final declaration. "You've got my number."

Bobbie tied the sash of her lightweight raincoat and slipped her feet into a pair of heels.

It had started raining nearly an hour before—appropriately, too, since the threads of lightning had begun to flash only minutes after Reno stormed out of her cabin. He had given her a lot to think about in the near hour since then, but now that Bobbie had made her decision, she wasn't about to let a summer shower keep her from letting Reno Tanner know exactly how she felt. And what she'd concluded.

Ignoring the mess she was leaving behind, Bobbie locked her cabin and headed for the main building. Yes, she told herself, walking resolutely through the lobby and to the private elevator. Dinner could wait. Her packed suitcases could wait. Everything else could wait.

Once upstairs, she realized there was no music this time. There was total silence now, and only one open doorway on either side of the long hall. She walked quietly to the entrance to his sitting room.

How wonderful he looked, Bobbie thought as she stood there unnoticed, simply watching him. He was stretched out on the sofa, the huge piece of furniture still too short for his height. His bare feet were propped up on one of its leather arms, his hands behind his head to add extra cushioning to the arm at the opposite end.

There was no lamp shining; only the room's one large window provided any light at all, which was faint because of the early evening storm. Even so, she could tell that his hair was damp, that he had showered and shaved and put on a fresh shirt and a pair of comfortable-looking old Levi's.

He turned his head then and spotted her.

"Please," she commented quickly, "don't get up. I'll just stand for what I need to say."

"Bobbie," he said, his voice deep and low as he complied with her request by rising slightly, bringing up his knee and moving into a different position where he balanced himself on one elbow. "I need to say one thing first. Before you start."

"All right." She took several steps into the room, keeping her hands in the pockets of her coat as she gave her head a toss, shaking the droplets of light rain from her hair. "Go ahead."

"I keep bragging about all this patience I used to have, and…" He took in a deep breath and slowly let it out. "If that sounded like a lecture, it was because I was angry. So I just thought I'd tell you, Bobbie, I have no idea if any of what I said was right. And if I was wrong, I apologize."

"Actually, I think you were some of each," Bobbie said, smiling hesitantly. "Overall, though, I'd say you were more right than you were wrong, so you don't need to apologize. I don't think I can apologize, either—not properly, anyway—but in this particular case, whether you think I owe you an explanation or not, I'm determined to give you one."

"Okay," he replied. "Then I'll keep quiet. I won't interrupt you this time, the way I kept doing the other night."

"That's the night I've been thinking about a lot, actually. About your suggestion that I might be trying to prove something to Harrison. I don't believe you were totally right then, either, but you've made me realize what I have been doing all these years." She reached up, touching her fingertips to her lips. Almost immediately, though, she put her hand back in her pocket. There was no other way to do this. She simply had to swallow her pride and say it.

"I was humiliated because of having to call off the wedding. And more than that, much more than that, I was hurt because he didn't love me. I was hurt because he didn't want me for me. So after that, I guess I set out to prove my own worth—without my inheritance, without my father's money and power. Not to Harrison, I don't think, but to all those people who had to be told that the wedding had been canceled. And not just to them, either, but to—" She lifted her shoulders. "It sounds foolish now, but I guess I felt I had to prove it to the world at large."

When she frowned in self-recrimination, Reno gave her an assuring smile and said, "I think I have to interrupt here, just to say that that doesn't sound foolish to me. It sounds perfectly reasonable."

"Well, anyway," she continued, shrugging her shoulders once more, "I think that's what I wanted to do, and I don't think I've ever stopped. But you've made me realize that I can now, that I've proven myself—to myself—and that's all that matters."

Suddenly aware that she had started pacing, Bobbie stopped and faced him again. "When you turned down my proposal today, Reno, it felt as if you were rejecting *me*. But now I know that you weren't. I mean, even though I haven't been able to see myself as anything but a businesswoman, you don't think that way at all, do you?" Her hand touched her breastbone. "You really do see more than that, don't you?"

"Oh, yes," he answered, laughing quietly. "Yes, honey, I see a lot more than that. And regardless of the way I've been acting, I can assure you I like everything I see."

"Thank you," she whispered. "And there's something I want to assure you of, too, Reno. I never thought you were anything like Harrison. You aren't. Not one bit. In fact, I think I knew that from the minute we met. It wasn't you I refused to trust, though. It was my own instincts about . . ."

She glanced away and then back at him, knowing she had to explain. "It was my own instincts about men in general. You see, Reno, along with not having very much luck with men, I haven't had very much experience with men. So when I heard you on the phone today, I acted horribly because of me, not because of you. I guess it was the timing. I had just admitted to myself how I felt about you, and after hearing what you said to Susan—" She forced herself to keep her eyes on his. "Well, to be perfectly honest with you, I had no idea what it was like to deal with that sort of thing. To feel . . . disgustingly jealous."

Seeing the pleased expression on his face, Bobbie smiled sheepishly. "There. I've said it. Are you happy now?"

"Yeah." He gave her a wink then, a slow, heart-stopping, deliberate wink with a grin to match. "I'm happy now. In fact, I'm downright flattered." He leaned back, his eyes never leaving hers. "And while we're still on the subject, Bobbie, what was it you had admitted to yourself? Just how do you feel about me?"

"Well," she said slowly, "I like everything you are, it seems. I like your seriousness . . . your intensity. The knack you seem to have for making me confront emotions I've never confronted before." As she spoke, his beautiful blue gaze continued to hold her captive. "And I like your teasing. I guess my own life has been too intense for too long. I've never really known what it's like to have fun . . . but I know I want to learn."

She wanted to say something else, too, she realized. She wanted to say, "I love you, Reno," but she knew she couldn't. Not now. Not yet.

Bobbie moved toward the window as she said, "You asked me to make up my mind about what I want, Reno, and I have. I want to stay awhile. I want to stay . . . long enough to come up with another proposal for you."

"And is that the only reason?" he asked. "The proposal?"

"No," Bobbie answered truthfully. "I want to spend some time with you." She swallowed hard. "If that's all right, of course. If that's still what you want."

"That's exactly what I want, darlin'." He stood then and advanced toward her. "So for right now—for tonight—why don't we keep this strictly personal? Why don't you take your coat off? Make yourself comfortable?"

"I will," she said, nervous all of a sudden, "in just a minute."

He was standing so close—close enough to make her breath catch in her throat, close enough to make her body start quivering for him—but apparently he didn't plan to touch her until she gave him the word. Or at least some kind of a sign.

Bobbie liked that. She liked it a lot, in fact. But at the same time, she realized she didn't know quite what to do next. Earlier, Reno had made it clear that the next move would have to be hers. That she would have to let him know exactly what she wanted. "Either fish or cut bait," he'd said, and Bobbie knew without a doubt which choice she had made. But the flush of self-confidence she'd experienced while soaking in the bathtub just before leaving her cabin was rapidly dwindling.

She glanced out the window. "It's not raining any more."

"I know," he whispered.

"Was . . . was your granddaddy a fisherman?"

"Yeah," Reno answered, obviously confused by the changes of topic. "As of a matter of fact, he was. Why?"

"Well. I thought maybe since he had something to say about everything . . ." Somehow, she managed to reach for Reno's hand, bringing it to the top button of her raincoat. "It's about those two choices you gave me. Before you left my cabin."

"Yeah?" he murmured, his gaze still locked with hers. "What about them?"

"I thought maybe your granddaddy would've known." In a slow, gentle movement, she tilted her face toward the window. "Is the fishing good? After a rain?"

"Oh, yeah," Reno whispered, his smile telling her he realized what she wanted to say, but that she didn't know how to put it into the proper words. "Yeah, it sure is. Granddaddy used to say that was the best time for fishing."

He unbuttoned her coat and opened it, smiling devilishly as his eyes raked her body and he saw what she was wearing beneath her raincoat.

And when Bobbie saw the look of pleasure on his face, the unmistakable flame of desire in his dark eyes, she realized there was no reason to feel self-conscious.

She reached up, her fingers skimming the bodice of her new black teddy. "And what would Granddaddy have said about this?" she whispered, watching as Reno's gaze roamed the filmy scrap of silk and lace.

He slid the raincoat off her shoulders, letting it fall to the floor. "Nothing," he said quietly, his voice sounding almost reverent as his eyes met hers once again. "Absolutely nothing. This would've rendered him speechless."

Reno groaned as she reached for his shirt. She kept her eyes on his while slowly, wordlessly, she unfastened each snap.

"And what would your straitlaced Grandma Louise have to say, I wonder?" he asked playfully, as if he were reprimanding

Bobbie for her shamelessly seductive behavior. "About this fishing trip you're suggesting?"

"The same thing she told my mother, probably," she whispered, returning his teasing smile. "'Close your eyes, dear, and think of England.'"

A low, husky laugh escaped his throat. "And do you plan to take her advice?"

"Oh, no," she murmured in answer, her hands sliding around his neck, her fingers threading through the soft thickness of his hair. "Absolutely not. My mother said that was the only bad advice Grandma ever gave her."

His thumb traced a seductive, burning path along the flesh of her shoulder, beneath one narrow strap of her teddy. Time seemed to stand still ... until his mouth took hers, his tongue hot and demanding and insistent, then gentle and sure and tender. When his arms went around her waist, crushing her breasts against the solid warmth of his chest, Bobbie heard herself moaning his name, felt herself drowning in the clean male scent of him.

Then, without another word, Reno swept her up into his arms and carried her across the room. The bedroom door must have been ajar, she realized, because he simply pushed it open with his bare foot.

He set her down beside the bed. It was growing darker outside, but a soft flood of light spilled into the room from the adjoining bath. And Bobbie was grateful for the light. She wanted to see him. Her mind ... every one of her senses ... wanted to memorize everything about him and this moment.

Her hands went under the open front of his shirt, her fingers raking through the crisp wealth of hair on his chest before she smoothed the fabric off his broad, powerful shoulders. She touched the top button of his jeans then, but her hands, her fingers, were suddenly inept.

Reno smiled down at her, his hand moving over hers, his eyes assuring her that she didn't need to worry, that he would take over from here.

"It's okay," he whispered, leaning to brush her earlobe with a light kiss, with the seductive heat of his breath. "Next time,

Bobbie. There will be a next time, honey, so it's okay. Why don't you just relax?"

She wrapped her arms around him, holding him tight, clinging to him. "Oh, Reno," she whispered feverishly. "I don't think I can! I'm aching for you. I—"

"And I'm aching for you," he murmured, his breathing as heavy and irregular as her own, his voice a tender caress despite that. "I've been aching for you for a long time now. Too long. So we're not gonna rush right through this, are we, darlin'? That's not what you want, is it?"

"No." The feel of his arousal pressing against her softness, pulsating against her warm flesh, was somehow assuring. Soothing. "No. That's not what I want."

"Good," he whispered, holding her against his heat and his strength until their breathing calmed . . . if only a fraction.

At last he drew back, his gaze burning into hers, his hand traveling in a slow, sensual journey along the V at the top of her breasts.

"Reno?" she said quickly, realizing she had to speak now. While she could still breathe. While she could still think. "There's something I have to ask you before..." She placed her hand over his, stopping its movement. "I'm sorry. I—"

"What is it, Bobbie? You can ask me anything."

"Well. I was wondering if you might happen to have..." She glanced away momentarily. Toward the nightstand. "You see, I don't take anything for..."

He reached up, brushing his knuckles across her cheek. "I sort of figured that. So don't worry, darlin'. I've got everything taken care of." When her eyes questioned him, he said, "After I left your cabin tonight, after I simmered down a little, I made a trip to the drugstore in the lobby."

How wonderful he was, she decided once again. He had considered her needs—even before she had.

Reno lifted one palm then, flashing her a smile. "And don't worry. No one saw me."

And, she thought, how wonderful he was to sense that his teasing would help her relax. "No one?" she asked, her tone playfully suspicious. "How can you be certain of that?"

"Because," he whispered secretively, "I sent the attendant on a break, and then I made sure no one else was around when I took care of my transaction." He gave her a wink and a smug look. "I own the place, remember?"

"You're sneaky, cowboy," she murmured. "And very, very sure of yourself."

"Not especially that," he answered, his smug tone replaced by one of sincerity. "But a guy can always hope, can't he?" A smile touched his lips as he asked, "You want to know what I like about you?"

"Yeah," she answered, drawing out the word.

"I like your seriousness," he said, repeating the phrase she had used to describe how she felt about him. "Your intensity. The way you worry so much about what people might think."

"Is that all? Just those three little things."

"Oh, no," he murmured. "I love your enthusiasm... especially when it's mixed with that unbelievable streak of innocence." His fingers moved to the row of black, silk-covered buttons, slowly undoing them as he kept on talking in the same hushed tone. "One minute you shock the hell out me—please the hell out of me—when I see this is all you've got on under that coat. And the next minute, when you're trying to ask me what I might or might not have in my nightstand drawer, you're blushing like a virgin."

She raised herself up, holding his face between her hands, her expression suddenly pensive and her voice almost breathless. "Maybe that's because when I'm with you, Reno, I feel like a virgin. I feel as if I don't have the slightest idea what it's going to be like, but I'm dying for you to show me. I'm dying to find out."

"I guess we'd better do something, then," he whispered seductively. "I don't want you dying on me."

He stood back then, allowing her eyes the luxury of watching him undress. Allowing her mind to bask in the sight of him. To memorize each line and contour of his tall, strong, hard body.

As he removed the last scrap of his clothing, as Bobbie saw him fully for the first time, her breath caught in her throat.

Reno moved toward her again, sliding his hands under the narrow, silky straps at her shoulders. Her teddy floated to the floor, and her pulse pounded in her ears as she watched him studying her. Adoring her with his smoldering blue eyes.

"My God, Bobbie," he whispered. "You're even more beautiful than I thought you would be. Than I've been imagining you'd be."

He lowered her gently to the bed, and Bobbie lost herself in his eyes. In his heated touch. In the slow, sure expertise of his mouth on hers.

Time seemed nonexistent as his hands traveled smoothly, provocatively, along the length of her legs...up to her hips...to the sides of her breasts. He whispered her name, his voice low and husky, and she watched as his mouth descended to the roundness of one throbbing breast.

His lips closed over her, his mouth and his tongue drawing first on one tight, sensitive nipple and then the other. Moaning, she held his head to her body. And then she felt his hand as it slid downward again, as he found her moistness. Her heat.

He lifted his head, smiling into her eyes.

"Oh, darlin'," he whispered, "you are aching, aren't you?"

"Yes!" she answered, struggling for every gasp of air. "Yes, Reno. Please. Now."

He reached for the nightstand, and when she felt his full weight on top of her, when his beautiful, soulful gaze was back on hers, she seemed to be able to breathe again. Deeply. Fully.

Bobbie smiled up at him...in sweet, blissful anticipation...and then, at last, Reno was inside her. He moved slowly at first, listening to her cries of joy, watching her eyes.

Her hands moved down his back, past his hips, pulling him closer and harder against her.

His lips found hers quickly, and when she moaned into his mouth, his movements became faster, his thrusts more forceful. Incredibly, powerfully rhythmic. For one brief moment, Bobbie thought she was surely going to die...and in the next moment, she heard her own voice crying out, felt the heat of her rapid breathing as it pushed against his, felt her body react in violent, soul-wrenching, unrelenting waves of pure passion. Mind-shattering spasms of pure ecstasy that seemed to intensify as his muscles suddenly tightened beneath her grasping hands...as she heard the sound of his voice, as he groaned her name over and over again.

They held each other, their hearts beating wildly, their breathing gasping and ragged. Until finally, as their breathing began to subside, Reno felt the dampness of Bobbie's tears on his chest.

"Oh," she whispered, her voice catching on a sob. "Can I cry, Reno? Is it all right if I just hold you and...and cry?"

Smiling, he held her tighter. "Yes, darlin'," he murmured against her hair. "It's okay, Bobbie. Go ahead and cry."

Dear God, he thought, dragging the sweet scent of her into his lungs, feeling the soft, slight, quivering movement of her body as she continued to sob. He hadn't thought it was possible for a man his age to feel the way he'd felt tonight. From the moment he first touched her bare, perfect skin he had felt like a virgin himself, as if she was the first and only woman he'd ever been with. The only woman he ever *wanted* to be with.

And while he continued to hold and stroke her, while she continued to cry, he realized he'd been right: what was going on between them was about him and her and now. It didn't have anything to do with the past.

She seemed to trust him, at long last, and what she needed now was the present. Time for her to see for herself what kind of a man he was.

She had already promised to stay, so they'd have plenty of time—later—to talk about the past. His past. And when she knew him a little better, she'd understand what had happened.

And who knows? he thought. Maybe, given a little time, he'd have a better understanding of his own thoughts about it. Maybe he'd be able to store away the last shreds of the guilt he knew he'd been carrying around for too long....

He felt Bobbie stirring against him, felt the brush of her still-tight nipples against the hair on his chest.

She sighed heavily, and finally, he heard her soft, throaty voice as she whispered, "I've never felt like that before."

"Like what?" he asked quietly, his breath fanning her hair.

"I don't know," she murmured against his chest. "Like I could let go that completely. Like it was all right to be...just a woman. Like it was just you and me in this bed, and nothing else in the world mattered or existed or..." She stopped then, her quiet, brief laughter sounding self-conscious. "I guess I'm not making much sense, am I?"

"Sure," he said, brushing a kiss across her satiny hair. Thinking back to what she'd told him earlier, he knew exactly what she meant. "Let me tell you something, Bobbie. When it comes to me, you can be any kind of a woman you want to be. Because I like everything I see, remember?"

She lifted her face and gazed down at him, the tears still glistening in her eyes. And then she gave him the most glorious, wondrous smile he'd ever seen.

In that moment, he wanted to say, "I love you, Bobbie." But he knew he couldn't. Because she was a complicated woman, and considering the wild mixture of emotions she'd been experiencing over the past few hours, the timing wasn't right.

"Everything?" she finally whispered.

"Everything."

She slid her leg upward, and he groaned.

"But I'll tell you something else," he whispered playfully. "I've had a lot of fantasies about you in the past few days, and in not a one of 'em were you holding a briefcase."

"Oh?" she asked, teasing him right back. "What was I holding, then?"

"You want it in official-sounding terms?"

"No," she whispered, "I'll just see if I can figure it out for myself." Her fingertips grazed his knee. "You tell me when I'm getting warm."

"You're warm," he answered, his body reacting, tensing with desire as he felt the movement of her hand sliding upward...ever so slowly...along his inner thigh. "You're hot."

"No," she said as her palm closed over him. "*You're* hot."

Chapter Eleven

Bobbie stirred, shutting her eyes against the sunlight that flooded the room, and reached across the bed. Instead of touching Reno's firm, muscular body, though, her fingers made contact with a piece of paper. She forced her eyelids open, squinting until the words came into focus.

She laughed at the orders he'd scribbled, telling her not to get out of bed—under any circumstances—because he'd be right back, and when he got there, he wanted to know exactly where he could find her. "Okay, okay," he'd added as a final paragraph. "You can get yourself a cup of coffee—but that's all!"

Seeing the way he'd signed the note, Bobbie felt her heart take a sudden leap. "Love, Reno" wasn't exactly "I love you," she knew, but it was darned close.

Bobbie slipped into her black teddy. After pouring a cup of coffee that smelled heavenly, she returned to the bedroom and stood close to the window, smiling as she thought about the way Reno had teased her about that fishing business. After they'd shared a late meal he'd ordered for them the night before, she had casually pointed out that it was raining again . . . and that she wondered how it might be *during* the rain.

He'd acted thoroughly disgusted with her, grumbling and saying, "For God's sake, Bobbie. Are we gonna have to try it in *all* weather conditions?"

But, she thought, laughing out loud as she crawled back into bed, he hadn't acted cantankerous for long. In fact—

Just as she propped herself against the pillows, Bobbie heard several noises. The bedroom door was closed, but the faint, shuffling racket seemed to be coming from the elevator. And then the hallway.

What on earth was Reno doing out there? she wondered, setting her cup on the nightstand and crossing the bedroom. Before she reached the door, though, he was in the room.

"Hi there," he said, folding her into his arms.

"Hi there, yourself," she whispered. "Where have you been?"

"Out saving a damsel in distress."

"Oh?" she asked, doing her best to sound irritated. "Some damsel I should know about?"

"Yeah," he answered, his tone blunt as his gaze raked her silk-clad body. "If I'm not mistaken, honey, you didn't bring much with you last night. Not that I'd mind seeing you strut around in something like this all the time—" he moved his hands, rubbing the heels of his palms slowly, seductively, along the sides of her breasts "—but the way you worry about appearances, I figured at some point in life you might want some real clothes."

"Oh, good grief," she said, touching her fingertips to the lacy bodice. "I guess I wasn't exactly thinking straight when I . . ."

Her fingers made contact with his, and he leaned over and kissed her hand, sending tingly jolts of sensation up and down her entire body. "Well," she said breathlessly, "thank you. What did you bring for me?"

"Come on and I'll show you." As he led her into the hallway, he asked if she'd seen the rest of his home.

"No, I haven't," she answered, "but I'd like that."

He opened the door directly across from his bedroom, showing her a darling little-girl's room done in pink polished cotton and white eyelet, complete with a canopy bed and a small vanity. "Susan's," he said simply.

Skipping the door in the middle, he moved on to the one across the hall from his office. "I don't use this room very often," he said as she glanced around the library, "so you'll be able to spread out and work in here if you like."

Before she could say anything, he took her hand and back-tracked to the middle door. "My work crew's arriving today, too, and they'll be working on the cabins. Repainting them and doing a few minor repairs. They stay in the cabins and do the work on a rotating basis, so..." He opened the door then, standing behind Bobbie after they entered the bedroom. "What do you think?"

"Oh, Reno," she said, her gaze taking in the big beautiful room, the gorgeous old quilt on the bed and finally, lined up along the far wall, every piece of luggage she owned. The packed suitcases she'd left in her cabin the night before. "I...I understand your situation with the work crew, and I appreciate the offer, Reno, but I can't stay up here."

"Why not?"

"Because of Susan." She turned to face him. "I realize you're not suggesting anything...out of line, of course, what with her arriving today. And what with her living here, too. But what would she think of—" Bobbie cleared her throat, realizing she had already given this issue quite a bit of conscious thought. "Well, after all, Susan's just coming into your life. Full time, I mean. This is an important phase in your relationship with her, and she might not appreciate another female hanging around. Taking up your time."

"Hmm," he said. "I hadn't thought about it in those exact terms, but maybe you're right." He lifted a shoulder. "So I'll introduce you as a friend. Someone who's staying here for a while to come up with a business deal for me. It's the truth; we wouldn't be lying to her." He tilted his head and grinned. "You can be discreet, can't you?"

"Yes," she answered, grinning right back at him. "I think I can manage to behave myself."

"And I can, too. So what's the problem?"

"Well," she said after a moment's thought. "Nothing, I guess." Her tone became serious. "But I want you to know, Reno, I have no intention of taking any of your time away from her. I meant what I said about coming up with another proposal, so I'll be busy with that, anyway."

"Okay." He reached up and brushed her cheek. "As long as you're not too busy. I want you to spend some time with me. And I want you and Susan to get to know each other."

"I'd like that, too," Bobbie said. "I'd like it a lot, in fact." She snuggled against his side, under the shelter of his arm, as he led her across the hall to his bedroom. "When does she get here?"

He glanced at his watch. "I've got it all worked out. Breakfast arrives at eleven, Susan and the work crew at noon."

"Gosh," she said, pushing him onto the edge of the bed and standing over him. "It's only ten now, isn't it?"

"Uh-huh," he said, leering at her before he gestured toward his boots.

Bobbie turned around. Straddling one of his legs and then the other, she tossed his boots aside. She remained standing, her foot touching the side of his... just as it had that day in the creek.

Glancing up from his feet, she took his hand and matched his palm to hers. "You know what they say about men with big hands and big feet, don't you?"

"Okay, I'll bite," he said, his fingertips working slowly, provocatively against hers. "What do they say about men with big hands and big feet?"

"Well," she answered, lifting her eyebrows. "They say that's sort of a gauge. A way of sizing a man up, so to speak, before you actually... see him."

"Geez, Bobbie. Is that what you women talk about at your quilting bees?"

"Well, no. But I have heard the theory a time or two."

"I think it's an old wives' tale."

"Maybe so," she said, glancing down and back up again, "but in your case it seems to be true."

"I don't know about that," he said, taking his side of the bed and pulling her down next to him. "But I do know one thing."

"What's that?"

"You're mighty good for a man's ego." His smile changed to a dramatically weary look, and he threw his head back against the pillow. "But as far as his body's concerned, you're a killer."

"Why?" she asked, trying to sound offended as she propped herself up on one elbow.

Lazily he rolled over to face her, mirroring her position on the bed. "Don't play dumb, Bobbie. Maybe I'd be okay right now—if the weather hadn't changed so many times in the last twelve hours. What was it? Around 7:00 a.m., I think, when you woke up and noticed the damned sun was shining. A man can only do so much fishin', you know."

"Oh, yeah? And who was it who woke me up in the middle of the night just because the clouds had disappeared? Who was it who dragged me over to the window and said, 'Look, honey, the sky's clear as crystal now'?"

"Well . . ." He pulled her against him, and she drew a sharp intake of breath when, through the denim, she felt his hardness pressing against her flesh.

"Boy, howdy," she heard Reno murmur against her hair, "would you look at that?" His tone was full of awe as he added, "I think it just started snowing."

"*What?*" Her head spun around toward the window. She felt his laughter rather than actually hearing it, and turned back to glare at him playfully. "You are a cad!"

"I know. And you're just a poor, defenseless, gullible creature who falls for it every time." He kissed one corner of her mouth and then the other. "What do you say?" he whispered. "Let's take a shower—and see how it is *in* the rain."

Two hours later, just before the elevator doors opened, Bobbie laughed and pushed Reno away so that she could straighten her blouse and shorts. "You're unbelievable, you know that?"

"You started it," he said, taking her arm as she stepped into the lobby.

"Ha! How do you figure that?"

"By walking in front of me upstairs—on the way into the elevator. By wiggling that cute little ass and—"

"You're such a liar. My ass is definitely not little."

He stopped her, turning her around. "Okay. It's not too big, not too little. I'd say it's exactly right."

As they continued through the lobby, Reno glanced outside. "Ah," he said. "They're right on time."

"They?" she asked, reading the name of the orphanage on the side of the old bus that was slowly winding its way toward the main building. "You mean, that's your work crew? The kids from—"

"Yeah," he answered quickly, shrugging his shoulders. "What can I say? They're industrious little workers. Cheap labor, too."

"Uh-huh," Bobbie said with a broadening smile. "Sure."

Then, right there in the middle of the lobby, she wrapped her arms around his neck and kissed him.

"Wow," he whispered, obviously surprised that she hadn't given one thought to the desk clerk, who'd been watching them. "What was that all about?"

"That was my way of telling you I think you're the sweetest, most wonderful man I've ever known." Bobbie took his hand. "Come on, now. I'm anxious to meet your daughter. And all the rest of your cheap labor force out there." She reached up for only a moment, briefly touching his cheek. "Right after I meet all the kids, though, I'm going to make myself scarce for a while. I know you want to be alone with Susan. To tell her the good news."

"Just a minute," he said, pulling her into his arms, kissing her deeply, fully, lovingly.

"What . . . what was that all about?"

"That was my way of telling you I think you're the sweetest, most wonderful woman I've ever met." His hand slid down her back, past her waistline. "And I don't care what you say. I think you've got the cutest little ass I've ever seen."

"Not too bad for an old broad, huh?" Smiling, she broke away from his embrace and headed for the double doors.

"No," she heard him say from behind her. "Not too bad at all."

Bobbie set the swing in motion and glanced up from her notes, frustrated. She had come here to start thinking about a new proposal, but... Hearing a whinny, she looked across the creek and saw Reno and Susan walking toward Diamond Jubalee.

They stopped at the fence line and Reno lifted Susan, setting her on the top rail and then leaning his arms on it to form a steeple over her legs. Susan took off his straw hat, plunking it on her own head, and threw her arms around his neck to give him a great big hug and a kiss.

Jubalee moved closer to the two, and Susan giggled when the horse nuzzled her. She lifted both of her hands, laughing again as she rubbed the horse's nose with one hand and Reno's with the other.

Bobbie had always thought Thoroughbreds were supposed to be high-strung and finicky. But with Reno and Susan, Jubalee looked about as high-strung as a basset hound. If the horse could have accomplished the feat, he probably would've rolled over onto his back and let the little girl scratch his tummy.

There was no wonder Susan had captured Reno's heart, Bobbie decided as she stood and walked to the edge of the veranda, still watching the trio. The little girl was adorable in her own special, distinctive way.

Bobbie had been introduced to her only a few hours ago, and she had quickly memorized everything about her. She wore a tiny pair of eyeglasses that suited her perfectly—expensive-looking glasses Reno had obviously paid for—and her sparkly aqua-blue eyes had literally twinkled through the lenses.

Her strawberry-blond hair was so curly it could have been fashioned into ringlets. Right now, though, she had it up in pigtails, complete with fine, wispy little curls escaping all over the place, framing her impish face in a splash of soft color. And to top everything off, there was a smattering of freckles across the bridge of her turned-up nose.

And Reno did love her. It was obvious from the minute he'd grabbed her up a few hours ago—after she'd come tearing off that bus and run straight for his arms.

Bobbie could still visualize their welcome for each other, and the way he'd hugged all the other kids who came off the bus. In fact, she decided, sighing dreamily as her fingers touched her lips, she knew she would never forget that scene. Just as she would never forget the night before. And this morning. Just as she would never forget the way she had felt when he....

Reno turned his head then and spotted her standing there watching them. Susan turned around, too, and they both waved. After their final goodbyes to Jubalee, Reno helped the girl down from the fence. Hand in hand, they walked toward Bobbie, and instead of continuing to stare at them, which she was tempted to do, she started gathering her papers into a neat stack.

When they arrived on the veranda, Bobbie greeted them both.

"You're working?" Reno asked, gesturing toward the file folders she'd left on the swing.

"I was," she answered, giving him a pointed look as she added, "but I seem to be a little distracted today, so I thought I'd just give it up for the time being."

"Well, I have a couple of things to take care of myself. Back at the office." He glanced down at Susan. "Maybe you'd like to stay here for a while, huh?"

"That's okay," the girl answered quickly. "I'll come with you."

"That'd be fine, sugar, except that I have a few things to check on at the barn first. And Bobbie's kind of new at this ranching stuff. I thought maybe you could show her the ropes, tell her how we do things around here."

Bobbie had to stifle a groan. The man was so transparent, it was almost comical.

"Okay," Susan answered with enthusiasm. "I can do that." Still looking up at Reno, she said, "When we get back, though, can I come up to your office? We could play boss."

"Sure. I'll get your pencils sharpened, boss lady."

"Well," Bobbie said, laughing. "I like that. No stereotypical jobs for this young lady."

"No," he stated flatly, stooping down to give one of Susan's pigtails a gentle tug. "I think we're pretty clear on who's who around here."

"Bye, Daddy," Susan said, the new title sounding reverent as she squeezed his neck.

"Bye, boss." Still hugging Susan, he winked at Bobbie over the child's shoulder. "Then I guess I'll see you girls in a couple of hours, huh?"

Reno headed nonchalantly for his truck, and when Susan waved goodbye to him as he drove away, Bobbie noticed the scaled-down I.D. bracelet on her tiny wrist.

"May I see your bracelet?" she asked. When Susan held it up, Bobbie saw that it was engraved with the child's full name: Susan Tanner. "Oh, this is really pretty. Is it new?"

"Uh-uh," she answered, turning the bracelet one way and then the other so that she could watch the gold glinting in the sunlight. "Reno gave it to me a long time ago, when he told me he wanted to adopt me. He said if something happened and they wouldn't let him, then I could still keep this bracelet. He said that way, even if they didn't let him be my real daddy, I could keep this for always, so I'd always know how much he *wanted* to be my daddy." She stopped moving her wrist and held it closer to Bobbie, still explaining. "He said if I always wore this bracelet, no matter what, he'd be my daddy forever—by spirit."

"Oh," Bobbie whispered, smiling. "You mean, *in* spirit?"

"Yeah. Same difference."

"Yes, you're right. It's the same difference," Bobbie agreed, swallowing against the lump that had formed in her throat. She straightened then and smiled as she asked, "Is there something special you'd like to do right now?"

"You mean like—" the girl pointed across the creek "—go see Jubalee again?"

"Well," Bobbie said hesitantly. "I don't know if that's such a good idea. Jubalee really loves you, I can tell, but I'm not sure how Reno would feel about me getting that close to him. He's worth a lot of money, and I'm afraid he might get spooked or something. I just don't know.''

"Okay," Susan said after another quick glance at Jubalee. "Then . . . you wanta go see where our new house is gonna be someday?"

"Sure," Bobbie answered, her curiosity piqued. "I'd like that." They started down the veranda steps, and Bobbie turned toward the Jeep.

Susan grabbed her hand, holding on to it and tugging her away from the vehicle. "We can walk. It's just right over there." She pointed beyond the first two bends in the creek. "See that old shack? Nobody uses it anymore, so we're gonna tear it down." She looked up at Bobbie. "Reno—Daddy says we can't have that old thing in our yard. He says it's nothin' but an eye sorrel."

"An eye sorrel?" she asked, then laughed when she realized Susan had coined her own term for the rickety old building Reno must have called an eyesore. "You and your daddy," she said, shaking her head as she squeezed the little girl's hand. "You certainly do love horses, don't you?"

"Oh, yes," the child commented seriously as they walked along, steering clear of the fence line. "We're gonna have our own stable, and when it's finished, I'll prob'ly even get my own horse." Her eyes were big as half-dollars as she asked, "You want me to show you where the stable's gonna be?"

"Of course! I wouldn't want to miss that."

When Reno had turned down her proposal, she realized, the house undoubtedly had been just as important a reason as the stud farm had been. She had wanted to use that land, and he'd already promised his daughter they would build a home there.

And, she realized, the new house was one more reason for Reno's needing capital.

In that moment Bobbie made a silent vow to come up with another proposal. No matter how many hours it might take, she would come up with an idea that Reno liked every bit as much as he had the first one.

Susan kept a firm hold on her hand, grinning up at her as they neared the old "eye sorrel."

How heavenly it would be, Bobbie thought all of a sudden, if she could be a part of this beautiful new family.

Bobbie glanced around the dining room as she took her last bite of Sunday dinner. Children of all ages were present—not just the younger group she and Reno and Susan were sharing a table with—and even though all the kids seemed well-mannered, the room was a veritable beehive of activity and commotion.

In the thirty-plus hours since their arrival, Reno hadn't exactly been putting the whip to his work crew. The kids had spent the whole time having fun: ropin' and ridin' and feelin' free . . . and a little bit of everything else. And now, obviously, they were anxious to finish dinner and get on to the baseball game that had been planned for the cooler hours of evening.

Bobbie glanced across the table, returning Reno's watchful smile before she asked one of the kids at their table to pass her another napkin.

"You're coming to the game, aren't you?" Susan asked from the seat beside her.

"Oh, I'd really love to, Susan. But I'm not sure. I still have some work to do tonight." As much as she wanted to play baseball—especially with the breathtakingly handsome man across the table who had organized tonight's game—she had to keep reminding herself to give Reno's brand-new daughter the time she deserved with him.

"But Daddy says people shouldn't work on Sundays unless they have to. Unless it's for something really important."

"Well, he's right, but this is for something really important. You see, I'm trying to come up with an idea your daddy needs for the ranch."

"An idea? That's all?" The child looked as if she couldn't believe something as simple as an idea could be considered honest work.

"Yes," Bobbie answered with a laugh. "That's all. Just an idea for a business deal."

"That's right, sugar." Reno addressed his words to Susan while he shot a teasing glance at Bobbie. "I asked Bobbie to stay so she could—" he raised his brows "—make me a deal I couldn't refuse. And so far, she's been doing a pretty good job of it.''

Bobbie put her napkin down and rolled her eyes at him.

Susan's aqua gaze remained on Reno, too, questioning him. "And that's why she has to work all the time?"

"Yeah," he said. "But she doesn't work all the time. She likes to take off once in a while." He grinned at Bobbie as she took another sip of iced tea. "Sometimes she likes to just take off and relax. And go fishing. Right, Bobbie?"

Almost choking on her tea, Bobbie finally managed to set the glass down. Her eyes open wide, she was still coughing when Susan glanced up at her with curiosity.

"You like to fish?" the girl asked. "Daddy has a really neat fishin' pole. Maybe he'd let you use it sometime."

Bobbie heard the thud of Reno's glass as it made contact with the table. Unable to resist the turn of events, she watched him rub his jaw in an obvious attempt to regain control.

"Yeah," he managed to say at last, smiling playfully again as he met Bobbie's amused gaze and held it with his own. "I've been meaning to tell you, Bobbie. You can use it anytime you like. Anytime at all."

Her cheeks grew even warmer, and she cleared her throat as she simply stared back at him in disbelief. "Why, thank you, Reno. How very...generous of you." She stood then and picked up her glass. "If you'll excuse me," she said quickly, "I think I need a glass of water."

"I think I could use one myself," she heard Reno say as she took off for the kitchen.

Bobbie hurried across the room to the sink, and as soon as the swinging door closed behind her, she leaned against the nearest counter and covered her face with her hands, trying to muffle the sound of her laughter as she kept her eyes on the door.

Within seconds, Reno sauntered through the doorway. He stopped and looked at her, smiling innocently and lifting his broad shoulders.

She dropped her hands and made a halfway decent effort to glare at him. "That'll teach you, cowboy," she whispered across the kitchen. "The next time you decide to tease me in front of your daughter, maybe you'll think twice."

"Nah," he said, shaking his head and looking disgustingly sure of himself as he closed the distance between them. He reached to brush his knuckles along her warm face. And then he backed her up, pinning her against the refrigerator. "Look, honey. Why don't you just go ahead and admit it?"

"Admit what?" she asked, her tone coy as her hands went around his neck.

"That you enjoyed that as much as I did." His lips were close, within inches of hers. "That if you had your choice of sports tonight, you sure as hell wouldn't pick baseball."

"Okay," she whispered in admission, her fingers combing through the soft, dark hair above his collar. "You're right. I guess if I had my choice, I'd probably pick tennis."

"Uh-huh." His mouth came down on hers then, his tongue finally, slowly, tenderly parting her lips, and—

Quickly releasing her hold on Reno's neck, she looked past him. "Reno! Stop it, now. I thought you said you could behave yourself. If Susan catches us doing this, she might—"

"She might what?" he asked, glancing over his shoulder and then back at Bobbie. "Get the right idea? You worry too much, darlin'. She already likes you, I can tell."

"Maybe so, but there's a lot she doesn't...know yet, and—"

"Hell, Bobbie, I sure hope not. She's only seven!" His grin disappeared then, and he seemed to be deliberating over a serious issue. "I don't need to talk to her about that sort of thing just yet, do I?"

"No," she said, laughing at the suddenly grave look on his face. "I don't think so."

Her heart seemed to be melting as she watched him. It astounded her that a man this strong, this big and virile and masculine, could also be so very gentle. So caring and vulnerable.

Bobbie shook her head, pretending to chastise him. "For heaven's sake, Reno, I didn't mean about the birds and the bees. I was talking about what she doesn't know about *me*. I'm supposed to be nothing more than a friend and a business associate. Remember?"

"Oh, that," he said, breathing a sigh of relief that was almost audible. "You're probably right about that, for the time being. So..." He glanced down at her breasts and then gave her a rakish wink. "So I guess for the time being, you'd better try to behave yourself."

"I'll try," she said wryly, giving his collar a tug.

"Now. Are you sure you don't want to go to the baseball game? I'm pitching, you know."

"Get out of here," she whispered teasingly, pushing at his chest. "I wouldn't play baseball with you if you paid me. You pitch enough stuff my way as it is."

After Reno laughed and kissed her goodbye, Bobbie stood in the kitchen for several minutes, listening to the enthusiastic sounds of the kids leaving for their game.

Darn it! she thought. Here she was on a big, beautiful ranch with the man she loved, with the little girl she wanted to get to know, and instead of being out there with them tonight, letting Reno pitch his stuff, she was cooped up inside trying to...

Maybe that was the answer, she thought. Maybe Reno had said the key words yesterday. She knew so little about this "ranching stuff" that perhaps if she simply did some research into ranching, she'd be able to come up with an idea that better suited Reno's way of thinking.

That had to be it! Bobbie decided as she pushed open the swinging door. She'd go upstairs to Reno's library and get started. Right this minute.

And it probably wouldn't take any time at all. A day or so, maybe, and then she'd be out there playing, too!

Chapter Twelve

Dammit!'' Bobbie muttered, frowning as her eyes scanned the top of the desk.

There were nearly a dozen books open and spread out before her. Over the past three days she'd spent virtually every waking hour in this room—going through most of the books in Reno's library—yet she was no closer to an idea than when she'd started her research early Sunday evening.

At the moment she was reading about the King Ranch in South Texas, one of the largest cattle ranches in the world. Unfortunately, though, Bobbie realized as she glanced at the book again, she couldn't recall one piece of information she had read about the massive ranch. Instead of knowledge, she seemed to be gathering nothing but an ever-mounting sense of frustration.

Sighing, Bobbie slapped the book shut and picked up the telephone receiver.

Fifteen minutes later, after hanging up the phone, she was more confused and frustrated than ever. Why would Reno—

There was no mistaking the big, broad-shouldered, muscular form that suddenly filled the doorway, making the library seem about the size of a walk-in closet. "Reno! What are you doing here?"

"Looking for you," he answered, doffing his hat and hooking it on the rack nearby.

"Where's Susan?"

"She's with Hollis and Jubalee," he said, laughing and shaking his head as he crossed the room to stand beside her chair. "Where else?"

Bobbie returned his warm smile.

He braced one hand against the edge of the desk, his fingertip touching the magnifying eyeglasses perched on the end of her nose. "You sure do look cute in those things."

"Admit it, cowboy," she said with a mock frown. "You're just a pushover for girls who wear glasses."

"Yeah, that's probably what it is," he murmured, slipping the half-glasses off her nose and dropping them on the desk top. He leaned closer then, his fingers brushing her hair back as his thumb grazed the sensitive skin in front of her ear. And when he lowered his head to hers, he kissed her fully. Beautifully. Lovingly.

When at last he drew back from her, Bobbie put her hand to her chest as she fought to control her ragged breathing.

"What is it with you and libraries?" she finally managed to ask. "You make a girl wish she'd majored in library science."

He winked then, and Bobbie rolled her eyes as if she were disgusted with him. "And you're a terrible distraction, too."

"I hope so," he stated, wiggling his eyebrows before he tilted his head toward the shelves. "While I'm here, what do you say we try to find that Cletus Tanner book?"

"No!" she said, swatting his hand and pointing to the leather chair in the far corner of the room. "Now go sit down for a minute and try to behave. I need to ask you about something."

"Okay," he said grudgingly, turning to saunter away. "If you're sure that's what you want."

"I'm sure," she replied. Maybe she wouldn't be able to detect his scent from way over there. Maybe then *she'd* be able to behave . . . so that she could concentrate on the issue that had her so puzzled.

He leaned back in the overstuffed chair, propping his feet on the ottoman before crossing his boots at the ankles.

Bobbie nodded toward the telephone. "I just got through talking to my brother-in-law, and—"

"Is everything all right?" he asked, looking concerned all of a sudden. "Your sister's not having her baby yet, is she?"

"No, no," she answered. "Alix is fine. Little Charlie's not due till about the middle of next month."

"I thought you said they didn't know whether it was a boy or a girl."

"They don't, but they're naming the baby Charlie, anyway, after Joe's brother." What with Reno's relationship with his own brother being on shaky ground, Bobbie realized this probably wasn't the right time to explain that Charlie was Joe's late brother. In an attempt to get the conversation back on track, she gave Reno a scolding look. "Now stop interrupting me, because I'm really curious about something."

"Okay," he said with a laugh. "No more interruptions."

In a few carefully worded sentences, Bobbie explained that she, not Joe, had placed the call. Saying that she'd simply wanted to visit with her sister, who hadn't even been home at the time—and leaving out the part where she'd been dying to tell Alix that she was in love with a man she was absolutely sure was Mr. Right—Bobbie went on to remind Reno that her brother-in-law was a veterinarian, and to add that quarter horses and Thoroughbreds were his specialty.

"Anyway," she continued, "when I told him where Alix could reach me, he... Well, apparently Joe doesn't know you, but he knows of your horse, and he said something about Jubalee that I don't understand."

"What?"

"He said that, like a lot of other people he knows, he sure would like to have the opportunity to buy into your horse. I didn't really understand that, either—I know so little about racing—so when I asked Joe to explain, he told me that if you wanted to, you could easily syndicate Jubalee."

"That's right. I could if I wanted to, but I don't want to. So what is it you wanted to ask me about?"

"Well...that, I guess. I mean, if you need money, why don't you just syndicate Diamond Jubalee? I don't understand all the fine details, of course, but I got the distinct impression my brother-in-law was talking about big money. Really big money."

"He was," Reno said, his tone blunt. "But if you'll think back, Bobbie, I think you'll recall that I've already told you how I felt about that."

"When?"

"When I took you out to Cal's house that day. You asked me about it, and I told you I had no intention of doing anything of the sort."

Bobbie glanced away, trying to remember everything they'd said that day on the veranda. After she'd seen Jubalee for the first time. And suddenly it dawned on her what Reno must be referring to. "But I was talking about selling him, and obviously, this isn't the same thing. This is just . . . letting people own shares in him, isn't it?"

"Yes, but the way I look at it, that's basically the same thing as selling him."

"Reno, I understand that you love that horse, but . . ."

"But what?"

"But I don't understand why you're so dead set against syndication. Your attitude seems unreasonable, especially when you could have all the money you could possibly use. I mean, you'd still be Jubalee's rightful owner. And you could still build the stud farm, couldn't you?"

"Yes." He shifted positions and frowned, rubbing his firm, tight jaw. "Look, Bobbie, maybe I haven't made myself clear. But I thought you knew that that's why I invited you here in the first place: to come up with a solution for me, something that you and I would both profit from and something that would leave me with an alternative. What I'm looking for is a choice—because I don't even want to think about syndicating Jubalee."

She simply stared at him. "And what if I can't come up with something? What then?"

"I don't think I'll have to worry about that, Bobbie. I have the utmost confidence in your abilities, and God knows you've been working hard enough on this project. You'll come up with something."

"And if I don't?" she asked, her voice rising. "What then?" *What about us?* she thought, a sense of alarm building from somewhere deep inside her. *What about me, if I fail you?*

"I don't know," he answered. "I'll cross that bridge if and when I come to it."

Bobbie hadn't missed his wording. *I'll* cross that bridge, he'd said.

"All I know," he went on, "is that I'm not about to syndicate. That horse is mine and mine alone."

Still staring at him, her eyes wide and disbelieving, Bobbie realized her stomach was tied in one giant knot. Why on earth was he so mule headed about that stupid horse?

She lifted her chin and cleared her throat. "Well, then . . . I take it that's the end of our discussion, in which case you'd better leave now, Reno. Obviously, I still have a lot of work ahead of me."

Reno sat watching her for what seemed an endless number of seconds.

"Fine," he said at last. "If that's what you want." Then he stood, grabbing his hat before he left the room and closed the door behind him.

Bobbie squeezed her eyes shut and dropped her face into her hands.

She had done it again. Obviously, Reno had no trouble making a clear division between personal things and business, yet she had gotten them scrambled together again. Old habits might be hard to break, she told herself, but where Reno Tanner was concerned, that particular habit didn't even apply . . . and come hell or high water, she was going to break it.

And, Bobbie decided as she stood and pushed in the desk chair, if she didn't understand Reno's attitude about Jubalee, then that was fine. Maybe she didn't have to understand everything about him. Right now, maybe it was enough just to understand that she loved him and wanted to do everything she could to help him.

The library door swung open before she reached it, and within seconds she was in his arms, both of them whispering "I'm sorry" at the same time.

"It's just that I'm so frustrated," Bobbie murmured, the words spilling out almost on top of each other. "I've been trying so hard, but I don't even have the start of another idea yet, and I'm afraid I might not—"

"Maybe that's the problem right there, honey. Maybe you're too close to it. Maybe you're trying too hard." He held her at arm's length and smiled down at her. "Why don't you take a day off? I've been wanting you to spend some time with me, remember? And with Susan, too."

"That's exactly why I'm so frustrated," she admitted. "I want to be with you, and I want to get to know Susan, but—"

"So why don't you?"

"Because I can't, Reno. Because I have to get this done, and I think my mind is at least on the right track now." She took his hand, guiding him toward the big leather chair as she nodded at the books littering the entire desk top. "This research will help me see something; I'm just sure of it. And actually, I think it might help Susan, too."

"How?" he asked, taking a seat in the overstuffed chair and watching Bobbie as she sat on the ottoman in front of him. When he put his hand on her thigh, she reached out to run her fingers along his bare forearm, along the hard muscles and the generous growth of dark hair.

"Think about it for a minute," she answered, covering his fingers with her own. "Susan's a sweet, innocent, lovable little girl who's finally gotten what she's always dreamed of: her very own daddy. So it's bound to be better for me to stay in the background right now."

He shook his head and smiled. "The old Roberta Powell logic, huh?"

"Yeah," she said, stretching out the word.

"Well, maybe you're right. But my instincts tell me there's another side to that coin."

"What?"

"You've spent a little time with her already, and with a little more, she's bound to see how much you two have in common."

"And what do we have in common?" Bobbie asked, studying his arrogant grin.

"Well, you both look cute in glasses." He looked straight into her eyes. "And you're both crazy about *me*."

"You sound mighty sure of yourself, cowboy."

"Sometimes I am. So why don't you just go ahead and admit it?"

"Okay," she said offhandedly. "All right, I'll admit it. I'm a little bit crazy about you." She lifted her face another few inches. "There. I've said it. Are you happy now?"

"Yes," he answered, rubbing her leg. "Very. And I'll tell you something else, too."

"What?" Bobbie lifted his hand, pressing her lips against his palm before returning it to her lap.

"You mark my words. It won't be long before Susan starts feeling the same way about you that I do." When Bobbie grinned, he said, "Well, not exactly the same way, of course, but..."

Unable to look away from him, Bobbie returned his intimate smile and the pressure of his hand. Reno hadn't told her exactly how he felt about her, but for some reason, she was content with that.

Yes, she decided. Even though he hadn't said the words she yearned to hear, Reno had been letting her know with his eyes. Those intense, teasing, dark blue eyes. And even though she wanted desperately to be alone with him, in or out of his bed, she could wait for both that and the words.

For now, she assured herself, what she had of him was enough. Because she knew that his child had to be put first. And because she knew that this man—this strong, caring, wonderful man—was definitely worth the wait.

Placing her palm against his cheek, Bobbie said, "Well, your instincts are pretty darned good, but I'm convinced she needs this time alone with you. I'm sure that all she wants right now is you, Reno."

"Well, maybe you're right." He sighed deeply and then rolled his eyes and laughed. "And if you are, maybe she'll get her fill of being alone with her old man soon enough. After tomorrow, she may be ready to throttle me."

"Why? What's going on tomorrow?"

"I promised I'd take her shopping, and tomorrow's the only day I can get away. School starts early next week and she needs everything: clothes, supplies, the whole nine yards."

Seeing the look of confused desperation on his ruggedly handsome face, Bobbie couldn't help laughing.

"It's not funny," he said. "What do I know about stuff like that? Girlie things and frilly dresses and—"

"Oh, my. I'm afraid you're already in trouble." When his eyes questioned her, Bobbie said, "I have a niece, remember? And from what I've seen, little girls don't even *wear* dresses anymore."

"They don't?" he asked, looking both surprised and puzzled.

"Well, once in a while, I guess. But for school, they usually wear jeans. Or skirts and blouses. Or even shorts, if there's not a rule against them. Have you checked with her school yet? To see if they have a certain dress code?"

"No." He shook his head, looking bewildered by the entire concept. "No, I haven't. I guess I'd better do that before we leave tomorrow." His spine straightened, as if another concern had cropped up in his mind. "I thought we'd just drive into Abilene. Does that sound all right, or do you think we ought to fly to Fort Worth?"

"Abilene's perfect, and don't look so worried. She'll pick out what she likes, and you'll do fine. Just let her drag you around all day—from one end of town to the other. Your job won't be that tough. All you'll have to do is whip out your American Express a lot, and let them run it through the machine until you can't even read the little numbers anymore." She flipped her hand. "Oh, and you'll have to stand outside the dressing rooms and let her model everything she tries on. When she does, just ooh and ah a lot. And before you leave town, be sure to ask her—specifically—if she needs any of those girlie things you mentioned."

"Like what?" he asked, looking almost panic-stricken.

"Like frilly little nighties," she whispered, "and panties. And don't forget about socks and shoes. She'll need several different kinds of shoes." Bobbie laughed and patted his hand. "It'll be great fun. You'll love it."

He grimaced. "Chinese water torture sounds like more fun than this fool shopping business. In fact after what you just told me, I'm wondering how the hell I managed to get myself roped into this in the first place."

"If you don't know," she said with a laugh, "I'll be glad to tell you."

"Okay, smarty britches," he said, trying to sneer. "Tell me."

"Why don't you just admit it? When it comes to kids, you're a soft touch."

"I am not," he said defensively.

"You are too. Take that little work crew you've got, for instance." She shot him a playful look of scorn. "How many kids get paid to take a vacation? You're not exactly what I'd call a tough taskmaster."

"I am, too. I make those kids work for their keep."

"You do not! So just stop acting so tough, because even if they haven't got your number, I have. And I think it's terribly sweet of you, paying those kids good money to have fun."

"They're painting cabins," he retorted, "as we speak. You call that fun?"

"The way they're doing it, yes. I looked in on them this morning and they were having a ball—slapping paint all over each other, laughing to beat the band."

"There's nothing that says they can't feel good about putting in a good day's work, is there? And they were doing a good job, weren't they?"

"Oh, yes. The cabin looked great, but I'm still trying to figure out how—what with all that paint on the kids themselves." Her hands on her hips, she tilted her head and gave him a knowing smile. "And while we're on that subject, Mr. Slave Driver, on top of their wages, not to mention giving up nearly a full week's worth of paying guests, just exactly how much do you figure you're spending on the paint alone? How many gallons would you say they used for each cabin?"

"I'm not sure, exactly," he said, his tone noncommittal as he lifted his shoulders. Almost immediately, though, he raised his index finger. "But don't forget, those are big cabins. You need a lot of paint for cabins that big."

"You're right," she admitted. "They are big. And maybe you could get me to fall for that, *if* I hadn't ever seen the outside of those cabins, and *if* I hadn't counted paint cans this morning." Bobbie propped her chin on her hand and smiled up at him. "I could be wrong, cowboy, but I'd say sixteen gallons was just a tad excessive, wouldn't you? Especially for a rock cabin—with no wood on it except for the trim!"

"Well," he said finally, giving her a devilish grin. "You're forgetting the porch—and something tells me that exact amount of paint is a bit of an overstatement, but okay. So you've got my number. So what?" He shrugged his shoulders. "Those kids don't, and I reckon that's all that matters."

"And I reckon you're right."

"And how'd we ever get onto that subject anyway?" he asked, reaching for her. "Come here, darlin'."

"Why?"

"Because," he whispered, his voice husky as he pulled her onto his lap. "I've missed you."

"I've missed you, too."

Time seemed to be suspended as she lost herself in his kiss. In the taste and warmth and strength of him. The texture and the scent of him.

At last she moaned . . . and simply snuggled her face against his chest. And then she heard the sound of his deep voice.

"Oh. Hi, sugar."

Glancing up, seeing Susan standing just inside the library door, Bobbie started to move away from Reno's lap. But he held her firmly in place, his forearms clamped securely over her hip, and she simply watched Susan watching them.

"Hi, Susan," Bobbie said, still trying to figure out the lack of expression on the little girl's face. "How's Jubalee doing today?"

"He's fine."

"Why don't you come over here?" Reno said, patting the outside edge of the chair's leather arm. When she walked over to stand beside the chair, he put his free arm around her and pulled her close to him. "Give your old daddy a hug, will ya?"

After Susan complied enthusiastically, she leaned her elbows on the arm of the chair and simply glanced back and forth—peering into Bobbie's face and then Reno's—time and time again.

What on earth was she thinking? Bobbie wondered. She wasn't frowning, wasn't smiling, wasn't... Nevertheless, it was almost as though Bobbie could see the gears turning inside the girl's mind.

After several more seconds, Susan reached toward them. But all she did was take Reno's wrist, turning it so that she could study the face of his watch.

"Come on, y'all," she said, letting go of Reno's arm. "We better hurry. It's almost time for the party."

Bobbie rolled over for the hundredth time and finally gave up the struggle to get to sleep. The kids from the orphanage would be leaving in the morning, before dawn, so their big farewell party had ended a few hours ago. It was now midnight, and Bobbie was still trying to figure out the many curious glances Susan had given Bobbie and Reno ever since she'd walked in on them that afternoon.

The evening's festivities should have been enough to hold the girl's interest. But all during the dinner party and throughout the rodeo that most of the kids and the ranch hands participated in, Susan had been too busy keeping an eye on Bobbie and Reno to do much of anything else.

Well, Bobbie thought as she switched on the lamp and got out of bed, worrying about it would do her no good, especially when Susan hadn't really seemed upset.

Yes, Bobbie decided as she stepped out into the hallway, what she needed now was to try to get some sleep. Her alarm was set for early in the morning, and if she wanted to be up and dressed in time to see the kids off, she would have to search the kitchen for something that might—

She stopped short, listening to the muffled sobs and then groping her way through the darkness to the bedroom next to hers.

"Susan?" Bobbie whispered, feeling her way across the little girl's room. "What's wrong, sugar?"

She knelt down, trying to make some sense of what Susan was choking out through her tears, rubbing her back as the sobs turned into deep, jerking gasps. She only caught a few words, but it was enough for her to know that Susan was crying because a harsh realization had finally hit her: after tomorrow, the children she'd grown up with—her closest and dearest friends—would no longer be living with her.

"There, there, sugar." Poor baby, Bobbie thought, trying to keep from crying herself as she lifted the child and held her close against her chest. "It'll be okay. You'll see." She smoothed her soft, fine, curly hair and simply held her, not knowing what to say as Susan clung to her.

After several minutes of being rocked and soothed in Bobbie's arms, Susan drew back, still sniffling. "Can I . . . Would it be okay if I sleep with you tonight?"

"Why, sure. I'd like that." When Bobbie placed her palm on Susan's pajama top, she realized that the girl's tears had thoroughly dampened her nightclothes. "We could have a slumber party. I even have a pretty pink nightie you can wear."

"You . . . you do?"

"Yes, and I have some bubbles, too. Would you like to take a bubble bath? Maybe that would make you sleep better."

Bobbie felt Susan shake her head and then heard her whisper, "I'm not allowed to use bubbles."

"Oh?" she murmured as Susan leaned away for a brief moment, searching for her eyeglasses. "Why not?"

"'Cause I might get a blabber infection."

Grateful that they were sitting in the dark, Bobbie covered her mouth to keep from laughing at the child's term for a bladder infection. Reno's daughter had a wide vocabulary for her age, but she also had a knack for hearing certain words incorrectly and then repeating them.

"Oh, yes. That happens sometimes, doesn't it?" Bobbie agreed. "I remember now; my niece isn't allowed to use bubbles, either—for that same reason." She took Susan by the hand then, guiding her through the hallway and into her own bedroom.

Minutes later, Susan emerged from the bathroom wearing the pink shortie gown Bobbie had found for her. By the way she kept running her little hand over the silk—not to mention the awestruck look on her face—it was obvious that the child had never worn anything but utilitarian nightclothes.

"Oh!" Bobbie said, watching as Susan gave her a beaming smile and made one quick twirl. "That really looks good on you."

"It does?"

"Yes. That's the perfect color for you, don't you think?" She turned Susan toward the mirror, standing behind her as she asked, "See how good it looks with your hair?"

Susan studied her own reflection, tilting her head first one way and then the other, her eyes wide behind her tiny glasses. And in that moment, Bobbie realized how badly she wanted to know this child. She couldn't push herself on Susan, but she did need to let the girl know that along with being interested in Reno, Bobbie was interested in *her*.

Yes, Bobbie decided, in this case, it was definitely up to her to make the first move. She reached for the two safety pins already set out on the dresser, keeping her tone light as she said, "I just thought of a good idea."

"You did?" the little girl asked. "What?"

"Well," Bobbie said as she knelt in front of Susan, pretending to be greatly interested in adjusting the nightgown's straps, "I know your daddy's supposed to take you shopping tomorrow, but I have my car here, so maybe you and I could follow the bus back to Abilene in the morning. Maybe we could have breakfast somewhere and then go to a few of the malls. I'm sure we'd really enjoy that."

When Susan didn't respond immediately, Bobbie added, "I'll understand, of course, if you'd rather have your daddy take you shopping. But why don't you sleep on it? You can give me an answer in the morning, okay?"

"Okay."

"Here," Bobbie said quickly, changing the subject in order to keep the atmosphere casual. "Would you like me to help you take off your bracelet before we go to bed?"

"No, thank you," Susan said, her tone serious as she turned around and crawled into bed. "I don't *ever* take my bracelet off. I wear it all the time."

"Oh, of course." Leaving the bathroom light on, Bobbie switched off the bedside lamp and smiled as she took her place next to Susan. "I should've known that."

Realizing that Susan had to be exhausted, Bobbie tried to get the ball rolling by acting exhausted herself: stretching and yawning and closing her eyes. Each time she stole a peek, though, Susan was simply watching her. Studying her.

Finally Bobbie yawned in earnest. Maybe she hadn't worded her suggestion just right, she thought sleepily. Maybe she should have...

Bobbie felt a slight, gentle movement near her feet as she snuggled closer to the pillow. She heard a noise then, a familiar noise from across the hall that announced the arrival of morning. Just as she opened her eyes, squinting against the light shining in from the bathroom, she heard Susan's voice and saw the girl move off the edge of the bed.

"Daddy's making his coffee now. I'll be right back."

Bobbie shot straight up in the bed. Her eyes had been open only a fraction, but she had seen it nonetheless. And it hadn't been a vision or a dream.

No, she told herself, smiling broadly as she tossed back the covers. What it had been was little Susan Tanner, grinning as she headed for her daddy's office in a silky-pink cloud of dust.

Less than twenty minutes later, Bobbie was fully dressed and pacing the floor, not knowing exactly what she should be hoping for but simply hoping, anyway. She heard the elevator doors open and close. And then she heard the unmistakable sound of Reno's boots as he approached her bedroom. After a brief knock, he opened the door.

"Where's Susan?" she asked from where she stood, peering beyond his body.

He leaned against the door frame, crossing his arms in front of his chest. "I sent her down to Annette's office to take care of something for me."

"Well?"

"Well, Bobbie," he said slowly. "It's bad news, I'm afraid."

"Oh, no," she said dejectedly. "What? Bad news about what?"

After shaking his head, he let out a short laugh. "It's about that little pink nightie, darlin'. I hope you're not real attached to that thing, because even if you are, I reckon you've just kissed it goodbye." He winked as he gestured toward the elevator. "She insisted on wearing it down to Annette's office just now."

"I don't care about that stupid nightgown!" she said, lifting her hands into the air. "For heaven's sake, Reno, how can you think I—"

Before Bobbie could finish her question, Reno had crossed the room and taken her into his arms.

"You big dumb jerk," she whispered against his neck. "Tell me what's going on here, will you?"

Bobbie felt the rumble of laughter in his throat, and in a couple of hushed sentences, Reno told her how Susan had "let him down easy," informing him that he had far more important things to do today than to take her shopping. "I got the distinct impression she got a better offer."

"Well," Bobbie murmured. "What can I say? I live to shop."

"Yeah," he said. "Sure."

"I do," she protested, then shot him a wry frown. "And besides that, I knew if you took her, you'd be draggin' in here late tonight, moaning and complaining about girlie stuff, and I'd have to listen to you for hours."

"Actually," he said, "I already had tonight planned, and we were only gonna do one part of that."

"Which part?"

"Well, I thought Susan and I would get home as early as possible. I figured she'd be worn out, and after you and I put her to bed, we could do that part where you listen to me for hours."

"About girlie stuff?"

"No," he answered slowly, quietly, shaking his head.

"About what, then?"

"About just exactly how crazy I am about you." He leaned closer, his lips brushing provocatively along the sensitive flesh of her throat. "In official-sounding terms. So why don't you girls try to come draggin' home early tonight?"

Home, Bobbie thought. What a lovely word. What a beautiful sound.

Her heartbeat was racing, pounding against his hard chest. "Why don't you just . . . tell me right now?"

"No way, honey," he murmured, his breath hot against her ear. "If I tell you now, you're liable to back out on the shopping trip."

Laughing, she pushed him away. "That's blackmail, cowboy."

"I know." He winked then, and Bobbie's knees went weak.

The elevator doors opened, and Reno patted Bobbie on the bottom before he turned and left the room. After making sure that Susan was getting dressed, he went to his office.

Yeah, he thought, opening the wall safe and pulling out some cash, he'd waited long enough to let Bobbie know exactly how he felt about her. This was no longer just about him and her. It was about their future. And in order to let her know what he had in mind for the future, he knew he had to tell her about his past. About Glendelle.

And for that kind of a discussion, he knew they needed more than a few minutes of privacy. Beyond that, with a woman as complicated as Bobbie Powell, the timing needed to be just right.

No, he reminded himself, he sure as hell didn't want Bobbie getting any wrong ideas. He didn't want her thinking he was in love with her only because his kid had taken to her. Or because Bobbie had offered to commandeer some fool shopping trip she knew he'd been dreading.

Still smiling, Reno counted out a handful of large bills, making a guess at what his girls would need for their big day on the town. He shook his head then, laughing at his own stupidity about "girlie things," and decided he'd better double the amount.

Less than an hour later, Bobbie glanced toward the passenger seat and returned Susan's grin. They were directly behind the slow-moving bus, which was a good thing since Bobbie wasn't familiar with the road the driver had taken upon leaving the Hideaway. Moments ago, they had driven past two picturesque old windmills and a rustic-looking watering tank. She would have remembered those if she had ever seen them before.

Perhaps she'd actually been on this route, though, Bobbie thought with a smile. Maybe she didn't recognize it because it wasn't 7:00 a.m. yet, and her eyes still seemed to be adjusting due to precious little sleep the night before. And beyond that, when Reno had taken her on the tour of the ranch, she'd been so distracted by his presence that for all she knew, they might have taken at least some of this route. And last but certainly not least, after the words Reno had whispered to her only this morning, she couldn't seem to think too clearly about anything except what he'd promised was in store for tonight.

If Susan hadn't come bounding out of the elevator exactly when she did, Bobbie thought as she stifled a laugh, she probably would have grabbed Reno by the collar and screamed, "Yes, I love you, too! And no, I don't need any time to think about it. I want to spend the rest of my life with you! I want to marry you—right here, right now. Today!"

The bus driver tapped his brakes, bringing Bobbie out of her daydream but leaving her smiling. The road made a sharp bend to the right, and while negotiating the turn she noticed that Susan was almost ready to fall asleep. Her seat belt was fastened, and she was snuggled against the door and clutching a stuffed animal—the cute, cuddly longhorn calf they'd forgotten to carry into Bobbie's bedroom the night before.

Still smiling, she glanced beyond Susan and spotted a real, honest-to-goodness, full-grown longhorn bull within a few hundred feet of the car. And when her gaze returned to the road, she saw a sign that announced they were getting ready to cross Longhorn Creek.

Strange, Bobbie thought, that she should see three related items in a matter of maybe three seconds. She tilted her head at the silly notion . . . and just then, out of the corner of her left eye, she caught sight of three other things way off in the distance.

Pulling to the side of the road, Bobbie brought the car to a stop, rolled down her window and motioned for the bus to keep going.

"Susan," she whispered, reaching over to touch the sleepy child's hand. After Susan opened her eyes, Bobbie pointed to the left. "Sugar? Do you know if those windmills are on the ranch? Are they on your daddy's property?"

Glancing to the left, Susan simply nodded that they were.

Bobbie rubbed the girl's arm until she drifted off to sleep. As quietly as possible, she got out of the car and shut the door. Then she stood in the middle of the road, staring at one of the most serene sights she'd ever laid eyes on: three gorgeous old windmills on a long, high mesa, and two more on the lower mesa alongside.

Bobbie glanced at her wristwatch. Judging by the time they'd left the Hideaway, they had to be close to the northwest corner of the Diamond T. And with the creek and the windmills and the longhorns grazing nearby, this— Of course! she realized all of a sudden. Reno's instincts had been right all along. Her original proposal was good, and with this spot, it would work! She knew it would. Before now, she had just been too set in her thinking.

The longhorns were an omen, Bobbie decided as she spun around and quickly searched for the nearby herd. And why hadn't she thought of them before? she wondered. They were the symbol of Texas. Of the land itself, and of the ranchers who had made this state what it was today.

Now, in fact, she recalled a caption under a picture she'd seen in that book about the King Ranch, about—

As she stared at the longhorns, Bobbie saw that the sun was just beginning to rise behind the watering tank and the two windmills she'd seen earlier. She pivoted again, realizing how beautiful these two mesas and their clusters of windmills would be at sunset. Yes, she thought, conjuring up an image of evening. It would undoubtedly be a breathtaking sight.

Bobbie decided then that she wouldn't share her idea with Reno just yet.

No, she thought, a radiant smile on her lips. She wouldn't dream of stealing his thunder tonight—for his sake as well as her own. She would tell him about her idea later, after she'd had time to bring it completely together in her mind and on paper.

In her mind, it was nearly complete already, so she wouldn't have to wait long. And how wonderful it was, she realized. How amazing it was that everything had happened in this exact way in order to do just that: to bring it all together for her.

Bobbie brought her hands up, covering her face, laughing with joy. She had wasted the past few days worrying about coming up with an idea to help Reno...and worrying about how his daughter would feel about her...when she hadn't needed to worry at all.

Lifting her face to the sky, Bobbie wanted to shout. It was a glorious morning. A glorious, beautiful, sunshiny day that was literally overflowing with promise for the future.

Her smile was as broad as it could possibly be as she turned and headed for the car. Today was going to be the most wonderful day she had ever had in her entire lifetime. There was nothing that could possibly spoil this glorious day!

Chapter Thirteen

Thanks, Annette." Releasing the intercom, Reno glanced at his wristwatch and punched the lighted button on his phone.

"Quint," he said into the receiver, leaning back and giving a short sound of amusement. "What's got you callin' before ten in the morning? I thought you never set foot in that place before—" Reno tilted his chair forward. "It's not about the adoption papers, is it?"

"No, no. The signing's all set up for Monday, as planned." Quint cleared his throat. "No, I'm calling about something else entirely. Are you holdin' on to your hat, old buddy?"

"Not hardly." Reno leaned back again and smiled. "Believe it or not, Quint, I don't usually wear one at my desk. So what's up?"

"Well, I'm calling about Glendelle. You know that letter you asked me to write?"

"Yeah, sure. I got the copy you sent me, in fact. It came in yesterday's mail." Reno stretched out his legs, propping his crossed ankles on the edge of his desk. "Thanks."

"No problem, but... Well, I figured I'd better let you know I got a phone call about it first thing this morning. Hell, I hadn't even pried my eyes open yet."

"At home? You mean to tell me she's harassing you at home?"

"No, not exactly. I was home, all right, but it wasn't Glendelle who called. It was her old man." After a couple of seconds, Quint asked, "Reno? Are you still there?"

"Yeah, I'm here. Sorry. I was just taken by surprise. I haven't had any contact with G. T. Phillips since the divorce, but that just doesn't sound like something he'd do. He never was one to meddle, and... Well, even if he had a problem with that letter, I don't understand why he'd be calling you about it. Especially at home." When Quint didn't respond, he added, "But listen, I'm glad you let me know. There's no sense in you having to deal with him. G.T. and I always got along pretty well, so I'll just give him a call today. I'm sure I can—"

"No, Reno. There's a lot more to it than that."

"What?" Again, no response. "For God's sake, Quint. Why don't you take a minute to pour yourself a cup of coffee?"

"No, it's not that. I guess I just don't know exactly how to..."

Reno glanced at his watch, trying to curb his impatience. It was only a couple of minutes till ten. When he'd tried to call a number in Abilene a little after 9:30, no one had answered. But surely the place would be open by ten.

"I don't want to sound impatient, Quint, but why don't you just spit it out?"

"Okay." Quint cleared his throat again. "It seems that G. T. Phillips stopped in at Glendelle's place late last night. And apparently that letter was sitting out somewhere—along with the voided checks."

"And?" Reno asked when Quint paused again.

"Well, Reno, I don't think you're gonna be too happy about this, but I don't know any other way to tell you. When G.T. called this morning, he was pretty hot under the collar. Asking all kinds of questions about the content of that letter. I didn't furnish him with any answers, of course, but from the sound of it, all he was trying to do was to confirm what he already suspected.''

"Which was?"

"It seems,'' Quint answered, his tone reluctant, "that right after the divorce—before it was even final, actually—Glendelle went cryin' to Daddy about how unfair you were being with her. And you know Phillips—he's always indulged her, all her life. So when he found out she was suffering in the financial department, he offered to give her some help.''

"So what's the big deal, Quint? That doesn't surprise me at all. She lied—as usual—and like you say, G.T.'s indulged her all her life. So what's his problem? You mean he gave Glendelle a little financial help, and now he's irritated with me about it?"

"Hell, no. He's irritated with *her*.'' Quint sighed. "Look, Reno. I hate to tell you this, but you need to know what's going on—in case you hear from either Glendelle or the old man.''

"Okay.'' Reno pushed his fingers across his scalp. "So what's going on?"

"Well, Phillips wanted to know exactly how long you've been paying Glendelle's monthly bills and how much allowance you've been giving her. But when I wouldn't give him any specifics, I guess it really didn't matter—because it seems he'd been led to believe you weren't helping her one iota. So all this time, Phillips has been giving her an allowance himself. A big one, evidently. In cash. Each and every month.''

Reno's grip tightened around the telephone receiver.

Quint coughed once before he added, "So I guess what it boils down to is that for the past three years, Glendelle's been playing both ends against the middle. And from the sound of it, Phillips is more than a little irritated with her. In fact, before he hung up he muttered something about this being the last straw. Evidently, as of last night, the old man cut her off completely. So my guess is that she's gonna be pretty desperate at this point, what with both of her financial sources pulling out on her over the course of only—''

After a few seconds of total silence, Quint spoke up again.

"Reno?'' he asked. "You still there, buddy?"

* * *

Bobbie hung up the phone and jotted another note to herself.

It was too bad that Reno's ex-wife hadn't come to work today, she thought, glancing out of Faye's office window to check on Susan once again. The orphanage's big play yard was filled with kids of all ages, most of whom Bobbie now knew or at least recognized, and she smiled as she leaned back to watch Susan jumping rope with two of the other children.

The little girl was certainly wide awake now, Bobbie decided, laughing as she thought about the way Susan had slept so peacefully earlier that morning. While Bobbie spent more than an hour exploring the entire corner of the Diamond T, driving over every bumpy road she could find, Susan hadn't even stirred. It wasn't until they'd reached the outskirts of Abilene that she'd woken up, which had worked out beautifully. Susan had been happy to hear Bobbie's suggestion that they stop by the orphanage for a while—since none of the stores would be open yet—and then she had directed Bobbie on how to get here.

Beyond wanting to give Susan some extra time with her friends, Bobbie had wanted to meet Reno's ex-wife. After Susan had run off to join some other kids for breakfast, though, Bobbie had inquired and found out that Faye wouldn't be in today. Although she normally brought her two youngest children to work with her, the director had said, both of them were sick, so Faye had stayed home with them.

Well, Bobbie thought as she picked up the phone again, with hope there would be other opportunities like this one. And in the meantime, it had certainly been nice of the director to suggest that she use Faye's telephone to make her business calls.

After glancing at her watch and realizing the department stores would be open by now, she placed the last in her series of credit-card calls. Fortunately, Judith Cavanaugh answered her private line on the second ring.

Bobbie spent a few minutes simply chatting with her friend and business associate, letting Judith catch her up on what had been happening in Bobbie's office while she'd been gone. Then she said, "If you have time, Judith, I've got an idea I'd like to pass by you. I'm convinced it'll work, but I might be a little too close to this one to be objective, and since I trust your judgment more than anyone else's, I'd sure appreciate your opinion."

After receiving a positive response, Bobbie filled Judith in on her plan for a secondary-residence retreat, mentioning its central location as well as the type of high-powered executives it would be geared toward. After that, she moved on to recap the telephone calls she'd made over the past hour. While Susan had played outside with the other kids, Bobbie had been busy talking with two separate individuals. Judith was familiar with the names Bobbie mentioned: an architect and a builder, both of them young and eager, innovative in their thinking and hungry for their first really big breaks. After Bobbie had outlined her general idea to each of them, they had each been excited about the possibility of becoming on-site people for the project in exchange for the opportunity, the experience and, of course, the fees they would receive from the residents themselves.

"It sounds fantastic to me, Roberta. I think you've got a real winner on your hands. In fact, if the opportunity arises, I might want to go in on this one with you. Do you need investors?"

"Probably so," she answered. "Naturally, I already have a few of my own in mind, but I think this project will need more." Bobbie had some additional ideas on that, too, but she wanted to discuss them with Reno first. Everything would be to his benefit, though, and she felt sure he would go for the additional investors in order to help with the paving of roads and the building of the main structures and the golf course. A bit more of his land would be involved than Reno had intended, but at least it was at the edge of his ranch. And in return, he'd be able to retain a piece of the financial action as well as having long-term participation in the project itself.

"Great, then," Judith said. "Be sure to keep me in mind."

After assuring her friend she'd be the first person contacted, Bobbie realized she had forgotten to mention one of the most important details of her plan. Briefly, she explained what Reno had told her about the beef from the longhorns, and then she told Judith about the caption she'd seen under a picture only the day before.

"Evidently," Bobbie added, "buying into the cattle-breeding business is kind of a social-status thing for a lot of people. And what with everyone being so health-conscious nowadays, I wondered if offering these potential residents the opportunity to invest in the longhorn-breeding business would give them extra incentive to live there." She laughed then. "I'm not sure if this makes much sense, Judith, but the idea of it really appeals to me. I have a vision of these people standing out on their weekend verandas, gazing off into the distance and watching their own longhorns grazing nearby. Somehow it all seems very...relaxing and serene."

"Oh, that does sound heavenly," Judith said, her tone reflecting her own excitement. "I think you're right."

Just then, the door flew open and Susan came skipping into the room. After promising to keep Judith posted, Bobbie hung up the phone and grabbed her clutch bag.

"I guess you're ready, huh?" Bobbie asked, smiling as the girl took her hand.

Susan nodded happily, her pigtails bouncing up and down.

"Well, come on then. Now that I've got all my work done, we've got some serious shopping to do!"

Reno frowned as the intercom buzzer sounded. "Who is it this time, Annette?"

"Sorry, dear," she said, "but it's Hollis. And no, it's not about Jubalee. But believe me, this one's urgent."

When Annette flatly refused to tell him what the call was about, Reno couldn't help laughing. Hell, he thought, picking up the correct telephone line. He could hardly blame her. The poor woman had spent most of her day screening his calls, and it had been the damnedest, craziest assortment he'd ever received. Everything from personal to business to—

"Hey, boss," Hollis said. "Sorry to bother ya, but I figured you'd wanta know. I was standing out there by the whirlybird a few minutes ago, just talking to Butch for a while, and... Well, while I standing there, I saw the Phillips plane comin' in for a landing."

Reno shook his head. Evidently G.T.'s secretary had relayed his message, and no doubt the old man had decided to return his call by way of a personal visit. "Thanks for the warning, Hollis, but I've been halfway expecting G.T. to show up today."

"Wait a minute, boss. I stood there long enough to watch, and it wasn't him who come climbin' off that thing. It was Miss Glendelle."

Reno let out a sigh of exasperation. No wonder Annette had refused to tell him, he decided. Of all the phone calls that had come in today, this one had to be the topper.

Mumbling another thanks into the receiver, Reno glanced at his watch and noticed it was already after four o'clock. "Hollis? I wonder if you could do me a favor. I'm supposed to pick up something at the jeweler's in Abilene, but they close at six." When Hollis agreed without hesitation, Reno added, "If you don't feel up to driving, why don't you see if Butch can get you there? That'd be fine with me."

"Sure, boss."

"And listen, Hollis," he said, forcing his thoughts back to an unrelated matter that had crossed his mind during one of the few lulls in the day. "There's something else I need to ask you, something I just want you to keep an eye on for me next week." Reno briefly explained what he needed, gave the jeweler's address, and hung up.

Well, Reno thought, propping his feet up as he leaned back. It had been one hell of an interesting day. And the strangest part was the fact that Reno wasn't supposed to have been here at all. It was a damned good thing Bobbie had offered to take Susan to town. He glanced at his watch again. And it was a damned good thing both Bobbie and Susan wouldn't be anywhere around for the performance Glendelle was no doubt fixing to stage.

What was *really* crazy, though, he thought, was that after Quint's original phone call, it had dawned on Reno that the news hadn't even surprised him. It was just like Glendelle to pull some conniving, underhanded trick like the one Quint had outlined.

Yeah, he thought, giving a short, bitter laugh. The woman had it down to a science, all right. He could just picture the upcoming scene: she'd be dressed to kill, batting her eyelashes and crying those phony tears she'd always been able to produce so easily, sidling up to him with a brand-new version of one of her old routines. Along with the usual I'm-so-sorry, this one would contain some pathetic little speech about how his letter had made her see the error of her ways. Hell, he thought, she would probably even claim she'd rushed out and joined Gamblers Anonymous.

More than likely, she had no idea Reno had been advised of what she'd done to her father. And that was fine, because he planned to save that information for just the right point in their confrontation—like maybe right after she moved from crying into screaming and making demands. Or, he decided, better yet, maybe somewhere close to the bitter end, when undoubtedly she'd switch back to the crocodile tears and start begging him for a loan.

The intercom sounded again.

Annette asked if she should escort Glendelle upstairs, and after Reno said, "Absolutely," he leaned forward and jotted himself a note.

Yeah, he thought as he stood and slipped the note into his desk drawer. When G. T. Phillips returned his call, Reno needed to suggest—subtly, of course—that maybe he should have a talk with his pilot about who didn't have privileges any more.

"Bobbie?" Susan asked as they reached the northwest boundary and drove into the ranch. "Can we take the other road and go see Jubalee?"

"Well," Bobbie answered reluctantly, glancing at her watch. They had made a whirlwind shopping trip and, unbelievably, it was only a little after five.

"It's okay," Susan said, giving her a look of assurance. "You don't have to be scared. I talked to Daddy this morning before we left, and he said it was all right for you to get close to Jubalee—as long as I go with you. He said, 'Just make sure Hollis is there, too.'"

"Oh," Bobbie said quietly, touched by the child's gesture. "Why, thank you, Susan. Why don't we do that, then? But just for a few minutes, okay?" Her gaze went back to the road as she added, "Because I talked to your daddy for a few minutes myself this morning, and he wants us home as early as possible." She reached over and tweaked Susan's nose. "He's probably dying for you to give him a style show."

After grinning excitedly, Susan picked up one of the boxes between them and opened it. "I think I'll show him this one first, 'cause I don't want him to have to wait till winter to see me in it." She pulled out the ruffly red nightgown, holding the brushed flannel against her cheek. "It's so *soft*."

"Yes," Bobbie said, "I'm sure he'll love that one. In fact, I think he'll love everything you picked out, don't you?"

"Uh-huh."

As Bobbie continued to drive, Susan busied herself opening every box, staring at each garment, fingering each fabric, and finally stacking and restacking the boxes in what Bobbie presumed was the correct order for modeling the clothes.

They had found at least half of what Susan would need, and Bobbie had promised to take her back to Abilene the following day. It would be a small price to pay...to get home early. And Susan had been thrilled at the prospect of going back again: doing more shopping and visiting her friends again and maybe even taking in a movie.

As soon as Bobbie parked the car, Susan dragged her toward the old foreman's shack, telling her she'd forgotten to show her something the other day. Before they even reached the site of the new house, Susan started pointing and naming off the various rooms they would have. "It's gonna be a really big house," she said at last, glancing up at Bobbie. "You like it here, don't you?"

"Yes, I do," Bobbie answered, amused by the question. "I like it a whole lot, in fact."

"I bet you could come here and live with us all the time. If you wanted to."

"Oh?" Bobbie asked cautiously. "What makes you say that?"

"'Cause you like it here, and we like you and you like us. And this is gonna be a really big house. You could prob'ly even have your own room.'' Susan glanced away as she added, ''Or maybe you could sleep in Daddy's room. With him.'' Her eyes were big and round and serious-looking when she peered up at Bobbie again. ''People can do that, you know—if they get married.''

Why, you cagey little devil, she thought, wanting to grab Susan and hug her. All this time Bobbie had been worried about how an orphaned child would feel about her horning in, when obviously Susan had been smart enough to realize she could have everything—a mother as well as a father, the perfect family an orphan probably dreamed about all the time.

Still watching Susan, Bobbie realized she needed to make a careful reply. ''Well, I think I'd really love living here with you and your daddy, Susan, but maybe it would be better if we kept that to ourselves for a while. I mean, maybe if we keep it a secret—just you and me—maybe after a while your daddy might think of that idea himself. Don't you think he might like that better?''

She stooped down, touching the wispy curls in front of Susan's ear as she added, ''It would be sort of like . . . the way he picked you out of all the other children in the whole wide world. Reno picked you specially, because he loves you so much, and it wouldn't be exactly the same thing, but I think that's sort of how he'd like to pick a wife, don't you?''

Bobbie continued to watch her, hoping and praying that she had chosen the right words.

''I'm good at keeping secrets,'' Susan whispered, bringing one finger up to her pursed lips.

''Good,'' Bobbie whispered back, smiling with joy as she hugged the girl. She straightened then and took Susan's hand. ''This can be our little secret, then. Okay?''

''Okay.''

Bobbie's heart seemed to be singing as, hand in hand, they crossed to the fence line.

Susan let go of her, darted a quick glance at Jubalee and ran inside to find Hollis.

Today was going to be perfect, Bobbie decided again. She just knew it.

"Hollis isn't here," the girl shouted as she raced toward Bobbie again. "So we better do what Daddy says." Susan stopped dead in her tracks, cupping her hand behind her ear. "Listen!"

"What is it?" Bobbie asked, hearing nothing but a faint noise in the distance.

"It's an airplane gettin' ready to take off."

"Is it?" Bobbie asked. "Was Reno planning to fly somewhere today?"

"I don't know," Susan answered, shaking her head as she added, "but that's not Daddy's airplane."

"How can you tell?"

"By the sound. It's a jet; it's different from Daddy's."

Bobbie simply grinned, staring at Susan as the noise became much louder. Children, she knew, paid more attention to their five senses than adults did, but—

"Uh-oh."

Bobbie pivoted to see why Susan's expression had turned grave all of a sudden. The plane had lifted into the air: a beautiful Lear jet with "Phillips Corporation" emblazoned across its side. How strange, Bobbie thought. Her father had once done business with a Mr. Phillips, but it had been ages ago, sometime before Bobbie had gone off to college.

"What's the matter?" she asked, still shielding her eyes and watching the jet.

"Glendelle was here," Susan said over the noise, "and that means Daddy's prob'ly not gonna be in a very good mood tonight."

Although Bobbie had never met Glendelle Phillips, she immediately recognized the name. Who could forget a distinctive name like Glendelle? But what in the world was Susan talking about?

Bobbie turned around just as Susan said, "Daddy must not'a picked her specially."

"What?" Bobbie asked, laughing.

"I met her once before—when she came here one time. She's not a very nice lady. I think Daddy was sorry he picked her. I think that's why they got a divorce."

"What?" Bobbie asked, her laughter gone as she spun around again, as her hand flew up to cover her mouth. The jet lifted higher and higher into the sky, and at the same time, her heart seemed to plummet all the way to the ground.

Dear God! she thought, sudden pain and confusion lashing at her insides. Why hadn't Reno told her?

"Bobbie?" Susan asked, tugging on her slacks. "Can I say bye to Jubalee before we go?"

Taking her hand from her mouth, Bobbie realized she had to keep her composure. "Yes, sugar," she whispered. "Why don't you go over and do that? I'll just . . . watch you from here."

She turned around at last, just as Susan climbed the rails of the fence and started calling to Jubalee, coaxing the horse toward the fence line.

Bobbie wanted to cry, but she knew she couldn't. No, she thought with determination, not now. Right now she had to try to figure out why Reno hadn't told her about Glendelle.

Her mind went back to that night in Fort Worth, when Reno had taken her to dinner, when she had asked him about his divorce. He had told her about Faye—ever so briefly, though, and only after Bobbie had virtually had to pry the information out of him. And then, instead of telling her the truth, instead of mentioning that there had been another divorce, he had quickly changed the subject. . . . Perhaps he had had his reasons for not telling her about Glendelle, Bobbie began to realize. Perhaps, as far as Reno was concerned, Glendelle Phillips Tanner hadn't even been important enough to mention!

A mixture of anguish and fear and desperate confusion seemed to be ripping right through her, stabbing at her heart. It was as intense as any physical pain could ever be. . . .

Bobbie stared at Jubalee, growing more upset by the minute.

For all she knew, she had fallen in love with a man who didn't take *anything* seriously. Except for that horse. That damned, stupid horse!

Chapter Fourteen

Even though the door to his office was shut, Reno heard Bobbie and Susan when they arrived on the second floor. He glanced at his watch, deciding that Glendelle must have left the ranch before they arrived.

Damn, but he was glad this business with Glendelle was over with—absolutely and completely. Today's confrontation would be the last, he knew, because before Glendelle left, Reno had made sure she knew exactly *why* there would be no more money: because he had finally let go of the last fragments of guilt. Once and for all.

Reno leaned back and pushed out a long, weary sigh. After everything that had happened today, he was tired. Bone tired. But nevertheless, he knew that tonight, by the time they finished dinner and got Susan to bed, he'd be more than ready to talk to Bobbie.

"Hi, Daddy!"

Reno smiled as he glanced toward the door to see Susan's exuberant face. "Hi, sugar. What have you got there?"

"A surprise," she squealed. Still clutching the white box, she raced over and threw herself against him, her arms pushing on his thighs. "And you have to come to my room if you wanta see me in it."

"Well, what are we waiting for, then?" he asked, lifting her up in the air and carrying her across the hall. After they entered Susan's bedroom, he noticed that several outfits were laid out neatly on the bed. "Hey, kiddo," he asked, "where'd your shopping buddy run off to?"

"Her room. She already saw me in my new clothes, and she said she was really, really tired."

"You wore her out, did you?"

"Uh-huh," Susan replied almost proudly, then whipped off her blouse. "See my pretty new T-shirt? Bobbie says it's not really a T-shirt, though. It's a..." Obviously trying to recall the word, she wrinkled her nose. "It's a camisole."

"Ah," Reno commented. "That's mighty fancy, all right."

Thanks to her new camisole, Susan showed no traces of modesty. Reno sat on the edge of her bed while she raced through one change of clothes after another, barely waiting for his comment of approval between each one.

"This is my favorite," she said, twirling around in a pair of pencil-slim jeans and a feminine-looking blouse.

"I think that's my favorite, too," Reno said. "So why don't you get busy and take your bath now? I want you to put this back on and wear it to dinner for me."

"Can I?"

"Sure," he said. "Why not? And while you're in the tub, I think I'd better go check on Bobbie, don't you?"

Susan nodded enthusiastically before disappearing into the bathroom.

Still smiling as he walked down the hallway, Reno knocked lightly and opened Bobbie's bedroom door. Even before he stepped into the room, his eyes caught her movement. She was inside the walk-in closet, working feverishly.

"What's this?" he asked, laughing as he shut the door behind him. "Don't tell me I'm in for another fashion—" When he turned around, he spotted the half-filled suitcases on the bed. "What are you doing, Bobbie?"

"I'm packing," she said quietly, her back still to him as she continued to pull clothes from her hangers. "I have to leave. I have to go back to Dallas."

"Why, darlin'?"

"Because I . . ." Slowly she turned to face him, her eyes red and swollen, her voice quivering. "Because I don't understand you, Reno. Because I want to—so badly—but I'm afraid I never will."

"Tell me what's wrong, Bobbie." He stayed where he was, sensing that she didn't want him to move any closer, that she didn't want him pushing her into any corners. "What is it you don't understand?"

A single tear rolled down each side of her face. "I don't understand . . . why you didn't tell me about Glendelle. I—I thought you loved me, and—"

"Oh, darlin'," he murmured, "I do love you. And I'm sorry you had to find out about Glendelle some other way. I was going to tell you myself. Tonight. After I told you exactly how much I do love you."

"Oh, please! How can you expect me to believe that, Reno? After what's happened? After you lied to me about her?"

"I didn't lie to you, Bobbie. I just hadn't told you about her yet, that's all."

"That's all?" Her eyes sparked with sudden fury. "What, Reno? You don't call that a lie?"

"No. In this case, I don't. I—"

"Well, I do!" she said, her voice rising. "And all those times I called you a liar, I thought I was joking, but I wasn't. You are a liar!"

"For God's sake, Bobbie, I wasn't lying to you all those times. I was teasing you." He raked his fingers through his hair. "I was trying to get you to lighten up a little—instead of taking everything so damned seriously."

"Well, pardon me, Reno," she said, her tone venomous. "Pardon me if there are certain subjects I don't seem to be able to take as lightly as you do!"

His spine stiffened as he watched the sarcastic look that had come across her face. "Like what, for instance?"

"Like marriage, for instance!" Her fists were balled up at her sides. "Tell me, Reno. How many *other* ex-wives do you have running around out there? Lurking in the bushes? How many other Mrs. Tanners have you conveniently failed to mention to me?"

"None," he yelled, "and don't start getting smart with me, Bobbie." He stared at her in disbelief. "So what was I supposed to do? Just say to hell with the timing? Just casually drop that little news flash into one of our conversations? 'Oh, by the way, honey, I'm thinking about making you Bride Number Three'?"

"Well, why not?" she screamed. "Especially since your attitude seems to be pretty darned casual when it comes to those brides of yours. Unlike your attitude about Diamond Jubalee, I might add! That damned stupid horse is the only thing I've ever seen you get—"

Bobbie's eyes darted to the door that had opened behind him, and Reno turned to see Susan standing in the doorway. She was wrapped in a towel, beads of water dripping down her legs.

"Daddy?" she said timidly. "Hollis is here. He says he wants to go to the bunkhouse for dinner and what should he do with your package?"

"Tell him to put it on my desk, sugar, and then you run on and get back into the tub."

"Okay."

After watching to make sure she did just that, and watching Hollis head for the elevator, Reno shut the door again and turned to Bobbie. She was standing over the bed now, flinging more clothes into her suitcases.

"Bobbie?" he asked quietly, softly, trying to keep the weary edge out of his voice. "Do you love me or don't you?"

"Yes," she whispered, turning to face him, her beautiful eyes moist with tears. "God help me, Reno. I do love you."

"Then don't leave. Stay and let's work this out."

"I can't," she replied, her voice almost pleading. "Don't you see? I have to go home...at least for a few days. I have to have some time to think. Maybe then I'll—"

"Dammit, Bobbie! Why do you always have to do that to me? Why do you always have to think everything to *death*?" He stood there, shaking his head in disgust. "What's it going to take for you to start listening to me with something besides your head?"

Seeing the look of anguish that was suddenly visible in her eyes, he stepped forward, closing the distance between them. But when he reached for her, she drew back.

"Please, Reno," she begged. "Please don't touch me. Not now. When you touch me, I can't—"

"What?" he asked, his anger quickly resurfacing, mixing with the weariness and then coming to a full boil. Raging completely out of control. "What, Bobbie? When I touch you, you can't *think*?"

She pressed her hand against her lips, not answering his question, and Reno headed for the door.

Turning once again, he glared at the open suitcases and then at her. "If you have to go strictly by what's stuck up there in your head, Bobbie...if you have to mull on that forever and calculate every move...then fine."

He yanked open the door.

"Finish your packing," he added firmly. "And go on home."

Seconds later Bobbie stood in the middle of the hallway, tears flowing down her cheeks as she watched the elevator doors close behind Reno, as she felt Susan's presence at her side.

"Bobbie?" the girl asked. "You're not gonna go away, are you?"

"Oh, honey," she whispered, not knowing what to say or how to explain. She was so confused right now, she didn't know *what* she was doing.

And dammit! she thought, how could Reno be so furious with her? He had *lied* to her, so why couldn't he understand that because of that alone, she was just plain scared?

She had fallen in love with him. And now...

Now, she thought sadly, squeezing her eyes shut, now it was all hopeless, anyway. Reno had left her no choice in the matter. And now she felt as if she was dying inside. As if her heart had been shattered into a million tiny fragments.

"But you *can't* go," the girl went on, her eyes pleading as she threw her arms around Bobbie's legs and clung to her. "Not...not now. Not yet! You promised to take me back to town tomorrow, remember? You said you'd take me to go visit my friends again."

Oh, God, Bobbie thought, holding the girl close, stroking the soft, fine hair of one of her pigtails. "You're right," she murmured. "I did promise you, didn't I? Well then . . . that's what we'll do."

Everything inside her seemed to be coming apart. She had wanted so badly to be a part of this little girl's life, but now that wouldn't be possible. All she could do now was give Susan one more day . . . no matter what Reno had told her to do.

She held the child away from her and forced herself to smile. "Your daddy had to go out for a while, Susan, but I'm sure he'll be back soon. In the meantime, we had a big day today . . . so why don't you go on to your room and rest for a while, until he gets back. I think I could use a little rest myself." Somehow, she managed to make her smile brighter, trying to look reassuring as she turned Susan around and swatted her bottom. "Run on, now. I'll be in after a while to check on you."

Over an hour later, after deciding she had shed every possible tear, Bobbie stood in the bathroom holding a washcloth to her swollen eyes. After applying some makeup, which wasn't much help, she changed into a fresh blouse and a pair of jeans. No matter how painful it would be to stay when she knew Reno didn't want her here, Bobbie had decided she was going to make this time as easy for Susan as she could.

Gathering every ounce of resolve she could muster, she opened her door and slipped into the hallway. Whether the mistakes had been hers or Reno's or both of theirs, there was no reason for an innocent child to—

Reno's office door was open, and she heard Hollis's voice. The man sounded terribly upset, and even though Bobbie hadn't heard all the words, she had heard one of them: Jubalee.

"No," Hollis was saying now. "I've already called everyone I could think of. No one's seen him! He's gone, boss, he's just gone."

"Dammit!" she heard Reno say in reply. "No one saw anything? Or anyone?"

"No, boss, they—"

"Glendelle's behind this—she has to be. I should've known better than to ignore her threats today." He paused. "Hell, she must've had someone lined up to come in here right about the time her plane landed in Fort Worth, to give her an iron-clad . . . Call Butch and tell him to have my plane ready to take off." Reno's voice was coming from the kitchen now. "Tell him I'll be there as fast as I can."

Bobbie was standing in the middle of the hallway when she saw Reno pass through the connecting doorway and go into the sitting room. And then she saw him heading for the gun cabinet.

"Reno," she yelled, racing to his side, grabbing his arm. "Don't do this!"

"Why not?" He yanked his arm away from her hold. But then, instead of reaching into the gun cabinet, he grabbed his key ring from the nearby table.

Thank God it hadn't been a gun he was after, Bobbie thought. But still, she realized all of a sudden, growing more alarmed by the second, there were guns in his truck. And considering the look in his eyes right now, and the way he felt about that horse . . .

"Please, Reno. This just doesn't make any sense. How do you know Glendelle's behind this?"

"Because she came here today for one reason, Bobbie: money. Because she begged me for a loan, and when I refused her, she said she'd find a way to get it from me." He turned and glared at her. "Now. Does that make enough sense to you?"

"No, it doesn't," she said evenly, glaring right back at him. "Why would Glendelle Phillips have to beg anyone for a loan?"

"Because she owes money to all kinds of sleazy, unsavory characters. Because she has a gambling problem, Bobbie—one that's gone from bad to worse over the past six years—and she's desperate right now."

"Okay, okay, but wait a minute." Oh, God! Bobbie thought. What if it *was* Glendelle? And if it was, what if Reno got there—with or without a gun—and ended up having to defend himself against some of those unsavory characters? The kind of people Glendelle could no doubt get to help her pull off something like this?

What could she say to stall him? To keep him from doing something that might turn out to be disastrous? Something that might even get him killed!

"Reno, please. Susan...Susan will be asleep by the time you get back. Please just calm down for a minute. At least long enough to say good-night to her. She's already upset today, anyway, after hearing—"

"Fine," he muttered, racing across the hall with Bobbie right on his heels, following him into his daughter's bedroom.

Susan wasn't anywhere to be found, and suddenly, they were both staring at the same gold object on the floor beside her bed: the I.D. bracelet that Susan never took off her wrist.

Never.

Bobbie gasped as Reno stooped to pick up the bracelet, as she saw the look on his face when he said, almost to himself, "If she's done anything to harm that child, I'll—"

"Please, Reno," she said frantically, struggling to fight back her own sense of panic and fear. "You've got to try to calm down! You can't . . ."

She ran after him again, grasping his arm, feeling helpless as she tried to think of what she could do. "But what about the elevator?" she asked as she scrambled toward it right alongside him.

He turned, grabbing her upper arms and yanking her body toward him. "I don't have time for this, Bobbie. I don't have time to give you answers to all your logical questions."

"But the elevator is secure! Glendelle wouldn't know the right numbers to—"

"For God's sake," he said, his voice almost plaintive. "The numbers are my birthday, Bobbie! How tough would it be for her to figure that out?"

"Please, Reno. Please let me go with you! Let me drive you to Fort Worth. You can't fly that plane when you're this emotional."

"No," he stated flatly. "If you want to be so damned cool, calm and collected, stay here. Wait by the phone." He let go of her arms and turned away from her. "Use some of that logic to bargain with—in case someone calls asking for ransom."

"Damn you, Reno!" she screamed as the elevator doors came open and he stepped inside. "Just because I don't react the same way you do, that doesn't mean I'm not just as—"

The doors closed, and Bobbie bit off the rest of her sentence before she pivoted toward Reno's office, realizing that staying by the phone was all she could do at this point.

"Oh!" Startled, Bobbie almost jumped out of her skin. She put her hand to her breastbone, trying to stop the short, quick gasps she was suddenly taking. "Hollis! You...you scared me." She hadn't remembered that he was still upstairs. That he had been in Reno's office all this time.

"I'm sorry, Miss Bobbie." He reached out, putting one arm around her while he signaled for the elevator to return to the second floor. "Now don't you worry about a thing," he added, his voice gentle as he made an obvious effort to hide his own anxiety. "I'll watch the phones myself—from downstairs. You take it easy for a bit. We're all upset right now, but things'll look brighter in no time. You'll see, honey."

"Thank you," she murmured, her pulse still fluttering wildly when the elevator arrived and took Hollis away.

She turned and headed for Reno's office. Just as she got through the doorway, though, Bobbie pivoted and simply stood there. Staring at the elevator.

No! she thought. It couldn't have been Glendelle. Glendelle couldn't possibly have sent someone in here with a long list of four-digit *guesses*. That number could've been any four digits under the sun.

But, she realized, there was one person who *would* know that number. And that same person resented Reno...and knew exactly how much Susan and Jubalee meant to him.

Bobbie swung around and started pacing the floor in front of Reno's desk, running her fingers through her hair time and time again. It was probably ridiculous, thinking that Reno's own brother might do something like this to him, but...

But what could she do right now? Bobbie wondered, a sense of alarm now churning, intensifying, deep inside her. There was nothing she could do to help Susan, and if there was any chance that Cal might have done this horrible thing, then she at least needed to think it through.

Still pacing, Bobbie tried to concentrate on the few things Reno had told her about his brother. He had said that their relationship wasn't good; that it had never been good; that they had parted in bad company.

And, Bobbie realized all of a sudden, when he was driving her to the airstrip that day, he had mentioned two pieces of information that were far more relevant to the issue at hand: Cal resented the fact that their father had left Diamond Jubalee to Reno. And, as of several months ago, Cal had taken off for parts unknown.

But considering the way his house was hidden—tucked away in that grove of trees—it was quite possible that he could have returned without anyone's knowledge.

And maybe she was crazy to think it, but it was also quite possible that the man had planned it that way. If Cal Tanner was as obsessed with that horse as Reno was, then maybe Cal had simply been waiting for Susan's arrival on the ranch, knowing that afterward it would be easy for him to take both her and Jubalee, and knowing full well that he'd be able to use Susan as a pawn to get Reno to turn Diamond Jubalee over to him.

Cal Tanner wanted Jubalee . . . and perhaps he didn't care if he had to frighten a poor, defenseless, innocent child in order to get what he wanted!

If Bobbie's conjecture was right, the very thought of it was absolutely revolting. Two grown men fighting over which one of them should own that high-priced animal. That horse was causing trouble for everyone!

Well, Bobbie decided, she wasn't about to sit here doing nothing. If Cal did have that horse, for all she cared, he could keep him. But she wasn't going to let him scare Susan to death with his ridiculous scheme.

Bobbie raced to her bedroom, grabbing her car keys. Before she turned toward the elevator, though, she realized that if she ran into Hollis and had to explain where she was going, he would try to stop her. The poor man had been witness to her yelling at Reno on two separate occasions in the same evening; undoubtedly he'd already decided she was stark raving mad . . . and this would only serve to confirm his thinking.

But if Hollis came upstairs to check on her, he didn't need to be adding Bobbie to his list of worries. Rushing back to the office, she snatched up a pen and scribbled a message for him— just in case. As she jotted the words "Cal's house," she decided that Reno ought to be darned glad she made a habit of using her head. Someone around here certainly needed to!

On that final reassuring thought, she poked the note through the paper spindle on Reno's desk and took off for the back elevator.

What seemed an eternity later, Bobbie finished negotiating the many turns that constituted the roundabout way to Cal's house. Approaching it from the west, she was able to pull off the main road and cut the engine before getting too close.

She shut the car door as quietly as possible and started to walk swiftly toward her destination. Her best approach, she had already decided, would be to come in from behind the trees at the back of the old carriage house, the one that had been converted to a combination garage and stable.

Darting a glance at her watch, seeing how late it was getting to be, she gave a silent prayer of thanks that it was the end of August. At least there would still be a little bit of daylight left, she told herself, quickening her pace. But as she neared a clump of trees and disappeared into their midst, she realized how very little time that would give her to do what she had to do...

Bobbie stopped dead in her tracks as she neared the carriage house. She heard a whinny come from the back of the stable. Oh, God, she thought. Her thinking had been right. No horses were kept in this stable, so it had to be Jubalee. And that meant Susan had to be nearby, too. But where?

In the stable? she wondered, resuming her stealthy approach. Lord, she hoped so. If Susan was being held somewhere inside the house, it would make Bobbie's task much more difficult. At least the stable, she knew, had Dutch doors on each end of its one row of stalls.

Finally she reached the structure. Pressing her back against it, Bobbie squeezed her eyes shut and covered her mouth with her hand. What if Cal was actually capable of harming Susan? What if he had—

She couldn't think about that now, she realized, slinking quietly along the outside wall until she reached the corner and peered around it. Seeing no one, she crept slowly toward the Dutch door.

"Jubalee?" she heard Susan asking from inside. "Did...did you hear somethin'?"

Bobbie stooped down, her pulse hammering as she squinted through the opening between the two halves of the door. She could see almost everything inside the long, narrow stable. She pushed her hand against her chest as she realized the only forms she could detect belonged to Susan, Jubalee and one other horse, a gray one.

"It's gonna be dark in a little while," Susan whispered, her voice sounding quivery and frightened. "I gotta..."

Ignoring the rest of Susan's words, Bobbie straightened and tried the knob. And surprisingly, it wasn't locked. She opened the door quickly, grateful that Cal had been foolish enough to leave them here without—

The little girl jumped and immediately gave a short, high-pitched scream. When Susan realized who was there, though, when she saw who was bending down with outstretched arms, she came running straight into Bobbie's embrace.

"I'm sorry," the girl was saying through her sobs. "I'm sorry, Bobbie. I promise I won't bring him back. I promise I'll leave him here and come back every day to take care of him. He won't be any trouble, I promise. You don't ever have to—"

"Susan?" she finally asked, holding her tighter. "Honey? Who are you talking about? Are you . . . are you talking about Jubalee?"

"Yes," she cried. "But please don't go away. If I keep him here all the time, you won't leave, will you? You don't ever have to come see him or—"

"Susan?" she asked, still holding her tight. "Are you saying *you* brought Jubalee here? All by yourself? All alone?"

"Uh-huh," the girl choked out.

"What did you do? Ride Lady Lee? All the way from the Hideaway?"

The girl simply nodded against Bobbie's chest.

"But why, sugar? Why did you do that?"

"'Cause you and Daddy were f-fighting about him. I took him away so you'd be happy again. So you'd stay here with us—with me and Daddy. Forever!"

Suddenly, Bobbie remembered Susan standing in the bedroom doorway, wrapped in that towel just as she, Bobbie, had yelled at Reno about the "damned stupid horse." Susan had relayed some message about Hollis being in a hurry to go somewhere, so she had known that Hollis wouldn't be with Jubalee.

"Oh, sugar," she whispered against the girl's hair. "No. We weren't fighting about Jubalee, Susan. Not really. We were..." Unable to stop the tears that were flowing from her eyes, Bobbie simply held Susan, rocking her back and forth, taking and giving comfort.

What *had* she been screaming at him about? she wondered. It hadn't been about Jubalee. It had been about her. It had been Bobbie fighting a battle of her own, fighting what Reno had been trying to tell her all along. For too long now, she had been afraid to listen to her heart. And because of that, she had been afraid to *believe* what her heart had been trying so hard to tell her about Reno Tanner.

"Bobbie?" the girl whispered raggedly. "You're all done with your business, but does that mean you can't stay?"

Bobbie smiled, shaking her head as she realized Susan was referring to what Bobbie had said this morning, after finishing her phone calls. That was undoubtedly the simple comment that had brought on Susan's talk of "sharing" their new house with her.

"I'm not sure if I can stay or not, honey," she answered sadly, realizing that it might be too late for her to try to convince Reno she finally understood what he'd been asking of her all this time. "We'll see, okay?"

"You mean, if you and Daddy don't fight anymore, we can all be together?"

"Well," Bobbie said with a smile, holding Susan at arm's length and brushing the moisture from her cheeks. "What that means is, people who love each other argue sometimes. So even though they don't always understand each other or get along perfectly every minute, people need to know that that's okay. They can still love each other very much."

"So does that mean you'll stay?"

Bobbie's heart seemed to be crumbling as she watched the sweet, searching look on Susan's face, as she realized how very, very much she would be losing if it was too late for her and Reno.

For now, though, she needed to push her own worries aside. Reno needed to be found. He needed to be told right away that Susan and Jubalee were both safe and sound.

"I'll tell you what," she finally replied. "Why don't we talk about that in the car? On the way home? Your daddy and I were both really worried about you when we—" Realizing she didn't want Susan knowing what they'd thought, she glanced down at the girl's wrist. "Why did you take off your bracelet, sugar?"

"It got knocked off my arm and I didn't wanta stop and put it back on. I was in a hurry to go . . ."

To go hide a multimillion-dollar Thoroughbred, Bobbie realized, schooling her grin. "Well, your daddy found your bracelet, so that's okay. But we need to get home now. We need to let him know you're all right. You and Jubalee both."

Susan agreed and then headed toward Jubalee's stall, getting ready to open it.

"I think we'd better leave him here for now, Susan. Why don't we walk over to Hollis's office? He's at the main building, so we'll just call him. I'm sure he'll be glad to come and get Jubalee."

"Okay," Susan said, tugging her toward the fine-featured chestnut stallion and coaxing Bobbie into using the palm of her hand to give him a proper goodbye.

"He is beautiful, isn't he?" Bobbie commented, almost to herself, and then she and Susan left the stable, only to meet Hollis a few steps outside the door.

The old man grabbed Susan and squeezed her like crazy, not able to say a word for several seconds. At last he set her down, asking her to go back and check on Jubalee again.

Once they were alone, Bobbie decided that since Hollis knew at least the basics of what had been going on between her and Reno, she might as well swallow the last of her pride and answer the question that seemed to be written all over his face.

Upon hearing what Susan had done—and why she'd done it—the old man simply smiled and shook his head in amazement.

"But hold on," he said, looking puzzled again. "How'd you know what the little one was up to? And of all places, how'd you figure she'd bring him here?"

"I didn't," Bobbie admitted, then sheepishly explained what she had suspected.

After a short, diplomatic sound of amusement, Hollis told her that Cal had always been "a fairly harmless fella." And then, without actually calling her a silly woman, he let her know just how foolish her idea had been. Cal had called Reno just today, as it turned out, from "somewhere over the seas."

"Yeah," Hollis added, "Reno asked me to keep an eye on things next week, 'cause he's sending some cleaning people over to get the place ready before Cal gets back. He said he thought they might be fixin' to finally work things out between 'em."

What wonderful news, Bobbie thought happily.

"But," Hollis added, patting her arm, "I reckon it's a good thing you got that crazy notion, anyhow." Smiling broadly, he peeked into the stable and nodded toward the two runaways.

In the next few moments, Bobbie and Hollis formulated their plans. As Jubalee's trainer, he was interested in giving the horse "the once-over"—just in case. And he would take care of getting Lady Lee boarded for the night. Since Bobbie was taking Susan back to the Hideaway immediately, she assured Hollis that she and Annette would start burning up the telephone wires to locate Reno in Fort Worth.

"Daddy!" Susan said unexpectedly from behind them.

With a sudden smile, Bobbie pivoted to see Reno standing inside the stable, his daughter now held snugly, securely in his arms. His eyes were squeezed shut, but when he opened them at last . . . when Bobbie met his gaze and noticed his tense form and the expression on his face . . . the smile disappeared from her lips.

She turned back to Hollis. "I—I think I should go ahead and drive back now, Hollis. They need a few minutes alone together." Tears welled up behind her eyes. "Please . . . tell him what happened, will you? And tell him not to be angry with her. It was all my fault."

As she rushed toward her car, Bobbie couldn't stop trying to figure out the expression she'd seen on Reno's face. Had it been anger? she wondered. Or worry or relief or a combination of all those emotions?

She couldn't blame him for the worry. She had been through that herself. That's why she'd come out here to rescue Susan from Cal's clutches in the first place.

All she could think of now was the fear they had both experienced earlier, when they'd thought Susan had been . . .

Bobbie got into the car, leaning her head against the steering wheel before she began to cry. A sudden, delayed flood of relief seemed to be washing over her: relief that a miracle had happened, that Susan and Jubalee were actually safe when so many things could have gone wrong.

Bobbie raised her head, blinking against the tears and the gathering darkness. Ever since she'd arrived here at the Hideaway, so many miraculous things had happened. Reno had been the first miracle. Just meeting him. Falling in love with him.

And of course there was the news about Reno's brother.

And, Bobbie realized with a soft, radiant smile, Reno's daughter alone had brought on an entire series of miracles in about twenty-four hours. If Bobbie hadn't found Susan crying last night, if she hadn't promised her that they would leave before sunrise this morning, then Bobbie never would have discovered the new site for her proposal. And if Susan hadn't caught her and Reno in the library yesterday, if that sweet, precious child hadn't been so willing to accept Bobbie's presence in her father's life and in their future . . .

But she had, Bobbie reminded herself. And back in that stable, in a matter of mere minutes, Susan had clearly shown Bobbie where she'd been going wrong. If that one little girl could possess so much bravery and faith—if she could be so willing to risk loving both Reno and Bobbie so unconditionally—then how could Bobbie not take a lesson from that? How could she not let herself be willing, at last, to love Reno and his child in the very same way?

Bobbie straightened, wiping the dampness from her cheeks before she turned the key and pulled the car onto the main road.

Yes, she thought. When she'd first found Susan in the stable, it had flashed through her mind that Reno had been right all along. There was no such thing as a sure thing when it came to love . . . or even to life itself. Yet that was what her head had been asking for: a sure thing.

As she continued to drive, she recalled what Reno had said to her when he stormed into her cabin, before they had made love for the very first time. "Some things just happen. Sometimes you just have to throw caution to the wind and let them happen." That was exactly what she needed to do now. Just as Susan had done, Bobbie needed to be willing to risk something of herself. To simply love Reno and let him love her.

By the time she arrived at the main building and parked her car around back, Bobbie had made up her mind. She was going to go upstairs and unpack while she waited for Reno and Susan to return. This time she wouldn't try to run away. This time she knew exactly what she wanted: to make things right between her and Reno Tanner, the man she'd come to love and respect despite their differences—because of their differences.

As soon as he arrived and put Susan to bed, Bobbie would have a talk with him. If he was still angry with her about the stupid things she'd said and done today, she wouldn't blame him . . . but she was prepared to stay and fight for him. For their future. If he wanted to fight with her, she'd fight fair this time. She wouldn't throw in things that weren't the real issues. Things like Glendelle. And Jubalee.

Bobbie smiled as she slammed the car door and turned toward the back elevator.

It had been a day overflowing with miracles already, she knew. Would one more miracle—the most glorious miracle of them all—be too much to ask?

Maybe so, Bobbie decided, but she wasn't about to leave without asking. Without trying everything possible to get what she *knew* was right.

Chapter Fifteen

Bobbie shut the closet door. She turned then, placing the last of her empty suitcases against the wall as she heard the elevator doors open and close, as she listened for the sound of Reno's footsteps.

After what must have been a quick search of his office and the sitting room, he appeared in her bedroom doorway.

"Bobbie," he said, a grave look on his face as his eyes moved from the row of luggage back to her. "We need to talk."

"I know," she said quietly, meeting him at the door. "Where's Susan?"

"Downstairs. With Annette." He took her arm and led her into the sitting room.

Her pulse was racing just from his light touch on her skin. "I—I don't know how to start this, Reno. I—"

"That's fine," he interrupted, "because I do." He ushered her to the nearest chair and then began pacing the floor across the room from her. "I've been wrong, Bobbie."

"No," she exclaimed. "It was me. If I hadn't—" Seeing the faint smile of exasperation that had come across his face, she clamped her mouth shut.

"You argue too much, woman," he said slowly. "Now why don't you just sit there and let me finish?"

"All right," she murmured. Her hands were trembling, and she steadied them against the denim covering her legs.

"*I* was wrong. On the way to the airstrip I realized I was in no shape to be driving, much less flying. And that's when it dawned on me that you were right, that for Susan's sake—for everyone's sake—I needed to use my head." Directly in front of the window, Reno stopped his pacing. "So I turned around and came back, knowing that no matter who was responsible, I had to call the authorities and let them handle it."

Pressing his hand high against the window frame, he stared out into the darkness. "The whole time I was driving back here, all I could think was what if something happened to Susan? What if I lost her because I hadn't taken the time to stop and listen to logic? And what if I lost *you* because of the things I'd said to you earlier, when I wasn't thinking? When I was tired and angry and emotional."

Not once, she noticed, had Reno mentioned Diamond Jubalee. How could she ever have accused him of loving that horse more than—

"Look, Bobbie. I realize this is no excuse, but..." He turned his head, his hand still propped against the window frame, his eyes intent on hers. "About Glendelle. I should've told you earlier, I know, but it was a long, complicated story and—"

"Reno?" she whispered. "I know everything I need to know about Glendelle. For now, anyway. If you want to—if you feel you need to—we can always talk about her later, can't we?" There was a lump in her throat that had to be swallowed. "Because right this minute, I think we should talk about . . . About you and me and now." *And forever,* she thought, her hopes soaring as she tilted her head and smiled up at him. "Don't you?"

"Yeah," he said, his baritone voice low yet infinitely clear. "And the first thing I need to do is apologize for yelling at you about using your head all the time. To tell you the truth, Bobbie, after what I'd been through with Glendelle's problem..." He stopped for a moment. "Well, I realize now that your sensible attitude was one of the things that attracted me to you in the first place. It's an appealing quality, to say the least, and one that certainly paid off tonight."

Shaking his head, he lifted his gaze toward the ceiling. "When I got back here and found your note, I didn't know what the hell was going on, but . . ." He gave her a stern, reprimanding look. "That was a crazy thing to do, Bobbie! I'm damned proud of you for going out there to save Susan, but you never should've taken a chance like that—especially without knowing who or what you'd be up against once you got there." He ran his fingers through his dark hair. "My God, Bobbie. What on earth ever possessed you to—"

"What is it you've always told me?" she asked, trying to erase the worry she saw on his face by grinning nonchalantly and lifting one shoulder. "No pain, no gain. Right?"

"Yes, darlin'," he answered, "but I didn't mean it quite that literally." He pushed out a long sigh. "Nevertheless, I'm damned glad you were using your head. Almost anything could've happened to her if you—"

Bobbie's quiet laughter interrupted him. "No," she said. "My head didn't have a thing to do with it. Oh, I thought it did at the time, but I realize now that it wasn't logic at all. I was scared for her, Reno—just plain scared—and because of that, I guess, I put all those things together and went out there on a hunch. It was nothing but a hunch!"

Seeing the look of puzzlement on his face, Bobbie wanted to laugh again. And at the same time, she wanted to cry. "Don't you see, Reno? For once, I think I listened to my heart." She flattened her palm against her chest. "I think maybe . . . finally . . . you and Susan have taught me to be brave in that respect."

"Well," he said, his beautiful blue eyes serious again. "You've taught me something, too, you know." He took a seat in the chair at the other end of the sofa, the chair facing hers. "Now that I know what's important to me—who's important to me—I've decided to go ahead and syndicate Jubalee."

"No!" She leaned forward all of a sudden. "You can't, Reno. I don't want you to do that."

"For God's sake, Bobbie. Why not?"

"Because you're the most generous man I've ever known. Because you share yourself with all of us—with me, with Susan, with all those kids from the orphanage—and if there's one thing in this world you don't want to share, for whatever reasons, then I think you have that right."

Her intense expression changed to a smile as she realized what she hadn't had the chance to tell him yet. "Besides, you don't *need* to." As briefly as possible, she told him about her idea: about the new location and her phone calls to the architect and builder, and even about the longhorns. "With a little work, it'll be perfect for the executive retreat. So there'll be plenty of money—without giving up Jubalee—and you'll still be able to build the..." Her voice trailed off as she realized he might be thinking she'd gotten business and pleasure mixed up again. "What I mean is, if you like my new idea. If you don't, I'll find something else. I'll—"

"No," he said, a slow grin spreading across his face. "I like it, Bobbie. I like it a lot, in fact. I'm sure it'll work." He rubbed his jaw. "That doesn't change my decision, though. I'll put the executive-retreat profits toward building the stud farm, but I still want to go through with my plans for Jubalee. The syndication proceeds can be put to use for the ranch itself, during lean times around here. And for plenty of other things, too."

"But your dad wanted Jubalee to be yours," she said. "Are you sure you want to make that kind of sacrifice?"

"Yes," he answered, his tone quiet but firm. "I'm absolutely sure. I realize now that...in spirit...Jubalee will always be my horse, no matter how many other people own shares in him. And when I think about all the good uses that money could be put to, I know I have to do it."

Glancing up at the picture of Reno's grandmother, at the children flocked around her, Bobbie smiled softly. She knew Reno wasn't talking about using the syndication profits strictly for the Diamond T.

"And besides that, Bobbie, I don't look at it as a sacrifice anymore." He shrugged his shoulders. "It's just a compromise. One of those compromises we all need to make from time to time, to do what's best for everyone."

"Well," she said, "now that we're talking about compromises, I have one of my own to make." It was her turn to put herself out on a limb, to take a risk by letting him know exactly how she felt about certain issues they'd never had the chance to discuss: how she felt about leaving Dallas, for one.

"Well," Bobbie said, starting over again, "since I feel so committed to this new idea, I'd like to see it through. I'm sure I could be valuable to you by handling the marketing and sales, so I want to volunteer my services. I could be . . . sort of a resident real-estate expert."

"Ah," he said, smiling with confidence as he leaned back and laced his fingers behind his head. "And is that the only reason you want to stay? Because of business?"

"Oh, no," she murmured. "I have a far more important reason. A very personal reason."

"What's that?"

"Because . . ." She ran her tongue across her suddenly dry lips. "Because I'm convinced my Mr. Right is here. Because I know we both feel the same way about his daughter, and about children in general, and about each other—especially about each other. So if he'll have me... Well, maybe there'll be other kids in our future." Her eyes stayed on his. "So you see, I can't possibly leave. Not when I'm hoping he has plans for us."

"As a matter of fact, he does." Reno leaned forward. "Come here, darlin'."

"Why?" she asked, her voice less than a whisper as she stood and crossed the room.

"Because I'm your Mr. Right, Bobbie." Reaching for her hand, he brought her down onto his lap. "Because I've known it for quite a while now, but I've been waiting for you to realize it on your own. And now that we both know, I want to touch you. And hold you."

His hand moved around her, grasping her neck so that he could bring her mouth against his. And when he kissed her, she realized how badly she was aching for him. For the familiar yet new sensations he would always set off inside her. With nothing but a kiss. With a word or a loving glance. With the strength and tenderness of his touch, the heat and depth of his soul.

When at last his mouth left hers, he reached behind the lamp on the table beside him, for a box she hadn't noticed was there. As he opened it, she realized it was a jeweler's box.

He held out her arm, and when he fastened the clasp, Bobbie turned her wrist first one way and then the other, watching the gold glinting in the lamplight, trying to read the inscription through the tears of joy that were suddenly pooling in her eyes.

"Bobbie Tanner," she whispered. "I like the sound of that. I like it a whole lot, in fact." His eyes drew her back. "I love you, Reno. I love you so much, I . . ."

"You want to know what I love about you?" he asked.

When she only nodded, he said, "I love the way you cry when you're happy." Using his knuckles, he brushed away the tears that had trickled down her cheeks even as she smiled. "I love the way you make me feel and the way you let me know exactly how you feel—no matter what." He sighed helplessly, grinning. "It seems that I love everything about you."

Realizing she couldn't speak, Bobbie laid her head against his chest. Her wrist was locked between their heartbeats, and she squeezed her eyes shut as she thought about the meaning behind this simple, beautiful token of love. They had learned so much from each other already, given and taken so very much. And regardless of what the future had in store for them, she knew they would continue to do so. Through the good times as well as the difficult ones, she would always be his, and he would always be hers.

He reached between them, covering her wrist with his hand.

"I'll never take it off," she murmured. "Never."

"Okay, then." She felt the rumble of laughter in his throat. "But first thing tomorrow morning, we make it official."

"But we can't, Reno." She lifted her head, her smiling eyes meeting his. "Not for a few weeks, anyway."

"Why not?"

"Because the timing's not right until then. Susan needs to get settled in school and start making new friends. And there's your brother to think about—and my sister: little Charlie's due in about two weeks, and I'd like to be there in case Alix needs me.

"And," she added, emphasizing the word as she gave him a disgusted frown, "I'm not about to get married and go off on a honeymoon with you until September twentieth, when you're absolutely, positively thirty-five years old. I don't want to spend my entire honeymoon listening to your comments about my cradle robbing. You'd be telling anyone who'd listen. Every bellhop and waitress and—"

"All right, then. What if I make you an offer you can't refuse? Like a nice, long honeymoon in the Caribbean? A cruise, maybe, and you could keep me locked in the cabin the whole time so I couldn't—"

"No way. I'm not falling for that." She winked at him. "And I stopped thinking about the Caribbean ages ago. I plan to keep you locked away in a cabin, all right, but I want it to be somewhere in south Texas."

"Why there?" he asked, obviously surprised by her choice.

"Well . . . I've heard this interesting saying." She glanced toward the window. "'If you don't like the weather in south Texas, stick around for a few minutes. It'll change.'"

"Hmm," he said, pretending to mull it over. "Well, that sounds fine to me. South Texas has a lot of great fishin' spots, too, you know."

"Oh," she commented. "I like the sound of that."

"Yeah, but I'm afraid we have a little problem here, honey. I mean, that part about waiting a few weeks for the honeymoon sounds logical, but I think we need to compromise on the getting married part. I think we'd better do that as soon as we can."

"Why?"

"You know that talk I was planning to have with our daughter? The one about the birds and the bees?"

Bobbie nodded, her eyes widening.

"Well, it seems she already knows something about that. In fact, on the drive back here tonight, she decided maybe she'd better clue her old man in on a few things. She was subtle about it, of course." He slowed his words, winking as he slid his hand up the length of Bobbie's thigh. "But basically she informed me that if a man and woman get married . . . and if they want to make baby brothers and sisters for the little girl they already have . . . and if they love each other a whole, whole lot, then all they have to do is sleep in the same bed."

Bobbie laughed, realizing there was at least one thing she already knew about being a mother. Never could little girls be counted on to keep secrets.

"Yeah," he added, lifting one shoulder. "She made it sound like there was nothin' to it. Like it was the most natural thing in the world."

"So tell me, cowboy. After Susan fed you all this information, just exactly what did you have to say to *her*?"

"I said I thought that was a mighty good idea, myself, and before I left her downstairs to spend the night with Annette, I sorta promised her I'd do everything I could to convince you to marry me...so we could get started right away. I promised her that—" he cleared his throat "—even if it took all night, I'd convince you that that was the logical thing to do."

"Well," she murmured, her fingers impatiently unfastening the snaps at the front of his shirt. "Since you put it that way..."

"What's this?" Feigning shock, he repositioned her in his arms and stood, carrying her across the room. "No arguments?"

"Of course not," Bobbie whispered, her lips brushing lightly against his, her voice a teasing reprimand as he pushed the bedroom door open. "For heaven's sake, Reno. How can I argue with logic like that?"

*   *   *   *   *

Silhouette Intimate Moments®

Let Bestselling Author KATHLEEN EAGLE Sweep You Away to De Colores Once Again

For the third time, Kathleen Eagle has written a book set on the spellbinding isle of De Colores. In PAINTBOX MORNING (Intimate Moments #284), Miguel Hidalgo is all that stands between his island home and destruction—and Ronnie Harper is the only woman who can help Miguel fulfill his destiny and lead his people into a bright tomorrow. But Ronnie has a woman's heart, a woman's needs. In helping Miguel to live out his dreams, is she destined to see her own dreams of love with this very special man go forever unfulfilled? Read PAINTBOX MORNING, coming this month from Silhouette Intimate Moments, and follow the path of these star-crossed lovers as they build a future filled with hope and a love to last all time.

If you like PAINTBOX MORNING, you might also like Kathleen Eagle's two previous tales of De Colores: CANDLES IN THE NIGHT (Special Edition #437) and MORE THAN A MIRACLE (Intimate Moments #242).

For your copy, send $2.75 plus 75¢ postage and handling to:

In USA

901 Furhmann Blvd.
P.O. Box 1396
Buffalo, NY 14269-1396

In Canada

P.O. Box 609
Fort Erie, Ontario
L2A 5X3

Please specify book title with your order.

IM284-1A

NAVY BLUES
Debbie Macomber

Between the devil and the deep blue sea...

At Christmastime, Lieutenant Commander Steve Kyle finds his heart anchored by the past, so he vows to give his ex-wife wide berth. But Carol Kyle is quaffing milk and knitting tiny pastel blankets with a vengeance. She's determined to have a baby, and only one man will do as father-to-be—the only man she's ever loved...her own bullheaded ex-husband!

You met Steve and Carol in NAVY WIFE (Special Edition #494)— you'll cheer for them in NAVY BLUES (Special Edition #518). (And as a bonus for NAVY WIFE fans, newlyweds Rush and Lindy Callaghan reveal a surprise of their own....)

Each book stands alone—together they're Debbie Macomber's most delightful duo to date! Don't miss

**NAVY BLUES
Available in April,
only in *Silhouette Special Edition*.
Having the "blues" was never
so much fun!**
